Big Lake Fugitive

By Nick Russell

Nick Russell
E-mail Editor@gypsyjournal.net

Also By Nick Russell

Fiction

Big Lake Mystery Series

Big Lake
Big Lake Lynching
Crazy Days In Big Lake
Big Lake Blizzard
Big Lake Scandal
Big Lake Burning
Big Lake Honeymoon
Big Lake Reckoning
Big Lake Brewpub
Big Lake Abduction
Big Lake Celebration
Big Lake Tragedy
Big Lake Snowdaze
Big Lake Fugitive

Dog's Run Series

Dog's Run
Return To Dog's Run

John Lee Quarrels Series

Stillborn Armadillos
The Gecko In The Corner
Mullets And Man Buns

Standalone Mystery Novels

Black Friday

Nonfiction

Highway History and Back Road Mystery
Highway History and Back Road Mystery II
Meandering Down The Highway; A Year On The Road With Fulltime RVers
The Frugal RVer
Work Your Way Across The USA; You Can Travel And Earn A Living Too!
Overlooked Florida
Overlooked Arizona
The Gun Shop Manual

Keep up with Nick Russell's latest books at
www.NickRussellBooks.com

Author's Note

While there is a body of water named Big Lake in the White Mountains of Arizona, the community of Big Lake and all persons in this book live only in the author's imagination. Any resemblance in this story to actual persons, living or dead, is purely coincidental.

Chapter 1

The Honda Civic was at least ten years older than the man behind the wheel and it didn't seem like it had been given much attention in all of those years. The paint was faded to some indeterminate color, there was a crack in the windshield on the passenger side, the springs were broken down in the seats, which were almost devoid of fabric, and the engine rattled and knocked climbing up the hills, making him wonder each time if the old car would reach the top. Going downhill was an adventure as well, given the Honda's loose steering, bald tires, and worn out brakes. But they say beggars can't be choosers. And neither can desperate car thieves.

He nursed the old rattletrap along U.S. Highway 60, fearing that every mile would be its last and it would give up the ghost. Twice New Mexico Highway Patrol cars had passed going in the opposite direction, and each time he felt the panic rising within him. Both times he had watched in the rearview mirror, his heart in his throat, expecting them to make a U-turn and their roof lights to come on, breathing a huge sigh of relief when it didn't happen.

Passing the Karl G. Jansky Very Large Array radio astronomy observatory, located on the Plains of San Agustin between Magdalena and Datil, with its large white dish antennas pointed toward the heavens, he remembered coming there on a field trip when he was in junior high school. God, how long ago was that? It seemed like forever. He would give anything to be able to roll back the hands of time and be a schoolboy again, before he made the mistakes that had landed him in his present predicament.

The Low Fuel light came on somewhere near Pie Town, but a search of the car's glove compartment and under the seats had only turned up a quarter, a nickel, and three pennies, along with three long forgotten foil ketchup packets from some fast food drive through window. He couldn't remember how long it had been since he had eaten and tore the ends off of them, sucking the rancid contents into his mouth. They did as much to fill his stomach as 33 cents would do to fill the Honda's gas tank.

He considered pulling into the gas station at Pie Town and trying to beg enough gas to get down the road, but he doubted that it would do him any good and was more likely to make the clerk remember him if somebody came in asking about any suspicious strangers passing through. Especially strangers with bruised faces and one eye swollen almost shut. He never even considered trying to fill the tank and driving off without paying. There was only the one road going anywhere through here, and the Honda wasn't exactly a getaway car. One of the local cowboys could have probably run him down without even kicking his horse into a fast lope.

Besides, his previous attempts at a life of crime had never worked out well, from the summer cabins he and his brother had burglarized when they were teenagers to that bust for possession last year, or his latest screw-up, which had led him into the mess he was in now. He still couldn't believe something as simple as driving a car with an expired license tag had ended up this way. Damn you, Claudia! If he would have known about the baggie of pot and the bong she had forgotten about and left in her backpack in the back seat he never would have gotten behind the wheel for that quick trip to the Circle K for a six pack and cigarettes. And now he was running for his life!

The Honda gave up the ghost a few miles past Quemado, sputtering to a stop with barely enough time to allow him to pull it into a wide gravel parking area that held two wooden picnic tables and a trash barrel. It could have been worse. Maybe the first cop that passed by wouldn't notice it as quickly as he would have if the car was on the shoulder of the road.

He felt bad about stealing the car but he had not had a choice. Still, he figured anybody who could only afford a car this beat up must be down on their luck, too, and he wrote down the owner's name and address from the registration he found in the glove box. If he survived all of this, he planned to send them some money to reimburse them for the loss of the car.

Not sure what to do, but knowing he couldn't stay there, he was debating whether to set off on foot or try to hitch a ride when a big Winnebago motorhome towing some kind of small SUV pulled into the parking area. A moment later the door opened and a small brown dog ran out, barking at him while it wiggled its rear end and wagged its tail as it approached.

"Hi there, little guy. How are you today?"

He squatted down and petted the dog, which licked his chin.

"Bosco, you leave that man alone! Come here."

The dog slurped his chin one more time, then ran back to its owner, an older man with a fringe of white hair and a friendly smile.

"Sorry about that. Bosco's never met a stranger."

"No problem, I love dogs. She's a sweetie."

"Yeah, when she's not being a pain in the ass. Now, you go do your business Bosco. We've still got a lot of miles to get behind us."

"Where are you headed?"

"Cottonwood. Going to spend a couple of weeks at a campground there. How about you?"

"Nowhere right now. My old car died and I'm kind of stuck."

"I'm not much of a mechanic, but I'll be happy to call a tow truck for you."

"No!" Then, realizing he may have sounded desperate, he added, "You probably couldn't even get a phone signal out here anyway. And to be honest with you, it would cost more to tow it than it's worth."

The man looked at the car and nodded. "Probably so. From the look of your face, you've had a run of trouble."

"Yeah. That was my own fault. I wrecked my dirt bike showing off for a couple of friends."

"You're lucky you got off that easy. Last year our grandson did the same thing. Broke his collarbone and a couple of ribs and punctured a lung."

"Ouch. Hope he's okay."

"Oh yeah. And as soon as he could climb on the darned thing he was riding it again. Obviously didn't learn any lessons from it."

"I think I have. I'm sticking to four wheels from now on. Well, I was until this old thing died."

The man looked at the Honda, then at the young man, and seemed to make a decision. "Can we give you a ride somewhere? I wouldn't want to leave you out here in the middle of nowhere."

"Boy, if you could do that, mister, I would really appreciate it."

"Where do you need to get to, son?"

"I'm trying to get home to Big Lake, over in Arizona."

"Don't know that I've heard of it. Where's that at?"

"Most folks haven't heard of it. It's a little mountain town about 25 miles from Springerville."

"Well, I know Springerville's on our way. We can get you that far, if that helps."

"Thank you, it would sure help a lot."

"Well, hop on in. You need anything from your car?"

"No, I don't think so."

"You travel light."

"Yeah, it wasn't a trip I planned to make anytime soon. Truth is, I didn't think I'd ever be going back there."

"Is that home to you?"

"I grew up there. Been gone a while."

"Well, sometimes it's good to go back home, even if you're not looking forward to the trip."

They followed the dog into the motorhome and the man said, "Jackie, this young fella's car broke down and we're going to give him a ride to Springerville. That's my wife, Jackie. Jacqueline's her real name, just like Jackie Kennedy. But I guess that was probably before your time. And I'm Stanley."

The woman smiled and looked at him tentatively, not entirely comfortable with her husband inviting a stranger into their motorhome. Especially one who looked so bruised and battered. He was afraid she might object and tell her husband it was best to leave him where he was and call for help when they could get a phone signal, but before she could say anything, her husband continued, "I don't believe I got your name, son."

"Weber. James Weber, Junior. My father's the sheriff in Big Lake."

4

Chapter 2

Sheriff Jim Weber had just left a long and frustrating meeting with the Town Council, where they had been discussing the budget for the Sheriff's Department. It was a battle he fought frequently. Even though the town was bringing in considerably more tax revenue than it had in past years, due to the large number of tourists who were visiting on a regular basis, the vacation cabins and condos that were springing up everywhere, and from the Cat Mountain Ski Lodge, the mayor and certain other miserly members of the Town Council never wanted to spend a penny unless they absolutely had to.

Mayor Chet Wingate had challenged the sheriff on every item in the budget, nitpicking and demanding to know what every expense was for.

"Sheriff, you have an item here I'd like to know more about. $3,895 for vehicle repairs. Less than two years ago every vehicle in your department was replaced. Didn't they come with warranties? "

"Yes, Chet, they did. But warranties don't cover acts of negligence."

"Negligence? How many deputies do you have that are so negligent they would cause $3,895 damage to a vehicle?"

"Just one, Chet."

"I see. What were the damages, and what did you do to discipline the deputy who caused it?"

"The damages included replacing the rear wheel bearings, rewiring the rear end of the car, replacing the trunk lid, and repainting. Those were caused when Archer backed down the boat ramp and put the rear end of his patrol car in the lake. I haven't decided what I'm going to do with him about that. Any suggestions, Mr. Mayor?"

"Well now, accidents do happen. I don't think there's any reason to fault a deputy for some little thing like that."

"Especially when that deputy is your son, Chet? You don't think he needs to be disciplined just like anybody else would be?" Senior Councilman Kirby Templeton rested his chin on his hand, elbow on the top of the dais, waiting for the mayor to answer his question.

"Moving right along," the mayor said, "$2,000 for ammunition? Are you planning to start a war, Sheriff Weber?"

"No, Chet, but every deputy has to qualify with their side arms, their shotguns, and their rifles. And, they kind of like to have some ammunition with them when they go on patrol."

"Well, how many bullets do their guns hold?"

"Depending on what they are carrying, their handguns hold anywhere from seven to fifteen rounds of ammunition. Their shotguns each hold eight rounds. And their tactical rifles each have a twenty round magazine."

"My God," said Janet McGill, the newest member of the Town Council, "It sounds like you are getting ready to start a war! Why in the world do your deputies need that many bullets, Sheriff? You're talking about over fifty bullets for each deputy. That's just insane!"

"Actually, Councilwoman," Weber said. "I didn't include the backup ammunition they carry with them."

"Backup ammunition? I would think if they can't hit what they are aiming at with fifty bullets, they shouldn't be carrying guns in the first place."

"That's not realistic at all," Weber told her. "Our people are spread thin and they never know what they're going to run into."

"This isn't a battlefield in the Middle East someplace, Sheriff Weber. This is Big Lake. Nobody needs that many bullets. And why do they have so many guns in the first place? A handgun, and a shotgun, and an assault rifle?"

"They are not assault rifles, Councilwoman. They are tactical rifles."

"That's not what they call them on the news."

"No, ma'am. But this is real life, not the news. At any given time, one of our deputies maybe called on to subdue a violent

6

criminal, to put down an elk that was hit by a car, or they might encounter a bear. They never know what might happen."

"And that justifies carrying an arsenal of guns and ammunition around with them?"

"Yes, ma'am. It does."

"Ridiculous," the councilwoman said, shaking her head.

"Janet, you spent your whole life living in the San Francisco area," Councilman Frank Gauger said. "And I can guarantee you, the police there are more heavily armed than our deputies are. But just because you moved to a small town a few years ago, doesn't mean you moved to the Garden of Eden. Sheriff Weber is right. It was only a couple of weeks ago that I heard a noise on my deck one night and looked out and there was a bear standing there."

"I saw a nature program on television that said all you have to do is make a loud noise and it will scare a bear away. There is no reason in the world to shoot one."

Weber could have differed with her, having encountered several bears in his time, including one that was devouring the body of a murder victim. At that time he had felt terribly undergunned with his .45 caliber semiautomatic pistol. But before he could say anything, Frank Gauger said, "Janet, maybe you should turn off the TV once in a while and go outside and see what life is really all about."

The councilwoman's face reddened and she gave him an annoyed look, but didn't reply.

"Okay, enough about the ammunition. Sheriff Weber, explain this bill for $318 for repairs to the ceiling in the Sheriff's office to me. What happened to the ceiling?"

"Archer happened, Chet."

"What are you talking about?"

"Archer blew a hole in the ceiling with his shotgun."

"How the hel... how the heck did Archer do that?"

"He was just being Archer, Frank. When he backed his car into the lake, we had to take the equipment out of it while it was in the shop being repaired. He brought his shotgun inside the office and Mary asked him if it was loaded. He said no. Then he proceeded to blow a hole in the ceiling to show her."

"Sheriff Weber, why do you seem to delight in picking on Archer? I find it very unfair of you," the mayor snapped.

"Trust me, Chet, I don't find anything about your son delightful in any way."

"The man's just reporting the facts, Chet," Kirby Templeton said. "You and I both know that it's always a crapshoot as to how much money Archer is going to cost this town every time he goes on duty."

"Maybe we ought to put some money in the budget for remedial training for him," suggested Councilman Mel Walker.

"Okay, that's enough," the mayor said. "I'm not going to sit here and listen to you all make Archer the whipping boy for everything that's ever gone wrong at the Sheriff's Department. Fine, Sheriff Weber, have it your way. The budget's approved, as is."

"Wait a minute," Councilwoman McGill said. "There are other items on the Sheriff's budget that..."

"I said the budget is approved," the mayor said rapping his gavel.

"Now you just hold on there a minute, Chet," Councilman Templeton said. "You don't get to just approve a budget on your own, we have to vote on it."

"Why? Whatever Sheriff Weber wants, you give him," the mayor said.

"Because that's the way it's done, Chet. We've all got a copy of the budget in front of us. You're the one that wants to look at every item. If you want to bypass that and make a motion to accept it as is, that's fine."

"All right then," the mayor said, "I make a motion to accept the sheriff's budget as is."

"Seconded," said Councilwoman Gretchen Smith-Abbott, the mayor's confidant and right hand in matters of the Town Council, as well as his lady friend on a personal basis.

Two Council members voted against the budget, Councilwoman McGill and Councilman Adam Hirsch, a short nerdy looking man who had had a grudge against the sheriff ever since high school. Weber wasn't surprised at their nay votes, but he didn't expect the mayor and Councilwoman Smith-Abbott to approve the budget without further argument. He made a mental note that as aggravating as bumbling Deputy Archer Wingate was, he did seem useful in ending the quarterly budget reviews. Even if a lot of the money allocated in the budget was spent to repair things Archer had broken or shot holes in.

~***~

When the sheriff returned to his office, his administrative assistant, Mary Caitlin, looked at him and said, "I just had the weirdest phone call."

"What? Is Hazel Fuller seeing hookers again?"

Hazel was an elderly woman who seemed to be obsessed with prostitutes. She was always calling the Sheriff's Department to complain about suspicious activity. According to her, ladies of the evening frequently solicited business at the boat launch in town, worked out of the library's bookmobile, and took jobs as convenience store clerks on the night shift so they could ply their trade with customers buying beer, cigarettes, or gasoline.

"Nope, it wasn't Hazel."

"Tell me that Arnold Fuller and Harley Willits haven't gotten into a shooting war."

Arnold and Harley were brothers-in-law who lived next door to each other. This was convenient for their wives, sisters who had a close bond, but the two men had been feuding about things for as long as Weber could remember. Harley made it a point to use his snow blower to clean his driveway and the street in front of his house after a snowfall. And when he was done with that he made a pass past Arnold's driveway and made sure to point the machine so that all the snow piled up behind Arnold's truck. Arnold, on the other hand, had watched patiently while Harley had planted and carefully tended a row of hedges to separate their two properties, then casually drove over them with his Toro riding lawnmower. And so it went, one hassle after another. Weber always suspected that if one of the old farts died, the other one wouldn't be far behind, because he would want to harass his nemesis throughout eternity.

"No," Mary said shaking her head. "This was somebody calling to see if your son made it home okay last night."

"Run that by me again, Mary. My son?"

"That's what he said. He wanted to know if your son made it home safely. Is there something you haven't told me, Jimmy?"

"If I've got a kid out there, it's news to me. Who was it that called?"

Mary handed him a pink telephone memo slip, saying, "I didn't put this on your desk because all you do is throw messages away when I do that."

Weber read the name on the memo. Stanley Sheppard, with a telephone number with an area code he did not recognize. "Name's not familiar. Where is 574, Mary?"

"I looked it up. It's in Indiana," Deputy Robyn Fuchette said, then asked, "So why is someone from Indiana that you don't know calling you about a son you don't know about?"

"Beats me," Weber said.

"So *is* there a Little Jimmy running around that we don't know about?"

"No."

"You're absolutely sure about that?"

"Well, as sure as I can be, I guess," Weber answered cautiously. Robyn had a jealous streak in her that she had done well to control in the last year or so, but with their wedding coming up, he wasn't sure how she was going to react. Was it possible that he had a child he didn't know about? Weber had had more than a few girlfriends, as well as a couple of one night stands in the past, so he guessed anything was possible.

Robyn gave him an impish grin and said, "Relax, Jimmy, I'm just pulling your chain. But I would like to find out what that phone call was all about."

"Me, too. Let me call this Sheppard fellow back and see what this is all about."

He went into his private office, sat down at his desk and called the number. The phone rang several times, and then he heard a click and a voicemail message: *Hey there, this is Stanley and Jackie. We must be on the road someplace or out having fun somewhere. Leave a message and we will return your call.* He left

10

his name and number and hung up, not knowing any more than he did before he made the call.

Chapter 3

"So, let me get this straight. Somebody calls and says they're worried about a son you don't know you have, and you're just going to sit here and eat dinner like nothing happened?"

"What should I do, Marsha? I called the guy that left the message and all I got was his voicemail. What would you do if it was you?"

Marsha leaned across the table and put her hand on his and said, "I guess I need to buy you a book, Jimmy. You really don't understand how boys' bodies and girls' bodies are different, do you? Trust me, if I had a kid, I'd know about it!"

"Yeah, I guess it's easier to squirt one in than it is to push one out," her boyfriend, FBI agent Larry Parks said.

"What would you know about it?"

"Hey lady, when it comes to how girls' bodies work, I've done a lot of research on the subject. Trust me, a lot of *hands-on* research. Now, how your minds work? Totally different story." He shook his head and waved his hands in dismissal. "*Nobody* understands that. Not even you ladies."

"Oh, yeah? A lot of research, huh? And I've still got to give you directions each and every time?"

"Don't blame me because you like to micromanage everything."

"Yeah, micro being the key word here," Marsha said.

"Now, that right there? That was hurtful," Parks replied, putting a hangdog expression on his face.

"Well, you know what they say. Sometimes the truth hurts."

"So, I asked Jimmy, and now I'll ask you," Robyn said. "Tell me, are there any Little Larrys running around?"

"I sure hope not," Marsha said. "One of him is enough in the world."

"See, there you go being hurtful again," Parks said, reaching across the table and pulling Marsha's chocolate pudding toward himself. "I'm going to need a second helping of dessert just to get through all this pain."

"Put that back and keep your hands to yourself or I'm going to show you what pain is."

"Back to the question at hand. In all that time you spent in the Navy, could you have left a trail of kids in your wake?"

"Not me, Robyn," Parks assured her. "I was a good sailor."

"The words good and sailor should never be used in the same sentence," Weber said.

"But it's true! Whenever we were in port and the rest of the crew was out drinking and chasing women, I stayed on board and wrote long letters home to mother."

"Yeah, right," Marsha said sarcastically.

"Okay, maybe I didn't spend *every* minute on the ship. I did go ashore at Subic Bay in the Philippines. But keep in mind that I was an innocent farm boy from Oklahoma. It sure didn't take me long to learn why the squids called it Pubic Bay. I saw things there that you wouldn't believe. Shoot, I was there, and *I* don't believe half of what I saw!"

"And did you learn anything from that experience?"

"I did, Marsha. I learned that if you sit down in one of those bars there and buy a dominatrix a few drinks, and the two of you are getting all cozy, never, ever suggest it's time to hit the sack."

Weber laughed so hard he choked, and Robyn had to pound his back to help him breathe. Wiping tears from his eyes, he said, "You are one sick man, Parks."

"See, it's not just me that thinks it," Marsha told Parks, then turned to Robyn. "Speaking of exotic foreign places, have you two decided where you're going on your honeymoon yet?"

"Not really," Robyn said. "We talked about Hawaii, but everybody goes there."

"You stay away from Hawaii," Parks warned. "Between those volcanoes that are burning the islands and sharks waiting by the beach to eat the tourists, it's no place to go."

14

"Nonsense, Parks. The volcano's only on one island. And people swim in the ocean there all the time and don't get eaten by sharks."

"That's only because they're not hungry at the moment. Trust me on this, Robyn. The first thing they taught me in sailor school is that only two things swim in the ocean, sharks and shark food."

"I was thinking about the Pacific Northwest coast," Weber said. "I spent some time up there after what happened with my sister, just trying to get my head straight. I don't think I've seen any place more beautiful in my life."

"They've got sharks there, too," Parks said.

"Enough with the sharks," Marsha told him. "Have you thought about Paris, Robyn? Now there's a romantic place to have a honeymoon."

"Yeah, and no sharks," Parks agreed, then added, "well, not unless your plane crashes into the ocean while you're flying there. Then all bets are off."

Weber's cell phone rang and he pulled it from his pocket. It was dispatcher Kate Copley calling from the office. He pushed the button to answer the call and asked, "What's up, Kate?"

"I'm sorry to bother you off duty, Sheriff, but a Mr. Sheppard called and said he was returning your call. I didn't want to give him your cell phone number, but I told him I would have you call him back."

"Thanks, Kate. I appreciate it."

He ended the call and Robyn looked at him curiously. "Everything okay at work?"

"Yeah. Kate called to tell me that that Sheppard guy called back. The one who called about somebody who's supposed to be my son."

"Well, call him back."

"Yeah, and put it on speakerphone," Marsha said. "I want to hear all the sordid details about your past debaucheries, Jimmy."

Weber ignored her and went into the living room and called Sheppard's number. The man answered on the second ring.

"Mr. Sheppard, Sheriff Weber in Big Lake. How can I help you?"

"Oh, yes, sorry I missed your call earlier. We're in a campground near a place called Cottonwood and we were out hiking. The cell phone service isn't very good around here."

"No problem, sir. I was confused by the 574 area code."

"Oh, that's from Elkhart, Indiana. We travel fulltime in our motorhome, and we just happened to be in the Elkhart area when we got our phones. The reason I was calling, Sheriff, is my wife Jackie and I were worried about your son and hope he made it home okay.

"My son?"

"Yes. We picked him up over in New Mexico when his car broke down and gave him a ride to Springerville. We were taking Highway 60 to Show Low and that was as far as we could take him. But we were worried about him, in the condition he was and all that. I'm sorry we couldn't bring him all the way home."

"Now I'm confused again, Mr. Sheppard. You picked up somebody who said he was my son?"

"Yes, sir. You're Sheriff Weber, right? In Big Lake?"

"That's me."

"And your son's name is James Weber, Junior, right?"

"Well, that's the problem, Mr. Sheppard. I don't have a son by that name. I don't have any kids at all."

There was silence on the other end of the line for a moment, then the man said, "That just doesn't make sense."

"No, it doesn't," Weber replied. "What can you tell me about this person, Mr. Sheppard?"

"He was young, early 20s. Seemed like a very nice young man. He was very polite."

"And you picked him up in New Mexico?"

"Yea, sir."

"Where at in New Mexico?"

"I'm not really sure. We've never been through this area before. I know we passed a place called Pie Town, because we laughed about the name. So it was west of there a ways. We pulled into this picnic area so I could let the dog out to do her business and he was there. He said that old car of his had died and I offered to give him a ride to Springerville."

"What does this kid look like, sir?"

16

"Like I said, early 20s. Average height and weight, dark hair. If he wasn't so banged up he'd have been a good looking young man."

"Banged up?"

"Yes. He said he got in a motorcycle accident, riding his dirt bike. Our grandson did the same thing not too long ago so we can sympathize. But you know what? After we left him off in Springerville, Jackie, that's my wife, she said he looked more like someone had beat him up than if he had been in an accident. She used to work in the hospital ER back home in Ohio before we retired, and she saw her share of people who had been in accidents and people who had been in fights."

"And you think maybe this kid lied about the motorcycle accident? You think he had actually been in a fight?"

"Well, that's what Jackie said. She said somebody who crashed a dirt bike was going to have a lot of scrapes and bruises on their arms. I know our grandson sure did."

"And this boy didn't?"

"No, it was mostly just his face. One of his eyes was closed up and black, his whole face seemed like it was one big bruise, and his lips were split. Oh, and he was missing a couple of teeth. I'll tell you what, Sheriff, whatever happened to him, if it wasn't an accident, it wasn't much of a fight. At least not on his part."

"What you mean by that?"

"I mean that whoever laid into that boy, if that's what really happened, beat the living hell out of him."

Weber talked to the man for a few moments longer, then thanked him for his time and said he would be in touch if he needed anything more.

"Now I'm thinking we were probably pretty dumb for picking somebody up like that," Sheppard said just before the call ended. "I guess he could have been a serial killer or something like that, for all we know. We just saw a kid in trouble and wanted to help."

"That's very good of you," Weber told him. "And I can understand why you would want to do that. If I really did have a son and he was in a situation like that, I'd sure feel grateful to somebody for helping him out. But at the same time, in this day and age you just never know."

When he went back into the kitchen everybody looked at him expectantly. He sat down and Marsha asked, "So?"

"So what?"

"Come on, Jimmy, inquiring minds want to know. What's the deal with your mystery son?"

"I don't know a lot more than I did before the telephone call," he told her, then shared the information that Sheppard had given him.

"So why do you suppose somebody is running around saying they're your son?"

"I don't know. This Sheppard fellow that gave him a ride said his car was some kind of beat up foreign job. He thought it might have been a Toyota, but he's not good on cars. I guess I could have dispatch call the Highway Patrol over in New Mexico and see if anybody reported an abandoned car along US 60 west of Pie Town."

"This whole thing is just weird," Robyn said. "Do you think it's something like an identity theft or what?"

"I have no idea," Weber replied. "I guess it could be something like that. Or just some wack-a-doodle, for all I know."

"Yeah, but if someone was trying to do an identity theft thing, why would they claim to be your son? I mean, saying they are you would be one thing. But your son?"

"It beats me, Marsha. But just so you know, while you've been worrying about all of this, Parks has been eating your dessert."

Marsha sent her boyfriend a seething look, and Parks paused with a spoonful of chocolate pudding halfway to his mouth. "Hey, don't be trying to divert attention to me, Bubba. You're the one with the bastard kid."

Chapter 4

"Got a message for you from a Sergeant Holmes with the New Mexico State Police," Mary Caitlin told Weber the next morning when he arrived at the office. "Apparently you called about an abandoned car or something?"

"Yeah, what did he say?"

"They did recover a stolen car abandoned on US 60 yesterday. Here's his number."

Weber poured himself a cup of coffee, then took the memo slip to his office and dialed the number. When Sergeant Holmes answered he identified himself.

"Oh, yeah. You were asking about any abandoned cars found on US 60?"

"That's right," Weber told him.

"We did find an old Honda Civic yesterday. A real beater. It was reported stolen from Indian Wells the day before."

"Where is Indian Wells? I'm not familiar with it, Sergeant."

"It's a few miles north of Alamogordo on US 54. Not much more than a wide spot in the road. A couple of convenience stores, two or three rundown mobile home parks, that's about it."

"Any idea on who took it?"

"Hard to say. Like I said, it was a beater. A 1983 that was about ready to fall apart. To be honest with you, I'm surprised it made it all the way to where it did. What's this all about, Sheriff?"

"I'm not sure, to be honest with you. I got a phone call from someone saying they had picked up a young man whose car broke down west of Pie Town and they gave him a ride to Springerville, which is about 25 miles from here. He told them he was my son, but I don't have any kids."

"That's strange."

"I thought so, too. What happened with the Honda?"

"According to the report I have here, the officer who found it ran the numbers and saw it was stolen and had dispatch contact the registered owner, a woman by the name of Jill Delarose. She's unemployed and living hand to mouth and said she didn't have the money to have it towed. So I guess it will eventually get sold for scrap and crushed. It's not worth much, if anything."

"I don't suppose your people ran fingerprints or anything, did they?"

"Come on, Sheriff. You know how it is. We're not talking about any kind of major crime here."

Weber was tempted to tell him that if you are just trying to get by, living hand to mouth, the loss of your car no matter how old and worn out it was, could be a major crime from your perspective. But he didn't. There was no use creating friction over what was probably a nothing case anyway.

"If it's important to you, I guess I could have somebody fingerprint it."

Weber realized that it would probably be a waste of time anyway. There was no telling how many people had been in and out of that old car, and without a set of prints to compare any they found with, it wasn't worth the effort.

"No, that's okay, Sergeant Holmes. I appreciate your time."

"Anytime, Sheriff Weber."

Robyn knocked on his door, then came in. "Did you find out anything?"

Weber shook his head. "Not really. New Mexico State Police recovered a stolen Honda that had been dumped in a picnic area between Pie Town and the state line. I guess it's a real junker, the owner didn't even want it back. Or couldn't afford to get it back, anyway."

"That's it?"

"That's it. We don't even know if it's the same car that this person calling himself my son was driving. I assume it is, given the location and timing, but who knows?"

Robyn sat on the edge of his desk and said, "Look, Jimmy, I know what you're thinking."

"You do? What am I thinking?"

"You're worried that if it turns out you do have a son you didn't know about, it's going to become an issue between us. But it's not, okay?"

"I really don't think I have a kid out there I don't know about."

"Probably not, but it's possible, right? I mean you have a certain history, shall we say?"

"Yeah, it's possible but..."

"All I'm saying is that the past is the past, Jimmy. So don't sweat it, okay? Now, if someone showed up here with a baby in her arms, that would be a different story. But anything older than three or four years is none of my business, as far as I'm concerned. That was before I was part of your life."

"I appreciate that," he told her.

"So, let's play what if, Jimmy. If you really do have a kid, are you going to teach him how to throw a baseball and start a campfire and all that dad stuff?"

"*If* I have a kid, and that's a very big if, from the way that Sheppard fellow described him, he's old enough to have learned all of that a long time ago."

"Do you ever think about having children, Jimmy? I mean, with me not being able to, do you think someday you'll feel like you missed something?"

Before he could answer, Mary knocked on his door and then pushed it open. "Jimmy, you'd better get out here. Archer just broke the window out on his patrol car."

Weber closed his eyes and sighed, then opened them and looked at Robyn. "Don't worry about it. I'm not interested in having any kids. Raising Archer is hard enough."

The sheriff stood with his hands on his hips, shaking his head as he looked at the pieces of tempered glass littering the parking lot and the inside of the patrol car.

"Do you want to explain how this happened, Archer?"

"I'm sorry, Jimmy. I didn't want you to yell at me."

"Why would I do that, Archer?"

"Because I locked my keys in the car."

"You locked your keys in your car, so you busted the window to get in. Is that what you're telling me? And you did this because you didn't want me to yell at you?"

"I know how mad you got the last two times I did it."

"That's true, Archer, because the last two times made a total of five times you locked your keys in your car. Now you're up to six."

"I'm sorry," Archer repeated, hanging his head.

"Archer, do you remember that I gave you an extra key for your car just in case something like this happened again? And do you remember I told you to keep track of that extra key?"

"Yeah, I remember."

"So why didn't you use your extra key to unlock the door?"

"I couldn't, Jimmy."

"Why couldn't you?"

"Because I put it on my key ring with my other keys. And they were locked inside the car."

Weber felt a headache coming on and tried to remain calm.

"Archer, do you understand how dumb it was to put your spare key on the same key ring with everything else?"

"I didn't want to lose it."

The headache was coming on strong.

"So instead of making me mad by telling me you locked your keys in the car again, you decided to break the window out?"

Archer nodded his head.

"You didn't think that would make me mad, too?"

"I thought that if I broke the window out I could go get it fixed before you found out about it."

Somebody was inside his head pounding on an anvil with a sledgehammer. He had stopped drinking long ago, but the headache was worse than the worst hangover he had ever had. Weber couldn't deal with it, and he couldn't deal with his sad excuse for a deputy.

"Archer, you don't just go down to the auto parts store and buy a new window and slap it in. They have to be ordered, and that takes time."

"I didn't know that."

Weber pulled his cell phone from his pocket and looked at the display. "It says it's 49° today, Archer. And the low tonight's going to be in the 30s. I hope you've got a lot of warm clothes to wear, because you're going to be driving around in a car with no window until it gets replaced."

"That's gonna be cold, Jimmy."

"Yes it is, Archer. What can I say? It's March in the mountains. Maybe you'll get lucky and a warm front will come through. Then again, we could have a blizzard. It's happened this time of year before." The sheriff didn't add that he was secretly hoping for the blizzard. Whoever was pounding that anvil had been joined by a friend with a drum set and cymbals.

"I don't suppose..."

"You don't suppose what, Archer?"

"I don't suppose I could use somebody else's car until my window gets fixed?"

"So then they would be driving around in a car with no window?"

"No, Jimmy, we could swap off when we change shifts."

Weber knew if he suggested something like that he would have a mutiny among the rest of his deputies. Archer's ability to damage vehicles and equipment was well known throughout the department.

"Dress warm, Archer. Dress warm."

He turned away and walked back into the building, Robyn following closely behind. "I think you handled that very well, *Dad*," she said.

Nick Russell

Chapter 5

Two days went by with Weber and his deputies handling the routine duties of the Big Lake Sheriff's Department. They were in a transition season, warm enough that much of the snow had melted and Cat Mountain Ski Resort had shut down their runs and the skiers were not filling the town's restaurants and shops, but it was still too cold for the fishermen to start heading to the mountains and for the summer people who came to town to escape the desert heat of Phoenix and Tucson to arrive. The locals enjoyed the slowdown and the respite from the flatlanders, recalling the good old days when things moved at a more relaxed pace. They conveniently forgot that in the old days some of them could not find work and barely eked by. Not that many of the new businesses that had opened in the last few years offered high paying jobs. Many were minimum wage positions for retail store clerks and food service workers. But at least it was something.

The slowdown didn't mean the deputies had nothing to do. Dolan Reed spent most of an afternoon trying to coax Mildred Harper's reluctant cat down from the highest branches of an oak tree. When the cat refused to cooperate, Dolan borrowed an extension ladder from a neighbor and crawled up to retrieve the cat. It repaid his effort by leaving scratches on his hands and both arms, destroying his uniform shirt in the process. Deputies Dan Wright and Jordan Northcutt were sent out with a folder full of warrants for people who had failed to appear in court on various misdemeanor charges like traffic violations and disturbing the peace citations. Word always spreads fast in a small town, and by the time they had arrested the fourth miscreant people started showing up at the Town Clerk's office to pay their fines and Judge Harold Ryman's courtroom on their own to avoid a visit from the deputies. Deputy Tommy Frost attended a two-day seminar in Phoenix on recognizing people with autism and how to interact with them when they came into contact with law enforcement personnel. Meanwhile, Archer Wingate was posted to the high school to slow down traffic when the students left at the end of the day. He spent much of the time napping in spite of the chilly air coming in from his car's missing window.

And, of course, there were the frequent flyers; people the Sheriff's Department came into contact with on a regular basis. Deputy Ted "Coop" Cooper stopped James Brunson for having an expired tag on the license plate of his beat up SUV, only to discover that the plate was from another vehicle, and that Brunson's drivers license was suspended. He also did not have proof of the state required mandatory insurance. Brunson never did care about things like that and made up his own rules as he went along. Coop cited him for the license tag and insurance violations and arrested him for driving on a suspended license.

Deputy Robyn Fuchette was called to the Town Pump, where an intoxicated customer named Levi Bischoff refused to leave the store when Virginia Ingram, the manager, would not sell him a twelve-pack of beer. Levi was generally a likable local young man who would give anybody the shirt off his back under most circumstances. Unfortunately, when he started drinking his personality changed. He became querulous and wanted to argue about anything and everything. He demanded that Virginia sell him the beer he wanted and had started calling her every foul name he could think of when she refused. But Levi quieted down quickly when Robyn appeared on the scene. They had tangled back in December when he started an argument at the Big Lake Brewpub and he had made the mistake of shoving her out of his way when she responded to the call to remove him. Thirty seconds later he had found himself face down on the floor, Robyn's knee in the small of his back while she locked her pink handcuffs on his wrists. The face plant and the night he spent in jail were bad enough, but having all of his friends tease him about how the petite woman deputy with the pink handcuffs had taken him down in the first place was too much to bear. He apologized sheepishly to Virginia and locked his car. Robyn gave him a ride home with orders to sleep it off before he left the house again.

Deputies Buz Carelton and Chad Summers responded to a neighbor's complaint about a loud argument going on at the

Prichard house and arrived to find Jerry and Melissa Prichard pelting one another with plates, cups, and saucers while they tried to outdo each other hurling insults. This was a regular occurrence, and more than once Big Lake's deputies had wondered how the couple had managed to stay together for over 25 years without committing serious bodily harm upon either of them. When Buz and Chad separated them, Melissa said she wanted her husband out once and for all. Jerry responded by claiming she wanted him gone so she could move in her latest boyfriend. Having heard it all many times before, Buz told them both to shut up, then he and Chad went into a huddle and decided the best way to solve the problem, at least for the time being, was to arrest them both for domestic violence. This stunned Jerry and Melissa because it had never happened before. Oh, sure, one or the other had sometimes been taken away in handcuffs, and the one left behind had promptly gone down and bailed them out of jail. No matter how bad the argument had been, they always left holding hands and cooing words of love to each other. Now, with both of them in custody, they weren't sure what to do. They asked if they could ride together in the back of one or the other deputy's vehicles so they could hold hands. Chad allowed them to do that, but drew the line at putting them in the same cell, saying they didn't allow conjugal visits.

So when Hazel Fuller called to report the peeping Tom, nobody gave it much thought. While the elderly woman's dedication to keeping Big Lake free from the scourge of prostitution was legendary, she also kept a close eye on her neighbors and reported anything else she considered out of the ordinary to the Sheriff's Department. When her neighbor Elaine Barwick traded in her ancient Ford Pinto for a new Kia Soul, Hazel reported it as a suspicious car in the neighborhood three days in a row. When a new UPS driver was assigned to the route and dropped off a package at her door, Hazel called to say she was worried it might be a bomb left by a terrorist. It wasn't; it was an order of multivitamins intended for someone else on her street and delivered to her house by mistake. If the local kids walked by her house, Hazel called to report loiterers. If they ran past while playing, she called to report that they might be fleeing from some pervert who was attempting to kidnap them.

Deputy Tommy Frost listened patiently while Hazel described the big, burly man she had seen lurking around her neighbor's house, looking in the windows the night before, and how she had spotted him again that afternoon sitting in his vehicle spying on the neighborhood with binoculars.

"Which house was he looking in the windows of, Ms. Fuller?"

"Juliette Murdoch's, right next door there," she said, pointing at her neighbor's house.

"And what time was this?"

"It must have been about 2 A.M. Yes, I'm sure it was real close to 2 A.M, because I got up to go to the bathroom and I looked out and saw him."

"Where was he, ma'am?"

"He was on the side of Juliette's, between our two houses."

"And he was looking in the windows?"

"That's what it seemed like to me. Of course, the blinds were all closed, so I don't think he could see anything. But he was definitely trying to!"

"Ms. Fuller, why didn't you call us then?"

"Because it was 2 A.M.! The last thing I want is a bunch of police showing up waking up all the neighbors. Besides, I wasn't wearing my glasses. And when I went and got them from the bedroom and came back he was gone."

"Do you think you may have dreamed this, Ms. Fuller?"

"Who do you think you're talking to, Tommy Frost? Do I look like some senile old woman to you, young man?"

"No ma'am, not at all. It's just sometimes I have a dream and it seems real to me when it isn't."

"Than I suggest you drink a glass of warm milk before you go to bed every night. Maybe that will help. But I know what I saw!"

"Yes, ma'am. Then you saw him back again today?"

"I assume it was the same man. He never got out of his car."

"Can you describe the vehicle he was in,

"It was dark colored. But it wasn't black, at least I don't think so. More like a real dark blue. Or maybe dark green."

"Was it a car, or a truck, or an SUV?"

"It was one of those things it looks like a station wagon but it's not. You know, like a truck only it's not."

"So an SUV?"

"If that's what you call it? Like what Sheriff Weber drives."

"Yes, ma'am. Did you happen to get a license plate number?"

"No, I didn't. I just peeked out and saw him sitting there with those binoculars of his."

"And just where was he parked at, ma'am?"

"Down there in front of the Alden's house. He was parked there for at least half an hour."

"Okay, when did he leave?"

"He was there when I called you, but he was gone by the time you got here. I don't know why it takes you people so long to come out when I call. Sometimes I think you just ignore me, or think I'm crazy or something."

"No, ma'am, not at all," Tommy lied.

"Well, I should hope not. I'm just being a good citizen!"

"Yes ma'am, and we appreciate that. I'll tell you what, I'm going to keep an eye out for that vehicle, and I'll tell the other deputies to keep an eye out, too. And if you see it, or the man you saw prowling around Mrs. Murdoch's house, you call us right away, okay? Day or night, it doesn't matter."

"I'll call," she told him. "But I won't hold my breath waiting for you people to get out here."

Nick Russell

Chapter 6

Except for the occasional ribbing he received from Mary Caitlin, Robyn, or Parks, Weber had pretty much filed the thing about his mysterious "son" away in the back of his head and didn't give it much thought. Whoever Stanley Sheppard and his wife had given a ride to, he had not made his presence known in Big Lake, if he ever made it that far after they dropped him off in Springerville.

Weber was just leaving Todd Norton's auto parts store, where he had gone to drop off a check for the replacement window for Archer's patrol car, when his cell phone rang. He pulled it out of his pocket, looked at the caller ID, and sighed.

"Good afternoon, Ms. Fuller. How are you doing today?"

"I'm vexed, Sheriff. That's how I'm doing!"

"I'm sorry to hear that, ma'am. What can I do for you?"

"That car was back here again."

Tommy had filed away his report on his visit with Hazel Fuller the day before, not bothering to share the information with the other deputies because nobody ever took her seriously. So Weber didn't know what she was talking about.

"I'm afraid I'm going to need you to tell me a little bit more, Ms. Fuller. What car we talking about?"

"The peeping Tom, that's what car I'm talking about! Tommy Frost was out here yesterday and I told him all about it. Don't you people ever talk to each other?"

"I'm sorry, ma'am, it's been pretty busy around the office lately. There was a peeping Tom? When was this?"

"I'm not going to go through the whole thing with you all over again, Sheriff. Talk to Tommy, he took a report. At least he said he did. I know you people think I'm crazy, but I know what I saw!"

"Okay, calm down," Weber told her. "I'll get with Tommy and figure out what's going on. In the meantime, there's a suspicious car hanging around your place?"

"There was, but he's gone now. I called your office and the dispatcher said she'd get somebody to come by as soon as she could. But that was twenty minutes ago. He's long gone now!"

"My apologies," Weber told her. "I'll talk to Tommy and we'll get to the bottom of this."

"I should hope so. I don't know what kind of pervert he is, but you need to lock him up!"

"Yes, ma'am. I'll call Tommy right now."

Weber pushed the button to end the call, then drove back to the sheriff's office. Judy Troutman looked up and waved from the dispatch desk when he walked in. "Did Ms. Fuller call you?"

"Yeah, she called, Judy."

"She called here saying something about a peeping Tom. I guess Tommy was out there the other day and took a report, and now she says he's back. When she called I had two units out on a roll over accident at the Y, and Robyn is in court testifying on the DelTondo case. I told her I'd get someone there as soon as possible, but she didn't take kindly to that."

"We've got instant coffee and instant oatmeal, but sometimes we don't have instant cops," Weber said. "What's happening with the accident? Any injuries?"

"One that I know of," Judy said. "Tommy called in to say the ambulance was on scene just as you walked in the door. They're going to transport the injured person to the hospital in Show Low."

"Okay. When he clears, ask him to drive by Ms. Fuller's place again, will you?"

"I will, but he's not going to look forward to that."

"He doesn't need to stop and listen to her babble, just do a drive by and see if he sees this vehicle she keeps talking about."

~***~

Two hours later Tommy showed up at the office and knocked on Weber's door. "Jimmy, I went by Ms. Fuller's place again and I didn't see that SUV she's talking about anywhere around. I'm sorry I didn't put the word out about it but, you know, it's Ms. Fuller."

"I know," Weber told him. "For all we know it was the UPS man again, or something like that. Don't worry too much about it,

32

okay? Hazel has never been right about anything yet that I can remember. What's going on with your accident victim?"

"He's going to live, but he's not going home tonight, or anytime soon. The EMTs said he has a broken collarbone and probably some broken ribs, too, along with facial lacerations."

"Any idea what happened?"

"He said he swerved to miss a couple of elk that were alongside the road and then overcorrected and lost control. Looks like he was probably doing at least 70."

"Anybody else injured?"

Tommy shook his head. "No, he was alone. A fellow from St. John's, name of Clarkson. I contacted his wife by telephone and she's on her way to meet him at the ER in Show Low."

"Good work, Tommy. Do me a favor and mention this mysterious car or whatever it is to the other deputies, just to appease Ms. Fuller, will you? Like I said, I'm sure it's nothing, but if she sees one of our units going by her place now and then maybe she'll chill out for a while."

As soon as Tommy left his office Mary Caitlin came in with a manila folder in her hand. She put it on Weber's desk and said, "Don't forget you have to go to the Friends of the Library meeting this afternoon. You should probably get a move on."

"Can't you send somebody else? You know I hate stuff like that. A bunch of old biddies who get together to gossip more than anything else."

"Hey, watch your mouth. I'm going to become an old biddy and sit around gossiping one of these days."

"You're never gonna get old, Mary. You'll be young at heart until you're 90. And even then, you'll still have the body of an 85-year-old."

"Oh, you sweet talking devil. But you're wasting your time. You can suck up all you want and it's still not going to get you out of going to that meeting. Now get it in gear, Jimmy."

"Hey, here's an idea. You're the one that said you're gonna become an old biddy someday. Maybe *you* should go and get a head start. Lord knows, if there's any gossip to be heard in this town you know all about it."

That much was true. Mary, an attractive woman in her 60s, was a walking, talking encyclopedia about the people who lived in Big Lake and their often complex family trees. Mary knew who was married to who, who had been in trouble with the law in the past, who was stepping out on their spouse, and everything else there was to know. But she wasn't a gossip by any means. She was happy to give Weber and his deputies information they needed about anybody when it came to fulfilling their duties, but otherwise she was closed mouth and respected other people's privacy.

"Are you trying to get rid of me already, Jimmy? Do you think it's time to put me out to pasture? Didn't you just say I was never going to get old?"

"That's what I said. *You're* the one who was talking about becoming a gossipy old biddy. I just thought this would be an opportunity for you to get your feet wet while you're still on the town's payroll. Kind of an on-the-job training type of thing."

"You know what, Jimmy? I grew up in Big Lake and I've been around cattle and horses and cowboys all my life. Not to mention being married to Pete Caitlin forever. So trust me, I can smell bullshit. And I'm not buying any of it. Get your ass in gear and get to that meeting."

Weber sighed and stood up reluctantly, picking up the folder. "I guess I need to get used to a woman ordering me around since I'm getting married."

Mary laughed and poked him in the ribs, saying, "What you mean *get used to it*? I've been telling you what to do since you were a youngster. And just so you know, I've been giving Robyn a few pointers now and then about how to keep you in line."

"Thanks a lot," the sheriff said as he walked out the door. "Nice to know you've got my back, Mary."

~***~

The Friends of the Library meeting was just as boring as he suspected it would be. After the reading of the minutes from the last meeting and a treasurers report stating that they had just over $900 in their fund, the president of the small group opened the floor to discussion.

Alice Fournier, who volunteered at the library as well as being active in the Friends group, suggested that it was time to get an Ancestry subscription, since so many patrons came in asking about genealogical research. After some discussion about the cost of the subscription, as well as whether the library had Internet access sufficient to support such activity, a vote was taken and Alice was authorized to go forward with the project.

Beatrice DeLong was next up, and she droned on and on for what seemed like an hour, talking about how much profanity had been found in the new paperbacks that had been appearing on the library's shelves. This launched a spirited debate about censorship and the First Amendment.

With that behind them and nothing settled, the next order of business was to discuss an upcoming reading by Wilbur Nehring of his autobiography, *Journal of a Cowboy*. Wilbur had grown up on a ranch near Big Lake, and at 82 he was still spry and sharp minded. Weber wasn't much of a reader, but he had picked up a copy of the book and found it fascinating. So many of the experiences Wilbur had had growing up generations earlier reflected Weber's own youth on his family's small ranch.

Once all of the details were worked out for Wilbur's reading, Dorothy Swafford announced that it was time for a question-and-answer session with the sheriff. Weber, who was never comfortable with public speaking, steeled himself for the barrage of questions that was sure to come. And they did. Beatrice DeLong asked Weber if there was anything he could do about the pornography appearing in the new paperbacks.

"It's not pornography," Cheryl Mason said. "You need to get with the times, Beatrice. Have you watched TV much lately? There is nothing in those books that isn't on TV every night during prime time."

"No, I don't watch TV, Cheryl. And that's the reason why!"

"I'm sorry, ladies, it's not our job to proofread all the books coming into the library to make sure that they meet everyone's different tastes," Weber said.

"What about the parking situation out in front? We have seven regular parking spaces and one handicapped space. There are times when they are all taken and people have to park across the street at Gaylord Kuykendall's place. He hasn't complained about it because his accounting business doesn't get that much traffic, but it just doesn't seem fair."

"That's something you'll have to take up with the Town Council," Weber said. "If there's room, maybe they can add a couple more parking spaces out front, or maybe on the side." Personally he didn't know how the small doublewide mobile home that had been converted into a library could hold very many people at one time as it was.

"Sheriff, what can you tell us about the DelTondo case? I understand his hearing was today."

"That's right, Mrs. Carver," Weber replied. "But I don't have any information about what's happening with that at this time."

"Do you think Judge Ryman is going to sentence him to the maximum?"

"I really can't say what the judge is going to do. That's up to him. I'm sure he'll be fair."

"Well, I certainly hope he put's that man away forever. There's just no excuse for what he did."

Anthony DelTondo had moved to Big Lake the year before, and quickly made himself known to the Sheriff's Department because he was a habitual drunken driver. The fact that his license was suspended, and that he had served six months in jail down in Pima County for his past offenses didn't stop him from drinking, or driving. A few months earlier he had stumbled out of the Antler Inn, climbed behind the wheel of his Ford pickup, and started home. He never made it. Instead, he had run a stop sign and broadsided a minivan with Allison Dubois at the wheel. The young mother of three, who was on her way home from her job at the Brennan's Dress For Less, was killed instantly. Robyn, who shopped at the store and had become friends with the victim, was the first deputy on the scene. After checking Allison's vital signs and realizing she was gone, it had been her job to pull DelTondo from his wrecked truck and place him under arrest, charged with vehicular manslaughter.

"Ladies, if there's nothing else that you need from me, I'd better get back to the office," Weber said, standing up.

"So soon? We were hoping you could tell us more about... well, about anything happening in town," Louise Carver said with disappointment in her voice.

"Most of it you can find out in the newspaper, just like I do," Weber replied. "Now, if you will excuse me, I've got some things I have to handle back at the office."

Weber got back in his Explorer, shaking his head, and looked at his wristwatch. "Well, that's two hours out of my life that I'll never get back," he said as he started the engine and drove away from the library.

Nick Russell

Chapter 7

It was late in the day and Weber was just climbing into his Explorer to go home when Tommy came over the radio and said, "Dispatch, this is Big Lake 9. I'm on Alderbrook Way and I just saw a dark blue SUV pulling away from the curb a few houses down from Ms. Fuller's. He's headed north toward Sycamore Circle."

Weber keyed his microphone and said, "Do you have a plate number on that vehicle, Tommy?"

"Negative. It's an out-of-state plate. I think New Mexico, but I had to turn around because I was going the other direction so I'm not sure. Do you want me to catch up and stop him?"

"Negative," Weber said. "Hold back but keep him in sight. I'm headed your way and should be there in a couple of minutes."

Weber didn't want to create a scene stopping some innocent person based on Hazel Fuller's paranoia, but at the same time, if there was a suspicious vehicle loitering around town, he wanted to know who was in it and what they were up to. He took Lincoln Avenue to avoid the traffic on Main Street, even though there wasn't much this time of year, and turned left onto Creekside Drive. A block later he came to Sycamore Circle. His timing was spot on and he was stopped at the stop sign at the intersection of Creekside and Sycamore Circle as a dark blue Chevrolet Tahoe with a New Mexico license plate drove past. The windows were tinted darkly and Weber couldn't see who was behind the wheel. A moment later Tommy's patrol unit came by and Weber swung in behind him.

"Let's go ahead and pull him over," Weber said into his microphone. "Those windows look pretty dark, we'll use that as probable cause."

They closed in on the back of the SUV and Weber saw Tommy's roof lights come on. The vehicle pulled to the curb and they both parked behind him. Tommy called in the license plate number to dispatch, and Judy Troutman told him to stand by, the computers were running slow for some reason. That wasn't unheard of. Getting out of their units, Weber said, "You take the driver's side, but be careful with those dark windows until we know who's in there." He approached the vehicle from the passenger side, looking carefully for any signs of danger.

When they got to the front of the Tahoe, both front windows were down. A large man who looked to be in his 50s was in the driver's seat, both hands on top of the steering wheel. Weber looked in the front passenger's window and didn't see anybody in the back of the vehicle.

"Good afternoon, sir," Tommy said. "I'm Deputy Frost with the Sheriff's Department. Are you the only person in this vehicle?"

"Just me, Deputy."

"Would you mind putting down the back windows so we can see, just for officer safety?"

"Sure, no problem. I'm taking my left hand off the steering wheel to do that. Nothing else, just putting down those windows."

Weber could tell the man had had experience dealing with law enforcement in the past. His movements were slow and deliberate, giving them no reason to suspect a problem. The windows rolled down and Weber had a better look in back.

"It's clear," he told Tommy.

"We appreciate your cooperation, sir," Tommy told the driver. "Can I see your license and registration, and proof of insurance, please?"

"No problem, Deputy. Before I do that, I need to tell you that my registration and insurance card are in the console, and there's a handgun in there."

Weber put his hand on his Kimber .45 semiautomatic pistol as a precaution. Arizona's gun laws were relaxed as to who could carry a firearm in their vehicle or on their person, and he didn't doubt that half the vehicles in Big Lake contained some kind of gun."

"Okay, instead of doing that, would you mind stepping out of the vehicle, sir?

"Whatever you say, Deputy. I've also got a handgun in a holster on my belt. I'm a cop."

"Okay, just step out and keep your hands in the clear, please."

The man reached his left arm through the window and opened the Tahoe's door from the outside, then got out, keeping his hands up and away from his sides. Weber crossed around the front of the vehicle as the man turned to face the Tahoe on Tommy's instructions. As he had told them, there was a pistol in a holster on his left hip. He put his hands on the side of the SUV and stepped back and spread his feet without being told to. Tommy stepped forward and removed the pistol from the holster, handing it to Weber, then he patted the man down. His trouser pockets held a wallet and a money clip with several bills inside. There was nothing in his jacket pockets.

Weber opened the wallet and saw a gold badge and an identification card from the Cañon Verde Police Department with the man's name and picture on it. A New Mexico driver's license was issued to the same man.

"It says here you are Police Chief Arthur Kramer from Cañon Verde, New Mexico."

"That's right."

"Okay, you can take your hands down and relax, Chief Kramer. I'm Sheriff Jim Weber and this is Deputy Tommy Frost. Sorry to pull you over, but your windows are tinted pretty dark. I think more than Arizona allows for."

"No problem, Sheriff," the man said reaching to shake their hands. "To tell you the truth, they're probably too dark for New Mexico, too. But they come in handy sometimes when I'm on a stakeout or something like that."

The dispatcher radioed back and Tommy stepped away while she told him who the vehicle was registered to, then nodded at Weber.

The sheriff handed the man's weapon, money clip, and wallet back to him.

"So what brings you to Big Lake, Chief Kramer?"

"Call me Art."

Weber nodded, then added, "Everybody calls me Jimmy."

"So am I getting a ticket for my windows?" Kramer asked with a smile.

"I guess we'll let that one pass," Weber replied. "Professional courtesy."

"I appreciate that, Sheriff."

"We appreciate your cooperation. It makes it easier for everybody when we walk up on a vehicle and the person behind the wheel goes out of their way to keep things safe for everybody. It doesn't always happen that way."

"Don't I know it. Last month I stopped a car with a couple of maggots in it and almost blew the one behind the wheel away when he reached down under his seat real quick. Turned out the asshole was just looking for his wallet, but I had no idea what he was going to come up with in his hand."

"Been there, done that," Weber said. He studied the man casually as they talked. The New Mexico police chief was a big man with dark hair slicked back and a thick mustache. He stood over six feet tall and was broad shouldered. There was a bit of a gut on him but he didn't look out of shape. He carried himself well and exhibited confidence that gave Weber the feeling that he was a man who could handle any kind of problem he might encounter on the job. But he also noticed something else about the man. Like a lot of police officers, Kramer didn't seem completely forthcoming. He knew that was a caution that many people who wore a badge showed around strangers, even fellow cops, until they got to know them.

"You didn't mention why you were here in Big Lake, Art. We've still got a few weeks before the fish start biting, and you don't look like much of a skier to me."

"No, if I tried that I'd probably spend more time falling on my ass than I did skiing," Kramer said with a chuckle. "Which one are you, Sheriff, a skier or a fisherman?"

"Oh, I've been known to wet a line now and then when I have time," Weber replied. "But I think if I got up there on the ski slopes I'd be falling down on my ass right beside you."

Weber laughed with him, then his face grew serious. "Getting back to my original question, why is a police chief from New Mexico here in Big Lake, Art?"

"Do you ask every stranger who comes to town that question, Sheriff? Or just out of town cops?"

"Well, right now I'm asking you."

"Would it be a problem if I said I'm just passing through? It's a free country, right? I mean, isn't that what all the pukes tell us when we bust them?"

"I've heard that more than once," Weber said, nodding. "But we're kind of off the beaten path here and we don't get that many people who are just passing through. And this little neighborhood you're in isn't even on the route through town."

"Hey, Sheriff Weber, I don't know what the problem is but I don't appreciate the interrogation."

"I didn't realize there was an interrogation going on," Weber said.

"Okay, maybe I was just a little oversensitive about all the questions," Kramer said. "Sorry about that. I didn't realize we were just three cops standing around shooting the shit."

"As far as I know that's all it is. Just three guys visiting."

"Fine. Sorry if I came off wrong. I'm usually the guy asking the questions."

"No problem," Weber told him.

"Well then, if it's all the same to you, I guess I'll be on my way. Nice talking to you, Sheriff Weber. And you too, Deputy."

He got back in his Tahoe, started the engine, nodded his head at them and drove away.

Tommy stood next to the sheriff as they watched the SUV go out of sight around the corner and asked, "What was that all about?"

"I don't know, Tommy. But whatever that guy is up to, he's not just passing through town."

Chapter 8

"So he drove off, just like that? With no explanation about why he was parked by Hazel's house?"

"Nope. Not a word."

"Maybe he was just passing through town like he said, Jimmy. Maybe it's just a coincidence that he was pulled over to the curb by her place. Maybe he was checking his cell phone or something like that. I guess it's possible, right?"

"Anything's possible, Robyn. But he was hiding something."

"What makes you think that?"

"A couple of things. The first is that instead of explaining why he was in the neighborhood, he answered questions with questions or changed the subject. And he went from him calling me by my first name when we started talking to him to calling me Sheriff when I began asking him questions. Not to mention the fact that Hazel reported the same vehicle more than once over a couple of days."

They were sitting on Robyn's couch after dinner. A rerun of an old sitcom was on TV but neither of them was paying much attention to it.

"But the guy's legit, right? He's the police chief of some town over in New Mexico?"

"Yeah, that much is true. I called Judy and asked her to find the number for the police department over there in Cañon Verde. I called and asked to talk to the chief and they said he was on vacation and was expected back in a couple of days."

"Where is this Cañon Verde, anyway? I don't think I've ever heard of it."

"Neither have I," Weber said. "It's in eastern New Mexico, a little north of Carlsbad. I get the impression it's about the same size as Big Lake."

"So what happens now? Do you give the guy the benefit of the doubt or do you check him out more?"

"I don't know," Weber said. "I hate to think bad of a fellow police officer, but something about him was hinkey. I'm going to have everybody keep an eye out for his vehicle in case he's still hanging around town and not just passing through like he claimed."

"But you don't believe that?"

Weber shook his head. "No, I don't. Not for a minute."

They had been sitting side-by-side holding hands, but Robyn moved to the far end of the couch and put her feet in his lap. "You know what's good to do when you're trying to figure out something like this, Jimmy? Giving me a foot rub."

"Really? And how does that help?"

"Because it's mindless work. You can do that and let your brain just do its thing, and who knows what you might come up with?" She playfully rubbed the heel of one foot along the inside of his thigh.

"Yeah, I can see how that might work," he agreed, pulling her socks off and beginning to rub her feet.

The foot rub didn't last very long. Five minutes after he started Weber's cell phone rang. Still massaging Robyn's instep with one hand, he picked the phone up with the other and looked at the caller ID.

"If I ever figure out who gave Hazel Fuller my cell phone number, I'm going to kick their ass."

"It's 7 o'clock. What the heck is she doing calling you at this time of night?"

"I don't know. Maybe hookers are doing business on her front porch or something."

Weber pushed the button to answer, but it wasn't hookers that Hazel was calling about this time.

"Sheriff, he's back."

"Who's back?"

"That same car. The one I called about before."

"Really?" Weber took his hands off Robyn's feet and sat forward. "Are you sure it's the same vehicle, Ms. Fuller?"

"Yes, it is. He's backed into the driveway of the McCleary place, four doors down. I know it doesn't belong there because they haven't come up for the summer yet. I don't know what he's up to, Sheriff, but it's no good."

"Okay, you sit tight. I'll be there in a few minutes."

He ended the call and stood up.

"I'm afraid your foot rub is going to have to wait, Robyn."

"The same car is back again?"

"Yeah. I'm going to go check it out."

Robyn sat up and began pulling her socks back on. "I'm going with you."

"No need for that."

"I don't care. I'm going."

"He's another cop, Robyn. I'm just going to go have a talk with him. I don't think there's any danger involved."

"Probably not," she said. "But if whatever he is up to is keeping you from rubbing my feet and us from... whatever he's up to, I want to know."

They were both out of uniform, but stuck their weapons in their belts before leaving her house. Not because they were meeting a stranger on a dark street, but because it was routine. If you are a cop, even a small town cop, credit cards aren't the only thing you never leave home without.

~***~

Weber pulled across the end of the McCleary driveway and got out of the Explorer. Robyn got out on her side and they approached the Tahoe. The front windows came down and Weber shined his flashlight on the man behind the wheel.

"We meet again, Chief Kramer. Why do I get the feeling you're not just passing through my town?"

"Yeah, that wasn't exactly true, Sheriff. Sorry about that."

"How about you tell me why you're really here?"

"I'm working."

"Really? Because when I talked to your office over there in Cañon Verde they told me you were on vacation."

"You checked up on me?"

"Yeah, I did."

"How about we call it a working vacation?"

"How about we cut through the bullshit, Chief? I don't appreciate you coming into my town unannounced and playing games like this."

Kramer sighed and seemed to contemplate his next move before saying, "Okay, I'm after a fugitive."

"A fugitive? Here in Big Lake? Does this fugitive have a name?"

"Yeah, Zachary Murdoch."

Weber knew who Zach Murdoch was. A few years earlier he had arrested Zach and his twin brother Josh for vandalizing vacant summer cabins. The twins' mother, Juliette, had been enraged, calling her sons' actions no more than youthful pranks and not something worth destroying their futures over. Their victims, who had to replace broken windows and doors and shattered plumbing fixtures, did not find it funny at all. Over time, Juliette had mellowed out a bit, and whenever the sheriff interacted with her in her capacity as the Chamber of Commerce director, things had been civil between them. The last he had heard, one of the boys had joined the military, and he had lost track of the other one. Weber figured they must be in their early 20s by now.

"I haven't seen Zach in a long time. What did he do?"

"What did he do? I'll tell you what he did, Sheriff Weber. He murdered a woman. Murdered her right in front of me, and then tried to shoot me before he escaped."

That surprised Weber. As foolish as Zach and Josh had been in vandalizing the cabins, when it came right down to it, their crimes had been exactly what their mother said, foolish pranks by bored kids with nothing better to do with their time. Judge Ryman, who always had a soft spot in his heart for young people, had put them both on probation, ordered them to pay restitution to the people whose cabins they had damaged, and specified that they had to earn the money themselves to do so. It couldn't come from their mother. He had also ordered both of them to perform 300 hours of community service and mandated that the time be spent mowing lawns and doing repair work on the homes of the elderly and less fortunate in Big Lake.

While some thought that might be no more than a slap on the wrist, Weber had seen both boys shoulder their responsibilities well, without complaining or trying to shirk the jobs assigned to them. He couldn't picture Zach or Josh committing any kind of violent crime, but he had been a lawman long enough to know that anybody was capable of anything under the right circumstances.

"And you think Zach is here in Big Lake?"

"I know he's not stupid enough to be anywhere around Cañon Verde, because if he was he'd be shot on sight. I figured this is as good a place as any to find him. You've been around long enough to know that when maggots get in trouble, a lot of them run right home to mama, expecting her to make it all better, Sheriff."

"And you didn't think it was appropriate to come to my office and let me know you were in town or what you're up to?"

"I'm sorry about that," Kramer said. "You're right, I should have done that first. My bad."

"So why did you lie to me when I asked you why you're in town?"

"I didn't exactly lie," Kramer said. "I just didn't tell you the whole story."

"No, you lied," Weber said. "You said you were just passing through town."

"It was kind of a white lie, that's all."

"Bullshit. That's like saying you're just a little bit pregnant. Either you are or you aren't."

"All right, let's say I was a little bit evasive. But I had my reasons."

"How about we stop wasting time doing this dance and you tell me what those reasons are?"

"Come on, Sheriff, it's a small town. You and I both know how things work."

"Apparently I don't. So how about you tell me how things work, Chief?"

"All I'm saying is that in small towns everybody knows everybody, and you have relationships with people. Take this kid's mother. The way I hear it, she's some kind of mover and shaker around here."

"She runs the Chamber of Commerce. I hope you're not suggesting that just because I know Juliette Murdoch I would do something to hinder a lawful police investigation. Because if you are suggesting that, you and I have another problem."

"Easy there, Sheriff Weber," Kramer said holding his hands up palms outward toward the Tahoe's steering wheel. "I didn't mean to offend anybody."

"Guys, are we going to stand here in the dark and the cold and talk about this all night?"

Kramer leaned down and looked at Robyn, standing on the passenger side of his vehicle.

"That's Deputy Fuchette," Weber told him. "And she's right. Do you have reason to believe that Zach Murdoch is at his mother's house?"

"I don't have any hard evidence that he's there, Sheriff. Just a hunch based on a lot of years of experience."

"Well, how about we go find out?"

"Just like that?"

"Yeah, just like that," Weber said.

Chapter 9

They walked up the street to Juliette Murdoch's house. It was a wooden-framed one-story building with an attached garage on the right side and a porch with a white railing. There were lights on in the living room and further back in the house.

"Robyn, how about you go around to the back in case this kid is in there and tries to slip out?"

She broke away from them and moved toward the rear of the house. Weber waited a couple of minutes to give her time to get in position, then turned to Kramer and said, "I know this woman, so let's don't come on like gangbusters, okay? Let me do the talking."

"It's your town, Sheriff. We'll do it your way."

They walked up the gravel path to the porch and climbed the two wooden steps onto it. Weber pushed the doorbell button and heard it chime inside. A moment later the porch light came on and Juliette Murdoch moved the blinds aside to look at them through a window next to the door. They heard the lock click and she opened the door.

"Jimmy, what are you doing here this time of night?"

"Sorry to bother you, Juliette," he replied. "This is Chief Kramer from Cañon Verde, New Mexico. Can we come in?"

She tightened her bathrobe around herself and said, "Well, I'm not really dressed for company... "

"We'll just be a minute. It's kind of important, Juliette."

"Okay, sure." She stepped back to allow them in. "What's this all about?"

"Juliette, is Zach here?"

"Zach? No," she said, shaking her head. "Zach hasn't lived here in almost two years. What's going on? Has something happened to him?"

"No, not that I know of. But there was an incident over in New Mexico that Chief Kramer here needs to talk to him about."

"An incident? What kind of incident?"

"Do you know how to get a hold of your son? I really need to talk to him," Kramer said.

"I've got a cell phone number, if that helps."

She turned and went into the living room and they followed. The TV was on but muted to some reality program and a cup of tea was sitting on a small table next to a blue fabric covered recliner. There was a cell phone on the same table and she picked it up and pushed the button to bring up the display.

"Here, let me write the number down for you." She pulled open a drawer on the table and took out a notepad and pen and wrote down the phone number, then tore the piece of paper off and handed to Weber.

"Juliette, would you mind calling him?"

"You're scaring me, Jimmy. Is everything okay?"

"We're trying to figure that out now," he told her. "Would you mind making that call?"

She nodded and pushed the button to call her son, then handed the telephone to Weber. It rang five times and then went to voicemail. "*This is Zach. You know what to do. I'll call you back when I can.*" Weber pushed the button to end the call and handed the phone back to her.

"When was the last time you talked to Zach, Juliette?"

"I don't know. It's been a week or two. He was doing construction work over around El Paso for a while, and the last time I talked to him he told me he was in New Mexico trying to get on with a pipeline crew somewhere in that area. Can you please tell me what's going on, Jimmy?"

"So he hasn't called or been around at all? That's what you're telling us?"

"No. Like I just told Jimmy, I haven't talked to him in a couple of weeks. Can you please tell me what this is all about?"

Weber felt a bit of irritation that Kramer wasn't following his directions to let him handle the interview, but before he could say anything else, the other man turned and started toward the back of the house.

"Where are you going? What's this all about?"

"I'm just having a look around to be sure, that's all."

"Can he do that without a warrant, Jimmy?"

"Why do I need a warrant, unless you've got something to hide? Do you know that harboring a fugitive is a felony, lady? If you don't tell us where he is right now you'll be sitting in prison right along with your son."

"Okay, that's enough," Weber said. "Chief, stand down right now. She said her son isn't here and she doesn't know where he is. That's good enough for me."

"And you're going to believe her, just like that?"

"Yes, I am."

Kramer scowled at him but Weber ignored him and turned back to Juliette. "I'm sorry about all of this. We'll get out of your way now."

"I really wish you could tell me what's going on."

"What's going on is that your son..."

"I said that's enough," Weber said sharply, and Kramer stopped midsentence and glared at him.

"Juliette, when I know something I'll be in touch. Again, sorry to bother you so late."

She nodded and they walked to the front door with her behind them. Kramer put his hand on the knob and opened the door, and Juliette said, "Oh, Jimmy, I forgot something."

Both men turned their heads to her, expectantly. "Your mother came by my office at the Chamber of Commerce today asking me for that cookbook she loaned me. She needs it back because she's making something special for your father's birthday this week. You can save her a trip into town if you take it now. Can you hold on just a second and I'll get it for you?"

"Sure."

She left them there and came back a moment later with a cookbook with a red and white checked cover. "There you go. And tell her I'm looking forward to that trip to Phoenix we were talking about. I'm making a list of all the quilt shops we want to visit."

"I'll do that, Juliette," Weber promised, taking the book from her. "Again, sorry to bother you so late."

They walked back to where their vehicles were parked, Robyn joining them along the way.

"I don't believe a word that woman said," Kramer said. "That kid's in the house, or else she knows where he's at."

"We don't have any evidence of that," Weber told him.

"I tell you, she was lying to us! Otherwise why wouldn't she let us search the house without a warrant?"

"If you showed up at my house this time a night unannounced, wanting to search it without a warrant, I would tell you to go to hell," Weber replied.

"So that's it? You're just going to take her word for it?"

"For the time being, yeah. Now, how about we go down to my office and you can tell me all about the charges against this kid? Then we'll take it from there."

"And meanwhile he hauls ass and is in the wind. What we need to do is we need to go back right now and knock that door down and find that murdering little son of a bitch and drag him out of there!"

"I don't know how you do things back home in New Mexico," Weber said. "But around here we don't go to the homes of solid citizens and kick in doors in the middle of the night. You've got two choices, Chief Kramer. We can go back to my office and talk about this, or you can get in your car and you can haul ass out of my town and not come back. Which is it going to be?"

"So that's the way you want to play it, Sheriff?"

"You heard me."

Kramer pointed his finger at Weber and said, "This kind of bullshit right here, that's why I didn't touch base with you in the first place. Like I said, I know how small towns work."

"And like I said, you've got two choices. I don't plan to stand around in the dark all night long waiting for you to decide. Which is it going to be?"

"Fine, have it your way. I'll follow you to your office."

"I'll tell you what, how about I ride with you and Deputy Fuchette here can drive my unit?"

"What, do you expect me to make a run for it or something?"

"Nope, that thought never entered my mind," Weber told him. "I just figured with it being after dark and you being from out of town, I'll keep you from getting lost."

"Fine, have it your way. Be sure to buckle your seatbelt when you get in, I wouldn't want you breaking the law."

Weber handed the keys to the Explorer to Robyn, then got in the passenger seat of the Tahoe.

Nick Russell

Chapter 10

"Okay, start at the beginning."

Weber, Robyn, and Kramer were seated in his office with cups of coffee. The out-of-town police chief seemed to have calmed down and wasn't displaying the anger he had after they left Juliette Murdoch's house.

"This Zach Murdoch kid is a real piece of shit. He was living with a girl named Claudia Bukowski. She's a druggy who makes her money peddling her ass to anybody who will have her. The guys around town call her Claudia Chlamydia. Sorry about that, ma'am," Kramer said, nodding to Robyn. "Didn't mean to be crude."

"I've heard worse," she told him.

"One of my officers popped Murdoch for driving on an expired tag. In the subsequent search of the vehicle he found drugs, so he arrested him. Murdoch claimed the drugs weren't his and said it was his girlfriend's car. That much was true, but he was in possession of it, so it was on him. He resisted arrest and there was a scuffle. The kid got the worst of it, and as soon as my officer got him to the jail he started whining and crying about being injured. Like a fat lip and a couple little scrapes were going to kill him. But I took him to the ER at our little urgent care center just to shut him up. This nurse on duty there, a real nice lady named Barbara Eibeck, always felt sorry for the young ones when they got in trouble. I can't tell you how many times I tried to tell her that there's no hope for that kind, but she wouldn't listen. She told me to take the handcuffs off of him, and when I told her that was against our protocol she insisted. I know I shouldn't have done it, but I did. And that's something I'm going to regret for the rest of my life, Sheriff."

"What happened?"

"It was all my fault. I shouldn't have taken the damn handcuffs off of the little bastard in the first place, but I did, just to make

Barbara happy. Then there was a problem out in the hallway because they brought in some drunk Mexican who was fighting with a couple of the other medical people on duty. I swear, I only stepped out of the exam room for a minute, and as soon as that beaner saw me, he knew it was time to stop that bullshit and he quieted right down. I run a tight ship and the drunks and the wetbacks know better than to get out of line whenever I'm around."

Weber had spent enough time around the man to believe that Chief Kramer wasn't above doling out some nightstick justice when he felt it was necessary. He couldn't completely fault him for that, because he had given a few lessons in proper citizenship to those who needed it in his time, too. But he suspected the police chief took pleasure in it, which was something Weber never had.

"That was all it took, just that minute," Kramer said. "When I went back in the room Murdoch was choking Barbara. I tried to pull him off of her but it was like he was on angel dust or some shit like that. I'm a big guy, but he was as strong as a gorilla. He dropped her and came at me and grabbed my weapon and started pulling it out of the holster. I think if he would have gotten his hands on it, he'd have killed me. When he couldn't get my weapon loose, he picked up the stool next to the exam table and slammed it into my chest, legs first. Like I said, he was really wired on something. A kid his size wouldn't have that much strength normally. He knocked me flat on my ass and was raising that chair up to brain me with it. I managed to roll out of the way and got my weapon out, but that didn't phase him at all. Tell you the truth, I should have shot the little bastard right then. And I was about to. But he threw that chair at me and took off running like a striped ass ape. By the time I got on my feet he was gone. I checked on Barbara real quick and couldn't find a pulse. I was yelling for help, but everybody was so busy with that damn Mexican out in the hallway they couldn't even hear what was going on. By the time I ran out and got somebody to take care of her, Murdoch was gone."

Kramer shook his head and closed his eyes for a long minute. When he opened them he said, "That woman's blood is on my hands, Sheriff. I never should've taken the cuffs off of him, and I never should've stepped out in the hallway to see what was going on with that drunk they were dealing with. I screwed up. I screwed up big time. She would still be alive if I'd have followed the procedures that I tell my officers to follow. So I take it personally. It may be wrong to do that, and the way I handled things when I got here to Big Lake may not have been professional, but that's the way it is. Barbara was a nice woman. I'm sure you work closely with the people at your hospital or medical center or whatever you have here, too, so maybe you get where I'm coming from."

"Yeah, I do," Weber told him.

"So, no hard feelings?"

The sheriff shook his head. "I've been known to take things personally myself," he said looking at Robyn, who had witnessed him stepping over the line a time or two in the past. "Look, why don't you get a motel room for the night and come back in the morning, and we'll figure out how to handle this. If Juliette Murdoch knows where her son is, maybe I can think of some way to get her to cooperate with us. If not, we'll go see Judge Ryman and see about getting a search warrant.

"Fair enough," Kramer said. "I'll trust your judgment, Sheriff Weber."

"Okay, how about we get together here at 8:30 in the morning? I'll buy you breakfast."

"Sounds like a plan," Kramer said, standing up and shaking his hand. He turned to Robyn and nodded and said, "Nice to meet you, Deputy. I just wish it was under better circumstances."

When he left Robyn looked at Weber and asked, "What do you think?"

"If what he said went down the way he told us, I'd probably feel the same way he does."

"So does this mean we go back to my place and you finish my foot rub?"

"No, I need to go back and talk to Juliette Murdoch again."

"Juliette? Why?"

"To find out why she lied to us," Weber said.

~***~

"What makes you think Juliette lied to you?"

"This cookbook," Weber said, holding up the book that she had given him before he left her house with Kramer.

"A cookbook? I don't get it, Jimmy."

"She said my mother stopped by her office and she needed this book back that she had loaned to Juliette, because she was planning a big dinner for my father's birthday this week. She also said that she and my mother were planning a trip down to Phoenix to go to some quilt shops or something like that."

"But your parents have been dead for a long time. She must know that, right?"

"Yeah, she knows it," Weber said. "Her mother and mine were friends. She was telling me that something wasn't on the up and up. She also kept calling me Jimmy. I think she's gotten over me arresting her kids back in the day, but we've never been on a first name basis."

It was almost 10 o'clock. They had driven by the Mountain Mist Motel to be sure that Kramer had checked in and was settled for the night, and now they were pulling into Juliette Murdoch's driveway. The same lights were on in the house, and when Weber rang the doorbell the porch light came on. The window blinds moved and she peered out, then opened the door and looked past him.

"It's just me and Robyn," Weber said. "I promise, just the two of us."

Juliette nodded nervously and stepped back to let them inside.

"I brought your cookbook back."

"I didn't know what else to do," Juliette said, shaking her head. "I'm sorry for lying to you, but he would have killed Zach if he found him here." Her eyes were red and puffy and it was obvious she had been crying.

"Where is he, Juliette?"

"He didn't kill that woman, Sheriff. I swear he didn't."

"Are we back to Sheriff, now? A little while ago I was Jimmy."

"I just... I just didn't know what to do! I was hoping you would pick up on that. Well, that and the cookbook, and that story about your mother coming to see me and all that."

"Where is Zach, Juliette?"

"I swear to you, he didn't kill that woman."

"You already said that. If it's true, he'll have his day in court and he can tell his story," Weber told her.

She shook her head. "No, you don't understand. He'll never make it to court. He'll never make it back to New Mexico. If that man gets his hands on him, he's going to kill Zach."

"Why would he do that, Juliette? The man's the police chief over there, not some kind of psycho."

"Oh, he's a psycho all right," she said nodding her head. "He's the one that killed that woman, not Zach. He did it! And then he tried to put the blame on Zach."

"Come on, Juliette, do you really believe it happened like that?"

"It's true. He killed that woman, not me. I swear I'm telling the truth, Sheriff. And my mom's right. If Chief Kramer finds me, he's going to kill me, too!"

Weber turned to see a young man standing in the hallway. He had to do a double take to realize it was Zach Murdoch. The boy he knew had grown taller and filled out, but that wasn't why he didn't recognize him at first. It was his mutilated face. One eye was swollen closed and his entire face looked like someone had used it for a punching bag. Used it long and hard. When he opened his mouth to speak Weber could see broken and missing teeth. He was shirtless and there were more deep bruises on his torso. Stanley Sheppard had not been exaggerating when he said that somebody had beat the living hell out of the young man he and his wife had picked up in New Mexico.

"Let me guess," the sheriff said. "You got a ride from somebody in a camper and told them you're my son, didn't you?"

Nick Russell

Chapter 11

"I was afraid once those folks with the motorhome saw how banged up I was they'd change their minds and leave me standing out there in the middle of nowhere. So I thought if I told them you were my dad it might make them feel a little better about me."

"Were you driving a stolen car that you dumped there in New Mexico, Zach?"

"Yeah, but I can explain."

"Turn around and put your hands behind you," Weber said, then realized he was in civilian clothes and didn't have his handcuffs with him. He turned to Robyn and asked, "Do you have any cuffs with you?"

"No," she said shaking her head. "I didn't think we would be arresting anybody."

"Wait, you can't arrest him," Juliette said.

"I have no choice, Juliette. He's a fugitive from justice."

"But he told you he didn't kill that woman!"

"I know, but that's for the court to decide. And he just admitted he was driving a stolen car."

"Please, Sheriff, just let me explain."

"Okay," Weber said, "but before you say another word I'm going to tell you your rights."

He didn't need a Miranda card, he had memorized the routine years ago. After informing the young man of his right to remain silent and telling him that anything he said could and would be used against him in a court of law, and that he had a right to an attorney and if he could not afford an attorney one would be appointed for him, and that he could refuse to talk at any time, Weber asked him if he understood all of that.

"Yeah, I understand."

"Okay, and you still want to talk to me?"

"Yeah, that's why I came here."

"You escaped from custody and stole a car so you could come here and talk to me?"

"Well, yeah. I knew that Chief Kramer was going to kill me. That's why I escaped. And I came here because I know I can trust you."

"What makes you think you can trust me any more than any other police officer, Zach?"

"Because... because back when me and Josh got in trouble you treated us right, Sheriff. We knew what we did was wrong, and you didn't rough us up or nothing like that. You didn't let us make any excuses for it, but you didn't treat us like we were animals or anything like that."

"Zach, breaking into some cabins and tearing them up is a lot different than killing somebody. "

"I didn't kill that woman! I swear to God, Sheriff, I didn't."

"I heard you the first time. You didn't kill her, Police Chief Kramer did. And you expect me to believe that?"

"My son's not a murderer, Sheriff Weber!"

Weber held up his hand to silence Juliette and said, "You need to stay out of this right now and let Zach answer the questions."

"You have to believe me, Sheriff. I'm not denying I was driving a car with some pot and a bong in it, but they weren't mine. It was my girlfriend's car, and if I had known about it I would've never driven it. I got busted for possession last year and I was only six weeks away from ending my probation. No way was I going to do something that stupid when I had been clean all that time. And yeah, I stole that other car. But I did it because I knew that if Chief Kramer caught me he was going to kill me. I just wanted to get back here and talk to you. I figured if I told you my story you could help me."

"Even if I did believe you, Zach, and at this point I don't, how do you expect me to help you out?"

"Just don't let Chief Kramer take me away and kill me. Please? Put me in touch with somebody so I can tell them what really happened to that lady at the hospital. That's all I'm asking. I'll confess to driving the car with Claudia's stuff in it and I'll confess to stealing that other car to try to get home. But I didn't fight with that first cop that arrested me and he's not the one who beat me up. That was Chief Kramer. And I swear, I never killed that woman."

"When did you get back to town, Zach?"

"Three days ago."

"Three days? You came here to ask me to help you, but you've been here three days and I had to come and find you?"

"That was my fault, Sheriff. Zach was so exhausted he slept for over twelve hours once he got here. He wanted to talk to you as soon as he woke up, but I kept telling him to wait. I was trying to figure out what to do next. I didn't know if I should call an attorney or what was best."

"What was best was to call me," Weber said with exasperation. "Jesus, Juliette, it's not like he was accused of shoplifting or something! This is serious."

"Don't you think I know that? My son's life is at stake. I wasn't going to jump the gun and let you take him and just turn him over to that animal."

She was shouting, and Robyn stepped between the two of them. "Just calm down, Juliette. There's no need to yell."

The other woman closed her eyes for a moment, then opened them and nodded her head. "You're right, I'm sorry. I'm just so afraid of what might happen to Zach. He really did want to call you as soon as he got here, Sheriff. I'm the one that told him not to. Just look at him. Can you understand why I did that? Why I didn't want that man to get his hands on him again?"

Weber looked at her son. There was no question that Zach's injuries were far more extensive than the fat lip and minor scrapes Chief Kramer had described. He didn't believe the young man's story. Not yet. But Chief Kramer had obviously not been upfront with him right from the start either.

"All right, here's what we're going to do. First of all, Robyn, I want you to call dispatch and see if there is an open warrant for Zach."

She pulled out her cell phone and dialed Dispatch. While she was doing that, Weber examined the young man's injuries. Usually after that much time bruises would have started to fade, but the beating administered to Zach had been severe. When Weber probed his side he winced and made a sharp yelp.

"I think you got some broken ribs. Does it hurt when you bend over or try to twist your torso?"

"Yeah, it hurts a lot," Zach replied.

"Try taking a deep breath."

The young man tried but stopped with a painful grimace.

"Sorry, I can't. It hurts too much."

"Open your mouth."

He did and Weber examined his ruined teeth.

"Okay, close your mouth. And you're saying that Chief Kramer did this when you were being arrested?"

"No, sir. That's not what I said. I didn't have any problem with the cop that arrested me. This happened after I got to the jail. Once I was in my cell."

"And why did he do all of this to you?"

"Because he's an animal, that's why he did it," Juliette said, then stopped and raised her hand and shook her head. "I'm sorry, I'll be quiet."

"Why did he do this, Zach? Were you giving them any trouble once you got to the jail?"

"No. I was doing everything they told me to do. They took my picture and fingerprinted me and all that, and then they put me in a cell. A couple minutes later Chief Kramer showed up and started asking me how much drugs me and Claudia were selling. I told him I didn't know anything about selling drugs and that the stuff they found in that backpack in the car was hers. He didn't believe me and kept telling me if I would cooperate she would be the one to go down, not me. I told him there was nothing to say because I didn't know anything about anyone selling drugs and I knew Claudia wasn't dealing. Then he said something dirty and... well, that's when things got bad."

"He said something dirty? What did he say?"

Zach looked at his mother, obviously uncomfortable, and she said, "Do you want me to go in the other room?"

"Yeah, Mom. For minute."

She patted his arm, then walked out of the living room.

"Okay, Zach, your mom's gone. What did Chief Kramer say that set this all off?"

"He said if I told him about Claudia selling drugs she'd be the one to go down instead of me. And when I told him again that I didn't know anything about that, and that I knew she smoked pot, but I didn't think she was selling drugs, he told me again that one of us was going to go down. Then he said that Claudia had a lot of experience going down, she'd gone down on most of the guys in town. And he said if I didn't cooperate, he was going to bring some other prisoners into the cell that would teach me all about how to go down, and that when they were done with me I'd be as good at it as Claudia was. I got scared and I called him a dirty name. That really set him off and he came in the cell and started beating on me."

"Did you resist, Zach? Did you fight back?"

"No! I knew if I did he'd kill me. Besides, I've only been in a couple of fights in my life and I got my butt kicked both times. I put up my hands and tried to keep him from hitting me in the face, and then he kicked me in the nuts and I hit the floor. Then he started kicking me. Kicking me and kicking me. Finally two other cops came in and pulled him off of me and told him that was enough. One of them looked me over and said I needed to go to the hospital and he was going to call the ambulance. Then Chief Kramer, he said no, he'd take me himself. The one cop, the one that arrested me, he didn't want him to do that. He said he would take me, but the chief wouldn't let him do it. He told him if he wanted to keep his job, he needed to get back on the street and mind his own business."

"What happened at the hospital, Zach?"

"He took me in and this nurse, the one who got killed, as soon as she saw me she asked him what happened to me. He told her I got injured resisting arrest. I could tell she didn't believe that because she gave him this look and called him a bar... a barbary or something like that."

"A barbarian?"

"Yes, ma'am, that's it," he told Robyn. "She called him a barbarian and told him that that was the last time that was going to happen. Then there was some kind of a fight or something out in the hallway because there was a lot of noise. Chief Kramer went out to see what was going on. That's when the nurse took out her cell phone and started taking pictures of me. Then Chief Kramer came back in the room and saw what she was doing and told her to stop. She said I wasn't the first prisoner he had beat up, but if she had anything to do with it I was going to be the last. She said she was going to go to the authorities and put a stop to it. Chief Kramer told her to mind her own damn business and to get me cleaned up so he could take me back to jail. She said no, that she was going to have proof of what he had done to me. He tried to grab the phone away from her and she slapped him. That's when he did it. He grabbed her by the throat and slammed her against the wall and started choking her. I was handcuffed to the bed and I tried to get up but I couldn't. I started to yell for help and he hit me in the side of my head with his elbow. It didn't knock me out but it really made me see stars. And all the while he was choking that woman. Then her body kind of went limp and he let go of her and she fell down. He leaned over and put his fingers on her neck like he was checking her pulse or something, then he stood up and poked his head out the door of the exam room like he was making sure nobody was there. He closed the door and unhooked my handcuffs and told me I was dead. He pulled out his gun, and I know he was gonna shoot me and blame me for killing her. So I jumped off the bed and grabbed this chair that was next to it and I hit him with it. I hit him as hard as I could and knocked him down. He dropped his gun and it slid under the bed. He was trying to get to it, and I knew if he did he'd shoot me, so I hit him with the chair again. Then I ran out of the room and there was an exit door right there at the end of the hall and I went through it and I kept on running."

Juliette had come back into the room by then and put her hand out to gently rub her son's back.

"Were you high that night, Zach?"

"No! I used to smoke pot, but I stopped a long time ago."

Zach looked at his mother apologetically. If Juliette was distressed over his admission of using marijuana, she was too concerned for his well being to show it.

"How long is a long time?"

"About six months."

"Have you used any other drugs, Zach?"

"No, never."

"How about angel dust, PCP?"

"No. Like I said, I smoked a little pot, but that was all. That other stuff," he shook his head, "no way would I mess with any of that."

"Zach, when you ran away from the hospital did you think about calling 911 and asking for help?"

"Who were they going to send? Chief Kramer and some of his cops? No, I didn't think about it, I just got as far away from there as I could as fast as I could. Out in the parking lot there were a couple of Mexican guys getting into a pickup truck and I asked them to please help me. One of them asked what happened to me and I told him that Chief Kramer had beat me up. He told me to get in, and they took off. He said usually the cops beat up on the Mexicans, but he knew white boys got some of it, too. They drove me out of town and dropped me off at another guy's house that they knew. They told him I needed help and that Chief Kramer had done this to me. I got the feeling he'd been in the chief's jail, too. He gave me a different shirt and said he would take me to Alamogordo. I'll be honest, Sheriff, I think he was probably some kind of criminal, because he had all kind of tattoos on him and he just looked pretty scary. But not as scary as going back and dealing with Chief Kramer. He drove me to Alamogordo and he was drinking all the while and talking craziness about going back and killing all the cops in town. By the time we got to Alamogordo he was really wiped out and I was almost as afraid that he'd wreck the car and kill me as I was about what would happen to me if I got caught. When he let me out I tried hitchhiking and after a couple hours somebody picked me up and they took me to this real tiny little place and dropped me off. They said they were going back to some ranch someplace. I didn't know what to do, and that's when I found that Honda with the keys in it. I hated to steal it, but I knew standing out there in the middle of nowhere trying to catch a ride, it was only a matter of time until I got caught. I copied the owner's name and address from the registration, and I really planned to send them some money to make up for it. It wasn't much of a car, but I guess it's probably all they had, and I really felt bad about it. But I didn't have any other choice. Then the car broke down and those people in the RV gave me a ride to Springerville, and I hitchhiked back to Big Lake. That's about all there is to tell. I hope you believe me."

Chapter 12

Weber didn't know what to believe. Zach's story sounded pretty outlandish, but at the same time, the young man seemed sincere. And there was still the fact that Police Chief Kramer had been elusive with him from the start. But no matter who was telling the truth, Zachary Murdoch needed medical attention before anything else was done.

"Here's what we're going to do," he told Zach and his mother. "There is a warrant out for Zach for first-degree murder in New Mexico. I can't just ignore that. But at the same time, Chief Kramer can't just take him back across state lines. There are procedures that have to be followed."

"Procedures? What kind of procedures, Sheriff?"

"Juliette, how about you go back to calling me Jimmy? There's been a lot of water under the bridge and I think we're beyond the formalities, don't you?"

She nodded her head and said, "I just don't want that man to get his hands on Zach. You've heard what he's capable of."

"I've heard Zach's side of the story," Weber told her.

"But you don't believe him?"

"I don't know what to believe at this point, to tell you the truth. But I do believe our justice system works. I'm not saying that there aren't bad cops out there, because there are. Whether Chief Kramer is one of the good guys or the bad guys remains to be seen. But like I said, he can't just take Zach and go. It doesn't work that way. There has to be a motion filed to extradite him, and Zach can fight that motion. When he does, there will be a hearing and he can tell his story. Meanwhile, if you can get anyone else to back up what Zach has told us, that will go a long way toward helping him."

"So you're saying that they might not be able to take him back to New Mexico?"

"No, Juliette, that's not what I'm saying. One way or the other, Zach is going to have to go back to New Mexico to answer the charges against him. But that doesn't mean he has to go back with Chief Kramer, and he doesn't necessarily have to go back to Cañon Verde. If what he's saying is true, if there's any way to prove any of this, the state authorities are going to step in and it will be out of Chief Kramer's hands."

"I'm just so terrified of what might happen to him."

"I understand that," Weber told her. "Right now, we need to get him to the Medical Center and get him checked out. I'm sure he's got some busted ribs."

"And then what happens?"

"Then I'm going to put him in my jail, and first thing tomorrow morning I'm going to start making some telephone calls and see if we can get to the bottom of this. Meanwhile, you need to find an attorney to represent Zach, okay?"

She nodded her head, then asked, "How do I know that Chief Kramer won't come to your jail and take him? Or worse?"

"That's not going to happen, Juliette. Not while he's in my custody. Zach said he came back here because he trusted me to do the right thing. You need to trust me, too. Can you do that?"

She looked Weber in the eye, seeking some kind of reassurance. Apparently she found it there, because she finally nodded her head.

"Okay. Yes, I trust you. I trust you to protect my son, Jimmy."

"All right, Zach, since I don't have any handcuffs on me, you need to promise me you're not going to try to run away or anything like that."

He shook his head. "I promise, Sheriff. I've run as far as I need to. I'm not going to give you any problems."

~***~

"Somebody definitely administered a real beat down to that young man," Doctor Priya Patel said an hour later after examining Zach Murdoch and wrapping his ribs. "I did my internship at an ER on the south side of Chicago and I've seen a lot of beating victims. Whoever worked him over really did a job on him."

Big Lake's newest doctor watched from out in the hall as a nurse helped Zach out of the examination gown and back into his clothing. Though he did not know her well, Weber liked what he had seen of the new doctor. She was a short, somewhat rounded woman with mocha skin, dark features, and amazingly white teeth who had excelled in medical school and came to Big Lake because as a single mother she wanted to raise her son in a small town away from the crime and pollution she had seen in the big city. Weber wasn't sure what the story was about her husband, but he had heard the man had died just about the time she was finishing her internship. In his observations of her, she was gentle and kind with her patients, cordial to the staff she worked with, and very professional when it came to practicing medicine.

"You wouldn't say this was result of a minor scuffle with a police officer while he was being arrested?"

She shook her head and looked at him sharply. "No, and I really hope you don't expect me to say something like that, Sheriff Weber."

"Not at all," he told her. "He sustained his injuries long before he ever got to town. I'm just trying to decide if the story he told me is the truth or not."

"I have no idea what story he may have told you," Dr. Patel said. "But whatever happened to him, it wasn't just a scuffle or anything like that. Somebody took the time to beat him. It was methodical and it was brutal."

"Did the x-rays show any internal injuries except for the broken ribs?"

"No, though I am surprised he didn't have a punctured lung to go along with everything else."

"Do you need to keep him here for observation or anything like that?"

"If he had just suffered his injuries I would say yes. But since it's been a few days, I don't expect him to collapse at this point. I would like to take another look at him in a couple of days to follow up, if that's possible. And he needs to see a dentist for his mouth injuries. May I ask what happened to him, Sheriff Weber?"

"To be honest with you, I don't know the whole story yet," he told her. "That's what I'm trying to figure out now."

Zach was dressed now and the doctor went to the door of the examining room. "That shot I gave you for pain is going to be wearing off in another hour or so. Because you're in police custody I can't give any kind of medicines directly to you to take with you, but I am going to give Sheriff Weber some pain pills for you. You need to take them every four hours as needed, all right?"

"Yes, ma'am," Zach replied. "I really appreciate it."

"If you begin coughing and any blood comes out, you need to get right back here. Do you understand that?"

"Yes, ma'am."

"I mean it. That could be a sign of a punctured lung. Sheriff Weber, your people need to know that, too. If he starts exhibiting any symptoms like that, get him back here right away."

"We will," he promised. He didn't know what kind of experiences she had had with law enforcement in the past, but he sensed a certain amount of skepticism on her part. But she nodded her head and went off to get some pain pills for the prisoner.

As he was waiting for her to get the meds, Weber's phone rang. The caller ID told him it was Dispatch.

"What's going on, Kate?"

"I'm sorry to bother you after midnight, Jimmy, but there's a disturbance at Juliette Murdoch's house on Alderbrook Way. Dan Wright and Coop are there, and apparently some policeman from New Mexico."

~***~

They made a fast trip to the sheriff's office and Weber took Zach inside.

"Kate, please put this young man in Cell Four. His name is Zach Murdoch, and if anybody comes in or calls asking about him, you don't know anything. I don't care who it is, you've never heard his name and you don't know anything about him. Got it?"

"Sure thing, Jimmy."

"You go with Ms. Copley," Weber told Zach. "And don't worry, things are going to be all right."

He started for the door then turned back to Kate and said, "Nobody goes back in the cellblock except our own officers. Nobody. As far as you know, it's empty back there."

"Got it, Jimmy."

But he was on his way out the door and never heard her.

Chapter 13

Flashing red and blue lights lit up the homes on Alderbrook Way and a dozen neighbors stood around in the cold night air bundled in robes and blankets when Weber and Robyn arrived. Juliette Murdoch's porch light was on and her front door was hanging askew. The mini blinds on the window next to the door were sagging down from one side. Deputy Ted "Coop" Cooper, standing on the porch, nodded to them.

"Sorry to bring you out so late at night, Jimmy, but we've got a mess on our hands here."

"What happened, Coop?"

"Ms. Murdoch called 911 and said someone was breaking into her house. Dan and I got here within half a minute of each other and the door was hanging open and there was a lot of yelling coming from inside. At first we didn't know if it was a domestic disturbance or what was going on. We went in and found that fellow there ransacking the place, and Ms. Murdoch was screaming and telling him to get out of there." Coop indicated the back of his police car, where Arthur Kramer was seated. "He was trying to get one of the bedroom doors open and started kicking it. We told him to back off and he ignored us, so Dan and I went hands-on and put him down on the floor and handcuffed him. He said he's a cop from New Mexico and he's after a fugitive. He was carrying a .40 Sig and identification saying he's a police chief from someplace in New Mexico, just like he told us."

"How's Ms. Murdoch?"

"She's pretty shook up," Coop said. "But I don't think she has any injuries."

Weber walked to Coop's patrol car and opened the back door.

"What the hell is wrong with you, Kramer?" he demanded. "I thought we agreed that we were going to handle this my way."

"Your way would've let that son of a bitch get away. I didn't come all this way to go back home empty-handed."

"The woman told you her son isn't there."

"I don't know what you've got going on with her on the side, but whatever it is, I don't believe a word that bitch says. Anyone that would give birth to a murdering piece of shit like her son wouldn't hesitate to lie to protect him."

"You need to watch your mouth," Weber told him. "You're skating on real thin ice with me. Can you tell me one reason why I shouldn't lock you in a cell and throw away the key?"

"Is that how you treat your brother cops, Weber?"

The sheriff had to resist reaching inside the car and throttling the contemptuous man. The more he saw of Kramer, the less he liked him. And the less he trusted him. He wasn't sure if he bought Zach Murdoch's story lock, stock, and barrel, but there was definitely more going on than Kramer had alluded to.

"Just because you have a badge doesn't mean you automatically deserve any kind of respect from me. You show up here and you don't have the courtesy to come by and let me know you're in town and why. You lied to me right from the start. We agreed we were going to meet in the morning, and then you show up here doing this? Mrs. Murdoch would have been within her rights to blow you away. And to top it all off, you fight with my deputies? No, you get nothing from me at this point, cop or no cop."

Kramer started to say something, but Weber ignored him and slammed the car's door.

"You want me to take him back to the office and put him in a cell, Jimmy?"

That was the last thing Weber wanted, with Zach Murdoch already there,

"No, not yet. Are you and Dan okay?"

"Yeah, it wasn't a big fight or anything like that. He started kicking in that bedroom door and we took him down and handcuffed him. He struggled a little bit, but like I said, it wasn't that big of a deal."

"Okay, hang tight. Why don't you see if you can get all of these looky loos to go back home. I'm going to go talk to Ms. Murdoch."

Weber and Robyn went into the house, where Juliette was sitting on the couch with her head buried in her hands.

"Give us a minute, Dan, okay?"

Dan nodded and left the house.

Weber sat on one side of the weeping woman and Robyn on the other.

"Are you okay, Juliette?"

She pulled her face up and looked at him. "Do I look okay? Now do you see what I was saying? What Zach was saying? That man's crazy."

"Are you injured at all? Did he hit you or anything like that?"

She shook her head. "No, he just kept pushing me out of the way when I tried to stop him. How's Zach? Is he all right?"

"He's fine," Robyn told. "He's got two broken ribs, but they wrapped him up good at the medical center and gave him a shot for the pain."

"Where is he now?"

"He's at the jail," Weber told her. "Can you tell us what happened here tonight?"

"I was in bed, trying to get to sleep, but I wasn't having much luck. I kept thinking about Zach and worrying about him. Then the next thing I knew there was this big crash and it felt like the whole house shook. Honestly, I thought somebody ran into the house with a car or a tree fell on it, or something crazy like that. I jumped up and ran out of my bedroom and he was there."

"Chief Kramer?"

"Yes. He kept shouting at me, demanding that I tell him where Zach was. I told him he wasn't here and he called me a liar and started turning furniture over and kicking doors open and it... it was a nightmare. I know if he would have found Zach he would've killed him on the spot."

"I'm sorry he came back here. I thought he would wait until morning like I told him to and that we would try to figure out something together."

"Please don't let that maniac get to Zach. Look at my house. He'll kill Zach if he finds him."

Weber looked around at the living room, which had been so tidy on their previous visits just hours earlier. The small table that had set next to her recliner was smashed into pieces, a door to a closet just inside the home's entrance was hanging open, winter coats and overshoes pulled out and thrown on the floor. Weber walked out of the living room and into a dining room, where two chairs were toppled over and some kind of porcelain vase was shattered, the dried floral arrangement it once held crushed and scattered about. A short hallway to the right led to two bedrooms and a bathroom. The blankets and sheets have been torn off of the bed in the master bedroom and the closet door was open. A second bedroom door was buckled inward from where Kramer had kicked it. In the bathroom the shower curtain was torn from the rod and laying on the floor. The man had definitely trashed the place in his search for Zach Murdoch.

He went back to the living room and asked, "Do you want to file charges against him, Juliette? If you do, I can lock him up right now for armed burglary and assault, since he pushed you."

"And what happens then? He gets locked up in the same jail where my son is?"

"I promise you, Zach is safe and nothing is going to happen to him while he's in my custody."

"You didn't answer my question. You'd lock him up in the same jail where Zach is?"

"They'd be in different cells, apart from each other. He wouldn't be able to hurt him."

"No, she said, shaking her head adamantly. "No. He'd find a way. I know he would. Please, just make him go away or something. I don't want him anywhere near my son!"

Chapter 14

When they were done talking to Juliette, Weber and Robyn walked outside. It looked like the neighbors were gone, either due to Coop dispersing them or the chilly night air driving them back inside.

"So what's the deal, Jimmy?"

"Take him to the office, but don't put him in a cell. Keep him handcuffed in the interview room."

"Okay."

"Keep an eye on him and don't leave him alone for a minute. If he has to take a leak, you go with him and stand in the doorway. I don't want him out of your sight. We'll be right behind you. This is important, Coop. *Do not* take him anywhere near the cellblock."

Coop, who had retired after 20 years as an Army MP before joining the Big Lake Sheriff's Department, was an experienced lawman who wasn't used to Weber emphasizing a point like he was some kind of rookie. He looked questioningly at his boss, but didn't say anything. His years in the military had taught him how to obey orders even if he didn't always understand why they had been issued.

"Dan, see if you can do anything to get that front door to work so Ms. Murdoch can close it, will you?"

"Sure thing, Jimmy."

"Thanks, when you're done there, go ahead and go back on patrol."

While he was driving to the office, Weber looked across to Robyn and said, "I guess I'll have to give you a rain check on that foot rub."

"No problem, Jimmy. I'll be holding a rain check for you, too."

They rode in silence for a moment, then Robyn asked, "Do you think Zach really did kill that woman over there in New Mexico?"

"I don't know what to think," Weber admitted. "What's your take on it?"

"Same as yours, I guess. He seems like he's pretty earnest, but you and I both know that some people can look you right in the face and lie and never blink an eye. His story is really out there. I mean, who's going to believe the police chief would murder a nurse like that in cold blood and then try to put it on him? That's the stuff you see on those made for TV movies. It's pretty far-fetched."

"Yeah, I know."

"But at the same time, this guy Kramer really rubs me the wrong way."

"He's not exactly a people person," Weber agreed. "I don't think he's the kind of guy I'd want to hang out with. But does that make him a killer?"

"I don't know. Does it?"

They were pulling into the parking lot at the Sheriff's office. "Let's go talk to him and see what we can find out."

Kramer, still handcuffed, was sitting at the long table in the interview room when Weber walked in and nodded to Coop.

"He give you any problems?"

"Nope. Hasn't said a word."

Weber set down across the table from Kramer and asked, "Do you want to explain what the hell happened over there tonight?"

"I told you, I went looking for that little puke."

"After we agreed that we would wait until morning and handle it then?"

"He's going to be long gone by morning, Sheriff. He probably already is, thanks to you."

"Can you think of one good reason why I shouldn't lock you up for that stunt you pulled tonight?"

"Come on, Sheriff! We're both on the same side here, remember?"

"Are we?"

"What's that supposed to mean?"

"I mean if someone came to your town and did the same kind of crap you've done here, would you let it slide just because they're a cop?"

"If someone came to my town looking for a fugitive, I'd be the one kicking in the door for them if that's what it took."

"Obviously we've got two different ways of doing things."

"Yeah, and your way is what's led to the pussification of this country."

"Pussification. That must be a word you made up, because I've never seen it in a dictionary."

"It's bleeding heart liberals like you that have turned this country upside down. There was a time when cops could kick ass and take names, and nobody said a word about it because they knew that's what it takes to get the job done. Now everybody in the world's got a cell phone recording everything that happens and putting it on the Internet so people like you can wring their hands and cry 'Oh my' and talk about how terrible it is."

Weber had been called a lot of things in his time as a law officer, everything from a Nazi storm trooper to a macho cowboy to a thug, and a lot of terms questioning his heritage and his relationship with his mother. But being called a bleeding heart liberal was a first for him and he wondered if anybody who knew him and the way he ran his department would ever use a term like that to describe him. He was pretty sure not.

"We're not here to discuss politics, Kramer. You've been way over the line since you got here. It's time for you to go back where you came from."

"I'm not going anywhere until I find Zach Murdoch. I can't believe you're going to let someone who killed a good woman get away with it instead of doing what it takes to bring him to justice."

"Yes, you are going," Weber told him "That's not a suggestion, that's an order."

"I don't take orders from you."

"You're starting to piss me off," Weber said. "Now, here's the way it's going to go. You are going to leave town, and you're going to do it tonight. I'm going to have Deputy Cooper here take you back to your motel to get anything you left there. Then he is going to take you back to Alderbrook Way to pick up your vehicle. You're going to get in that vehicle and you're going to start driving, and Deputy Cooper is going to escort you out of town. If you give him any trouble or if you show your face around Big Lake again, I'm going to charge you with armed burglary, assault and battery, resisting arrest, and just being an asshole in general. Do we understand each other?"

"Do you think you intimidate me, Weber? I've dealt with a lot worse than you in my time."

"I'm not trying to intimidate you, I'm just telling you the way it is. I *will* lock you up and I *will* charge you with anything and everything I can think of. I don't know how the people over in Cañon Verde feel about you, but I'm pretty sure there are a lot of them who don't have a very high opinion. I know a TV reporter who loves scandal, and when she hears about this she will be sure it goes national. When it does and the folks back home find out that their police chief has been arrested in Arizona and is facing serious felony charges like the ones I just lined out for you, you may be looking for a new job. Once you get done serving your time here, that is."

"Why are you doing this, Weber? What's this woman and this kid mean to you? Are you banging her or something?"

"You know what? Screw it. I'm done with your bullshit. Robyn, can you give Lisa Burnham down at Channel Six in Phoenix a call? Tell her we hate to wake her up in the middle of the night, but I've got a scoop for her that she needs for the morning news. Tell her this might be the story that's going to take her from that anchor's desk in Phoenix all the way to one of the networks."

"Will do," Robyn said, pulling her cell phone out of her pocket.

"You'd really do that? You'd ruin another cop's career over some murdering little piece of shit like Zach Murdoch?"

"No, I'd do it because you're a dickhead and an embarrassment to every good man and woman in the world who's ever pinned on a badge."

Robyn started pushing buttons on her phone and Kramer gave Weber a hateful look, then said, "Forget it. You win, for now. Murdoch is going to turn up someplace sooner or later. Guys like him can't stay out of trouble. And when he does I'll get him, and there won't be a damn thing you can do to protect him. I'm going to make sure he pays for what he did to Barbara Eibeck. And you can take that to the bank, Weber!"

"Just remember," Weber warned him. "This is your one and only chance. Show your face around Big Lake again and I'm going to take you down, Kramer. Take you all the way down."

The two men glared at each other and the air in the small interrogation room seemed to be laced with venomous hatred. Finally Weber said, "Coop, get him out of my sight. And if he gives you any trouble at all, just shoot his ass and be done with it, okay?"

"Whatever you say, boss."

When Coop left with Kramer, Robyn looked at the sheriff and said. "Are you as tired as I am?"

"I don't know. Are you so tired you could fall asleep sitting here?"

"I think so."

"Then yeah, I'm as tired as you are. Your place is closer."

She stood up and yawned and said, "Let's go."

Nick Russell

Chapter 15

Robyn had the day off, but Weber was in the office by 8:30 the next morning, his eyes gritty and his head aching from lack of sleep. He walked back to the cellblock with a takeout breakfast and a cup of coffee from the ButterCup Café and gave them to Zach.

"How's your pain level? Do you need a pill"

"No, I'm okay, Sheriff. What's going to happen now?"

"I'm not sure yet. I want to talk to some people and figure that out."

"Sheriff, I wasn't lying when I said I didn't kill that lady at the hospital. I never laid a hand on her. Chief Kramer did it, not me."

"Yeah, I heard you before, Zach."

"You've got to believe me!"

"Why, Zach? Why do I have to believe you? I mean, let's face it, you're not exactly an angel. There was that stuff that happened when you were a kid, and you're on probation for a possession charge, and then you got busted driving a car with drugs and paraphernalia in it. And you admitted to me that you stole a car to get here."

"I'm not denying that I used to smoke pot. I did, and I liked it. But when I got busted it cost me everything. A good job I really liked, and when I got fired and couldn't make the payments on my pickup it got repoed. Then the next thing I knew, I couldn't pay the rent and I got kicked out of my apartment. All that because I was stupid and liked getting high. I wanted to get a job with one of the pipeline crews, they're making big bucks. But you have to be clean, and they test your urine to make sure you are. If you had any kind of drug bust they won't even talk to you for six months. And I was almost there, Sheriff! I realized after I lost everything when I got busted that it just wasn't worth it. You get high and you have a good time for a little while, and then you pay for it for a long, long time. And yeah, I stole that car. I told you that right up front. But I had to! Look at me. Look at what Chief Kramer did to me. I mean it, he was going to kill me. That's why I took off."

Weber looked at the young man and tried to decide how much of what he was telling him was true. He still had a hard time believing that someone in Arthur Kramer's position would murder somebody and then try to pin it on an innocent kid, but at the same time, Kramer sure hadn't won any points with him with the way he had acted.

"Eat your breakfast, Zach."

~***~

As if being worn out and groggy from lack of sleep wasn't enough, Weber had more trouble waiting for him when he walked back into the main office.

"Sheriff Weber, we need to talk!"

"Really, Chet? I can think of a lot of other things I'd rather do than listen to you this morning."

"You've got some explaining to do, Sheriff."

For a moment Weber wondered if Kramer had filed some kind of complaint, but the mayor put that thought out of his head when he said, "I want you to explain to me why Archer has been driving around in a car with no window in it."

"Oh, you heard about that, did you? What did Archer have to say about it?"

"I didn't hear about it from him, I had to find out about it myself. I drove by the school yesterday and saw him with some kind of clear plastic taped over his car door. When I stopped to ask him about it he said the window had been broken and you told him he still had to drive the car."

"Did you have to wake him up first to ask him about it, Chet?"

The mayor ignored the question and said, "This is totally irresponsible on your part, Sheriff. How could you have one of your deputies riding around in a car like that when it's this cold?"

"Well, Chet, first of all, the window is being replaced this morning. And second of all, Archer is the one who broke it in the first place. Did he tell you that?"

"No, but what's that got to do with it?"

"I was trying to teach him a lesson that he can't go around breaking stuff all the time with no consequences."

"He's not a child, Sheriff."

"Are you sure about that? Because you could have fooled me, the way he acts sometimes."

"I'm not here to discuss your opinion of Archer's behavior, I'm here to talk about the fact that you let one of your deputies ride around in a freezing car all day long."

"Well, I could have suspended him until the replacement window came in."

"You think you can run things around here anyway you want to and just get away with it. But you're wrong, Sheriff Weber! I intend to take this matter before the Town Council at our next meeting."

"You do that, Chet. And when I present them the bill for the window that Archer broke, I'm also going to tell them that I'm suspending him for 30 days. How about that?"

"You can't do that. I won't allow it."

"You'd better read the Town Charter and bylaws, Chet. It gives me full authority to run this department in any manner I see fit. That includes hiring, firing, and disciplining deputies, as long as I'm within state law guidelines. But you go ahead and take your best shot, because you're going to do it anyway."

"There's no getting through to you, is there, Sheriff Weber?"

"Apparently not, Chet. Now, if you're done stomping your feet and throwing your little tantrum, I've got grown-up work to do."

He left the mayor standing there and walked out of the office and to the small park model trailer in the back of the parking lot that served as FBI Special Agent Larry Parks' office. He found his friend cursing at his computer.

"Are we unhappy with the technological world this morning, Parks?"

"You could say that, Bubba. Headquarters sent out some kind of automatic update last night, and somewhere along the line they seem to have changed all of my passwords. It took me over an hour on the phone with our techno-geeks to get that figured out, and now the darn thing won't send anything to the printer."

"I think the world was a lot better off when we used a notepad and a pencil," Weber said. "How about you take a break from that? I need to talk to you about something."

"What is it? Woman trouble again? I keep telling you, Jimmy, relationships between men and women are psychological. And more often than not she's the psycho and he's the one being logical."

"And you wonder why you're still single."

"Single? I'm not single. I'm in a healthy relationship."

"Healthy? I saw Marsha stab you in the back of the hand with a fork when you tried to sneak an extra piece of garlic bread at Mario's last week."

"Yeah, because she's trying to keep me fit and trim to survive all that lovin' she gives me. See what I mean? Healthy."

"Sometimes I get a headache just talking to you, Parks."

"Yeah? Well you'd better get used to them, because once you get married, you're going to be hearing a lot about headaches. Seriously, that woman I was married to got a headache on our honeymoon and it lasted until three days after the divorce was final!"

"Are you done now?"

"I guess so. What's up?"

"I've got a situation and I need your input."

Weber told him about his first encounter with Arthur Kramer and the feeling the man had been lying to him, and then he and Robyn going back to confront him when he returned to Alderbrook Way, and what had taken place when they paid an unexpected visit on Juliette Murdoch. Then he told him the rest of the story, about the cookbook, and going back to the Murdoch house again, where they found Zach and he told them his story. By the time he was done relating how Kramer had gone back and kicked in the door of the house searching for the fugitive, whom Weber had hidden away in the jail by then, and how he had ordered Kramer to leave town, Parks was shaking his head.

"Man, this could get ugly, Jimmy. Technically, aren't you hiding a fugitive?"

"I'm not hiding him, Parks, he's under arrest. I'm just not willing to let Kramer have him, because no matter what happened over there in New Mexico and how that woman got killed, I'm beginning to believe Zach's not going to be safe if I turn him over to Kramer, or any of his people."

"So what's your next move?"

"That's where you come in. Can the Feds take him into protective custody or anything like that?"

"Protective custody based on what? Wild accusations that a police chief killed somebody and is blaming it on him?"

"I know it's a crazy story, Parks, and I'm not sure I believe it either. But I do believe that Kramer is out of control for whatever reason. Maybe it's like he said and he's blaming himself for that nurse getting killed. But it doesn't matter what his motivation is, there's a problem there. Not to mention the fact that he beat Zach so badly that he had to take him to the ER in the first place."

"There is that. And the kid said that he didn't provoke him or do anything to earn that beating?"

"He says he didn't. But even if he did, so what? You and I, and every cop we know, has run into smart asses who mouth off. That doesn't mean we stomp them. Just do me a favor and come talk to the kid, okay? I just want your input on what to do next."

Parks looked at his computer and laser printer, which still weren't communicating with each other, and said, "What the hell, I'm not accomplishing anything here anyway."

They went back to the Sheriff's office and Weber was relieved to see that the mayor had gone elsewhere to spread his own special brand of misery and discontent. He took Parks back to the cellblock and said, "Zach, this is Special Agent Parks from the FBI. I want you to tell him everything you told me, right from the start when you got pulled over driving your girlfriend's car. And don't leave anything out."

He left them to talk and went back out front to find Juliette waiting for him.

"How's Zach? Is he okay?"

"He's fine," Weber assured her. "He's talking to Larry Parks from the FBI right now. We're trying to figure out our next move. How are you this morning, Juliette?"

"I don't think I got any sleep at all. I'm a nervous wreck."

"I understand. Look, for the time being Zach isn't going anywhere. I'm not sure what's going to happen next, but I promise you, Chief Kramer is not going to get anywhere near him until we get all this worked out."

"But then what will happen?"

"Juliette, I honestly don't know. I can't just wave my hand and make this all go away. Like I told you last night, one way or the other Zach is going to have to answer the charges against him. That's just the way it works. What I'm trying to do is keep him out of Chief Kramer's hands until we can figure out a way to get somebody on the state level to take the case."

There were tears in her eyes and she was trembling. Weber wanted nothing more than to put his arms around the woman and comfort her, but based on their past relationship and the current situation, it wasn't appropriate. Instead, he said, "Look, have a seat here, and once Parks is done talking to Zach you can go back and visit him, okay?"

She nodded her head, unable to speak.

Weber put his hand on her shoulder for a moment to try to comfort her, but he knew there was nothing he could do to set her mind at ease.

Chapter 16

"It's a wild story," Parks said when he had finished talking to Zach. "He makes this Kramer guy sound like one of those stereotype old-time southern police chiefs we hear about. But I think more of that happened in books and movies than in real life."

They were seated in Weber's private office drinking coffee.

"I know. It sounds pretty far-fetched. But there's no question that somebody really worked that kid over. And Kramer himself told me that happened before he ever got to the hospital. Of course, according to him, it was when he was resisting arrest and it wasn't any more than a fat lip a little bit of road rash. Nothing like what actually happened. So I believe there's some truth in that part of Zach's story, at least."

Parks nodded his head. "Yeah, he didn't get all of that with just a simple arrest."

"So what do you think? I really don't want to turn this kid over to that guy. Not after the way he was acting yesterday."

Parks crossed his arms over his chest and thought for a moment, then said "Well, we know he's guilty of interstate flight to avoid prosecution. That's a Federal charge. This is above my pay grade, Jimmy. Let me make some calls and see where we stand on this."

"I appreciate it, Parks."

~***~

Weber managed to get a half hour's sleep on the couch in his office and woke up feeling somewhat refreshed. When he was growing up he hated naps, but now he found them rejuvenating.

Mary Caitlin was at her desk and looked up when he came into the outer office. She got up and poured him a cup of coffee.

"Feeling better?"

"A bit."

"So what's going on back in the cellblock that's so hush-hush?"

"Yeah, our people need to know about it."

He gave her a quick rundown of the situation, and when he was finished Mary said, "I can't see Zach or Josh either one hurting somebody. Especially not a woman."

"Why do you say that?"

"Because I know them, and I know Juliette. And I know the way she raised them. Yes, I know how protective she was when they got busted when they were kids. That was the Mama Bear syndrome. But Juliette taught them to be gentlemen and those boys were always respectful of women, Jimmy. Holding doors and being polite and saying "yes, ma'am" and all that. I just don't believe either one of them could kill somebody, let alone a woman."

"I hope you're right," Weber told her. "Listen, if I'm not here I want you to pass the word along to everybody when they come on duty. But I want it done face-to-face, no radio traffic about it at all, okay? I don't want anybody to know Zach is back there until we know what our next move is going to be."

"Don't worry," Mary said, "I'll handle it. By the way, Paul Lewis called wanting to know any details you could give him on a disturbance at Juliette's place last night."

"What did you tell him?"

"I told him you'd get back to him."

Weber spent a couple of hours doing paperwork, then walked across the street to the *Big Lake Herald* newspaper.

"Hey, handsome," Margie Shores, the newspaper's receptionist and office manager greeted him. "Please tell me you came to sweep me off my feet and take me away from my life of drudgery and that we are going to spend the rest of our days drinking piña colada's on a beach somewhere in Mexico."

Weber had known Margie forever. They had been friends and classmates all through school, she had been his date for the Junior Prom, and he had brought Margie and his friend Keith Shores together. Over a decade later it had been his duty as a young deputy sheriff to knock on Margie's and door and inform her that Keith had been killed in a logging truck accident. She had never remarried, raising their daughter Jennifer alone and doing a fine job of it.

"You know I'd love to do that, Margie, but I get sunburned so easy."

"We'll take suntan lotion with us," the big woman said, hugging him as he came around the counter. "Lots and lots of suntan lotion, Jimmy. We'll stay in the hotel and just slather it all over each other and order room service."

"As much fun as that sounds, I'm going to have to pass. You and I both know this town would implode if I left for more than 24 hours."

She pouted and said, "So you're just here to see Paul. Don't tell me you guys have got some kind of homosexual thing happening and it's going to be the two of you rubbing suntan lotion on each other."

"I don't think they make that much suntan lotion, Margie."

She laughed and said, "He's back there somewhere. If you guys are going to do anything freaky, hang a towel or a necktie on the doorknob, will you?"

Paul Lewis, the weekly newspaper's editor and publisher, was on his hands and knees when Weber looked in his open office door. Seeing the fabric of his trousers stretched tightly across his roly-poly friend's rump, Weber said, "You know, Paul, I've never seen this side of you before."

Paul, a good humored little gnome who peered out at the world from faded blue eyes that hid behind wire rimmed glasses, looked over his shoulder and said, "Calm down, Jimmy, this isn't an invitation to play leapfrog. I dropped my pen on the floor and the damn thing landed just out of reach under my desk."

"Here, get up and let me get it," Weber said. "I've seen as much of your ass as I need to."

Paul put his hand on the top of the desk and heaved his bulk upright. Once he was out of the way, Weber retrieved the pen and handed it to him.

"Are you kidding me? All that work for a damn Bic pen? I thought it was a Montblanc your old man gave you when you graduated from journalism school. Or at least a Cross you picked up at the office supply."

"Give me a break. I'm a poor man and every penny counts."

"If I had your money, I'd give mine away."

"As it turns out, there's not a lot of money in newspaper publishing *or* police corruption, is there?"

"Nope, we both chose the wrong line of work, didn't we?"

Weber couldn't remember when he and Paul first became friends, but he was pretty sure they weren't much out of diapers. That was a long time ago.

"So what's this I hear about some big disturbance over at Juliette Murdoch's house late last night? Somebody said someone broke in or something?"

"Yeah, it's a crazy story."

"I'm all ears."

"Here's the thing, Paul, I need you to sit on it for a while."

"Are you kidding me, Jimmy? It's so slow out there that I'm reduced to writing stories about how busy local handymen are getting cabins ready for summer visitors. It's so boring even I don't want to read it after I write it."

"I know, but I can't go into a lot of detail right now. It's a sensitive issue."

"Sensitive in like Juliette has a boyfriend and they got into an argument and the cops got called?"

"No, you're letting your imagination and dirty mind take control, Paul. I really can't tell you much of anything. Not yet, anyway. But I promise you, when I can I'll tell you the whole story. And I think it's going to be one worth waiting for."

Besides being friends, they had always had a good working relationship, and Paul nodded his head. "Fair enough, Jimmy. But as consolation, you have to buy me lunch."

"What the hell, it's cheaper than suntan lotion."

"What?"

"Never mind. Let's go."

~***~

Coop wasn't scheduled to come on duty until 6 PM, but Weber drove to his house after lunch, hoping he was awake. He found him loading a ladder into the back of his Ford pickup.

"Hey, boss, what's up? You got me just in time, I was heading for Roberta's place."

"If you're planning to elope you're not going to need the ladder," Weber said. "She lives in a one-story house."

His deputy laughed and said, "Nothing like that. When that big windstorm came through here a few days ago it tore one of the gutters loose on her roof. I was planning to fix it."

Coop and Roberta Jensen, a blind woman from Big Lake who had gone to Tucson and earned a law degree before coming back and establishing a practice in her old hometown, had been seeing each other on a steady basis and it looked like the relationship was going somewhere.

"Did that guy Kramer give you any problems last night?"

"No, not really. He was too busy cussing you out to say much of anything else. He said he didn't leave anything in the motel so I did like you said. Took him back to pick up his vehicle, then I gave him his weapon and shield back and followed him out of town. But I've got to be honest with you, Jimmy, I don't think we've seen the last of him. He seemed pretty determined."

"Yeah, that's why I wanted to talk to you, Coop. I know I may have seemed kind of weird the way I wanted you to bring him in last night but not let him anywhere near the cellblock. I wanted to explain why."

After Weber got done telling Coop what was going on, his deputy whistled and shook his head. "I've heard a lot of wild stories in my time, Jimmy, but I think this one takes the cake."

"I know. And I don't know who's telling the truth and who's lying."

"Well, I can tell you one thing. I've never met him, and I have no idea what happened over there in New Mexico, but I think the kid's telling the truth when he says that Kramer would do him harm long before he got him back to wherever he came from. A couple of times last night when I was taking him to his vehicle he said something about he should've blown the little so-and-so away when he had the chance, and he damn sure wasn't going to hesitate the next time he saw him. I thought he was just blowing off steam at first, as pissed off as he was. But now I don't know."

"He said that? Just like that?"

"Those were his words exactly, Jimmy. He said the next time he laid eyes on Zach Murdoch he was going to be dead."

Chapter 17

Parks knocked on his office door and Weber waved him in.

"Tell me you've got something good for me."

"Well, there's good news and there's bad news. Which one do you want first?"

"Hell, just lay it all out."

"It took a while to connect with people because I was playing telephone tag, but I talked to the Special Agent in Charge down in Phoenix. He says that if Zach is already in custody there's no need for the FBI to get involved, even if he did cross a state line to get here. So officially, at this point, I can't do anything. That's the bad news."

"Okay, give me the good."

"He also suggested that I talk to Sandra Dunnsire. She's an Assistant U.S. Attorney down in Phoenix, and she and I have coordinated a couple of times when the Bureau had me working on undercover cases. I laid the whole thing out for her and she was skeptical. But as a favor to me, she did agree to a Skype interview with Zach. Once she hears what he has to say, we'll see what happens."

"When you want to do it?"

"I can set it up for an hour from now if that works for you."

"Call her back and tell her it's on."

~***~

They brought Zach into the interrogation room for the Skype interview. He seemed nervous when Weber led him out of the cell, but the sheriff explained to him what was happening and told him to just tell his story the same way he had related it to him, Robyn, and Parks.

Sandra Dunnsire looked to be in her late 30s, with reddish hair and a prominent nose. She asked Zach if he had been read his rights, and when he confirmed he had she told him the interview was being recorded. Then she asked him to tell her everything he could about his experience, starting from the time he was pulled over by the police in Cañon Verde while driving his girlfriend's car.

She made notes as he was talking and waited until he was done before saying anything.

"First of all, are you absolutely sure that you did not resist arrest in any way? You didn't struggle with the arresting officer, you didn't tense up when he tried to put his handcuffs on you, anything at all like that?"

"No, ma'am," Zach said. "Him and me, we never had a problem. He treated me just fine. The problem started when I got to the jail."

"And that's when you're saying Chief Kramer assaulted you?"

"Yes, ma'am."

"And you didn't fight with Chief Kramer or any of his officers once you got to the jail?"

"No, ma'am, I didn't."

"So what you're telling me is that Chief Kramer assaulted you after this conversation about your girlfriend selling drugs? Is that correct?"

Zach nodded his head, and she said, "Please answer verbally."

"I'm sorry. Yes, ma'am."

"How did it go from him asking you questions about selling drugs to him assaulting you?"

"He was saying some dirty things about Claudia, my girlfriend, and then things that would happen to me. And I smarted off to him. I guess that was a big mistake."

"What were those things that he said and you said back that led up to the physical assault, Mr. Murdoch?"

Zach told her the same story he had told Weber, how the chief had referred to Claudia using the term "going down" and how he had threatened to bring other prisoners to his cell, alluding to what they might do to him. "He said they were going to make me their bitch. When he said that, I was mad and I was scared, and I called him a son of a bitch."

"What were your words exactly?"

"I said something like 'you can't do this to me you son of a bitch.' And when I said that he just went ballistic. He came in the cell and started hitting me and knocked me down and then started kicking me. I think if those other cops hadn't pulled him off of me, he would have killed me right there."

She had him go through the story a second time from the very start, this time focusing on the events at the hospital. When he was done, she thanked him for his time and said she would be in contact with FBI Special Agent Parks.

Weber took Zach back to his cell and locked him in it.

"What happens now, Sheriff?"

"I don't know, Zach. I guess we wait and see what the lady has to say."

Back in the interview room, Sandra Dunnsire was looking at her notes. Weber and Parks sat quietly, and after a moment or two she looked up and asked, "What's your gut reaction, Parks?"

"I know his story seems pretty out there, but he didn't get torn up like he is as a result of a simple arrest."

"Sheriff Weber, according to you, Police Chief Kramer said that all Zach sustained when he was allegedly resisting arrest was a cut lip and a few minor scrapes?"

"That's what he told me," Weber replied.

"According to Special Agent Parks, you said that Chief Kramer was out of control when he allegedly broke into the Murdoch home, after you had been there with him earlier that evening?"

"That's right. Two of my deputies had to take him down and handcuff him. And according to Deputy Cooper, who escorted him out of town, Kramer told him that he should have blown Zach away when he had the chance, and the next time he saw him that's exactly what he intended to do."

"Wow. He said that to one of your deputies? Will that deputy swear to that in court?"

"Yes, ma'am, he will."

"I agree with you, Parks, the story seems way out there in left field. But based upon the way Sheriff Weber tells me Chief Kramer was acting, and that statement to one of the sheriff's deputies, I'm willing to give Zach the benefit of the doubt to some extent, at least. Are you familiar with the term 'color of the law'?"

"I am," Parks said.

"I've heard it, but I'm afraid you're going to have to refresh me," Weber admitted.

"Police officers and other people acting in an official capacity, like judges and prosecutors at the state, local, or federal level have a tremendous amount of power. But this power comes with limitations, obviously, and when somebody abuses that power under what's called the color of law to deny anybody their Constitutional rights, it's a federal crime. That can be investigated by the FBI and prosecuted by the federal government. So if Chief Kramer did assault this young man as he alleges, his rights were violated. And if Zach didn't kill the nurse and Kramer is trying to pin that on him, it's fabrication of evidence. Not to mention, of course, a murder charge at the state level. Is there any way that you can find anything to corroborate any of these events?"

"How? I doubt Kramer's going to admit to any wrongdoing," Weber said.

"No, but I wonder if there's anybody over there in Cañon Verde who would be willing to confirm anything Zach told us. Let me talk to my boss, Parks, and I'll get back to you within the hour."

~***~

She kept her word, and twenty minutes later Parks was back in Weber's office.

"Well, what's the verdict?"

"I don't think you're going to like it, but here it is. She said you should call the Cañon Verde PD and let them know you have Zach in custody. They have to file for extradition, and when they do, he can fight it. There will be a hearing, and at that hearing he can tell his story. That puts it on the official record, and if the judge is willing to believe it and believes his life is in danger if he is returned to Chief Kramer's custody, it gets kicked up to the next level for appeal. And when that door is opened with his testimony, she said she will then open an official investigation through her office."

"I don't like giving Kramer any information at all," Weber said. "But I figured we would have to at least start with the extradition process."

"Meanwhile, we have to come up with something to back up Zach's story. I just don't know if we'll be able to find anybody over there in Cañon Verde who will tell us anything."

"So it looks like we're believing Zach's story, right?"

"Let's just say I believe at least part of it," Weber said. "How about you?"

"What the hell, Jimmy, in for a dime, in for a dollar. You know me, no matter what you do I've got your back."

Parks didn't need to say it because Weber already knew that. More than once the FBI agent had backed him up when things got hairy. Weber looked at the clock on his wall and said, "It's almost 5 o'clock now. I guess I can wait until tomorrow to call over there and let them know we have him in custody. Meanwhile, I want to go have a talk with Judge Ryman."

Nick Russell

Chapter 18

The judge had already left his office for the day by the time Weber got there, but Cindy Oswald, the Court Clerk, said she was sure he was at home, because he had told her when he left that he had to fix a leaking pipe under his kitchen sink. When Weber got to the judge's house his wife Bonnie, a short woman with a swimmer's build that she had kept since her days competing in high school and college, led him into the kitchen. The judge was on his back with the upper half of his body under the kitchen sink.

"You know, Judge, Max Woodbury does that kind of work for a living."

The judge slid out, with a pipe wrench in his hand, and said, "Just a leaky pipe. Nothing I can't handle. I worked part-time for a plumber for a while when I was in law school. Bonnie, turn the water on and fill the sink up so we can see if that did it."

She leaned over the sink and turned the water faucet on waited a moment, then turned the water off and pulled the stopper from the sink. The judge watched carefully, then smiled and said, "See? Good as new, and I kept $45 in my pocket instead of putting it in Max's."

"You're a man of many talents, Harold Ryman," Bonnie said admiringly as he got to his feet and wiped his hands on a paper towel.

"So what brings you here, Sheriff?"

"Well, I got a report of a man practicing plumbing without a license and I thought I'd better come by and investigate."

"Guilty as charged," the judge said with a chuckle.

"Actually, I do need talk to you about something if I can have a few minutes of your time."

"Is this official business? And if so, can it wait until tomorrow?"

"It's kind of officially unofficial, if that makes any sense."

"We're supposed to be meeting Kirby and Angela Templeton for dinner."

"I won't take any more of your time than I have to," Weber told him. "But it is kind of important."

"We've got time," Bonnie said. "And I can always call Angela and tell her we're running a few minutes late."

"All right, let's go in the den."

The judge was an Arizona Diamondbacks baseball fan, and one wall of the small den in his house was covered in baseball memorabilia, including a poster-sized photograph of the judge posing with several team members while wearing a Diamondbacks hat and jersey. He sat down behind his desk and motioned Weber to a chair.

"Just so you know, I prefer to keep work and home separate."

"I know that," Weber told him, "and I wouldn't bother you here at home unless it was important."

"What's up?"

Weber told him the whole story from start to finish and when he was finished the judge asked, "So what is it you want from me, Jimmy?"

"I don't know what happened over there in New Mexico, Judge, but based on the way he acted here, going back to Juliette Murdoch's house like that in the middle of the night and kicking the door in, I honestly believe that if Zach Murdoch is released to this Chief Kramer, he's going to kill him."

"I heard something about a disturbance at her house, but I didn't know any details."

"He was out of control, Judge. And based on his statement to Coop that the next time he saw Zach he was going to blow him away, I honestly fear for the boy's life."

"And where do I fit into all of this?"

"This Ms. Dunnsire, the Assistant U.S. Attorney, says if Zach contests extradition, it gives him a chance to tell his story, and from there she will open a case on it."

"So you want me to agree to hold up the extradition, is that right?"

"I'm just asking you to hear his story with an open mind, sir, that's all."

The judge put his elbows together on top of his desk and rested his chin on his folded hands for a moment, studying the sheriff.

"You do know this is highly irregular, Sheriff."

"Believe me, sir, I wouldn't be here if I didn't feel it was necessary. I need to let the Cañon Verde police know that I have Zach in custody, and as soon as I do Chief Kramer is going to be here, trying to take him."

"Juliette Murdoch is a good woman, and despite their youthful indiscretions, I think she raised both of her boys with good morals. And I trust your judgment. If you say this man Kramer was out-of-control, I believe you. Do whatever paperwork you have to do to get the ball rolling, and we'll go from there."

They stood up and Weber said, "Thank you, Judge."

"We never had this conversation, Jimmy."

~***~

"How long is it going to take the U.S. Attorney to get moving on this? And can you guys delay Zach's extradition that long?"

"They say the wheels of justice grind slowly," Parks said. "But I think once there's an extradition hearing, Sandra Dunnsire won't waste any time."

They were playing rummy on Marsha's kitchen table, and as she dealt the next round of cards she asked, "How do you plan to go about getting any kind of evidence to support what Zach is saying?"

"I know a guy who works in the field office in Roswell, New Mexico," Parks said. "I've got a call in to him to see what he can tell me about things down there in Cañon Verde. And once Sandra opens an investigation, there'll be Feds crawling all over that police department. But no matter what, I think Coop's testimony alone about Kramer saying he would blow Zach away is enough to delay things for a while, at least."

"The whole thing just seems so convoluted," Robyn said. "We've got cops protecting an accused murderer while they're investigating cops."

"Do you think Zach Murdoch really did kill that lady and these guys are going off on a wild goose chase?"

"No, Marsha, that's not what I'm saying. Not at all. Kramer gave me the creeps just talking to him. He's one of those bad boy types that could just as easily have been the town bully as police chief. Or, in this case, it appears he's probably both. I'm just saying that it shouldn't be like that. We should trust the cops to be the good guys."

"In a perfect world, that would be true," Weber said.

"Yeah, and in a perfect world, Marsha here would be a rich blonde nymphomaniac. But just like this game, we play the cards we're dealt," Parks added, discarding three cards from the hand she had just dealt.

"Hey, don't pick on me just because I'm poor and a brunette!"

Marsha won the round and ignored Parks when he accused her of cheating. As Weber shuffled the cards for the next hand, Marsha and Robyn set out a tray of snacks and glasses of sodas for everybody.

"This thing has been hard on Juliette," Marsha said. "I stopped at the Chamber office late this afternoon to drop off some information on the Spring Fling Antique Fair and she looked like she had aged ten years."

"Stress will do that to you," Weber said.

"I know you guys had problems in the past and Juliette held a grudge for a long time after that thing with her boys, but she really is a nice person."

"I don't disagree," Weber told her. "And I never felt any animosity toward her. And she's really worked hard at the Chamber promoting the town."

Parks' phone rang and he looked at it. "This is my guy from Roswell calling back."

He pushed the button to answer the phone, then the speaker icon. "Hey there, Mayfield, thanks for getting back to me."

"No problem, Parks. Can you talk?"

"Yeah. I've got you on speakerphone because Sheriff Weber and Deputy Fuchette from Big Lake are here with me, if that's okay with you."

"No problem. Hi, Sheriff. Hi, Deputy."

They replied and Parks asked, "So what do you have for me about Cañon Verde and Chief Kramer, if anything?"

"I've only met the man once, myself, but Dennis Boyer, the other agent here, has been around longer and has dealt with him several times."

"What does he have to say?"

"Between you and me and the fence post, he thinks he's, and I'm quoting here, a flaming asshole."

"And what does he base that glowing opinion on?"

"Kramer is old-school, and not in a good way. If you're Hispanic, you're a beaner or a greaser, or a wetback."

Weber looked at Robyn, both of them remembering how Kramer had referred to the patient causing the disturbance at the medical center that took him out of the room briefly as a beaner.

"And it's not just the Mexicans he singles out," Mayfield was saying. "Kramer's got a reputation for roughing people up, as long as they're poor and don't fit into his picture of what makes you a good citizen. There have been lots of rumors, but nobody's ever come forward to make a formal complaint against him."

"Probably because they're all afraid of him," Parks said.

"Exactly. If you're a nobody going up against him, you're going to lose."

"How does he get away with it? I would think somebody would stand up to him," Robyn said.

"Chief Kramer's got a lot of support down there in Cañon Verde. If you're one of the well-to-do ranchers or business people in town, you're never going to have a problem with him. And a lot of them think he does a good job of keeping the place cleaned up. You won't see a panhandler or a vagrant anywhere around town. Kramer makes sure of that. And when someone causes trouble, he comes down on them hard. With both feet."

"Yeah, and maybe sometimes he uses those feet to excess," Parks said.

"What's this all about, Parks?"

"I really can't say too much at this point, just that it looks like there may be something going on involving Kramer. We'll know more in a day or so and I'll fill you in as much as I can then."

"Fair enough. For what it's worth, I'd love a chance to take a shot at him if you can come up with anything."

"One more thing before I let you go," Parks said. "Do you know anybody down there that can tell us anything more, off the record?"

"There was a guy... hang on a second, let me ask Boyer." The line was silent for a moment and then Mayfield came back on and said, "Drysdale. Lee Drysdale. He was on the PD down there for a while and he and Kramer had some kind of a falling out. This is all off the record, but the way I hear it he saw something he shouldn't have and stood up to Kramer about it. Word is Kramer fired him and ran him out of town."

"Do you have any idea where we could find this Drysdale guy?"

"Sorry, Parks, I don't. I know it happened about two years ago. I wish I could tell you more, but that's all I've got."

"That's a lot," Parks told him. "I appreciate your time."

"No problem. Like I said, Special Agent Boyer and I don't have any love for Kramer at all. If something is going to go down, we'd like to be a part of it."

"I'll be in touch," Parks promised and ended the call.

"Well that's interesting," Robyn said, picking up a pretzel and biting into it. "I think Zach was telling the truth. There *are* some bad things going on over there."

"Yeah, and we're going to get to the bottom of it," Parks replied.

"Hey, guys, I know I'm not a cop or anything," Marsha said, "but from my point of view, for what that's worth, just because this guy comes down on the people on the fringe of society or those who can't stand up for themselves, does that mean he would kill a nurse? That's a big difference from somebody standing on a curb trying to get a handout."

"That's true," Weber agreed. "But a guy like him, who has been able to do whatever he wants for so long, I think sometimes he gets it in his head that he's invincible and can do anything and get away with it. I think it's about time he got a wake-up call."

Chapter 19

"I tracked down Lee Drysdale," Mary Caitlin said the next morning. "He works at a Ford dealership in Las Cruces. Here's the phone number."

"You're good," Weber told her. "What did that take you, half an hour?"

"It doesn't take that much effort to do an Internet search, Jimmy. You'd know that if you ever got into the modern world and started using a calculator instead of an abacus."

"I don't need Google and all that stuff, I've got you," he told her. "Think of it as job security."

"Yeah, yeah, you keep shoveling it and I'll keep buying bigger boots so I can wade through it."

When she left his office Weber dialed the number for the automobile dealership and a friendly sounding young woman answered the phone to tell him that they were having a great day at Fisher's Ford and asked how she could direct his call.

"I need to speak to Lee Drysdale, if he's there."

"He sure is. Can I tell him who's calling?"

"Jim Weber."

"You just hang on for a minute, Mr. Weber, and I'll get Lee for you."

In less in a minute there was a click and a man's voice said, "Good morning, this is Lee. How can I help you?"

"Mr. Drysdale, my name is Jim Weber. I'm the Sheriff in Big Lake, Arizona. Do you have time to talk for a few minutes?"

"Is this about a vehicle, Sheriff Weber? Because right now we've got some incredible deals on F-150s, two wheel drive or four, whatever you need."

"Actually, this isn't about a vehicle, Mr. Drysdale. It's about your time with the Cañon Verde Police Department."

He could hear the change in the man's voice when he replied, "I'd rather forget about anything to do with that town or that job."

The guarded tone in his voice told Weber that whatever had happened in Cañon Verde was not something Drysdale wanted to talk about.

"Look, I'm not trying to cause you any problems. I just need to get some feedback on things there in Cañon Verde."

"Why is a sheriff from Arizona asking questions about Cañon Verde?"

"I can't go into a lot of detail, I just need to..."

"I've got nothing to tell you," Drysdale said, cutting him off.

"Please, I'm just trying to find out how things operate over there."

"Mister, I don't know who you are. You're just a voice on the telephone. And like I said, I've got nothing to say to you." There was a click and the phone went dead.

Weber stared at the phone for a minute and started to call back, then thought better of it. Whatever Lee Drysdale knew, whatever had happened to him while he was on the Cañon Verde Police Department, and whatever had caused him to leave his job was not something he was going to talk about. At least not to an unknown voice on the telephone. Instead, he called Cañon Verde and asked to talk to Chief Kramer.

"What can I do for you, Sheriff?"

The man's voice was not friendly.

"Actually, I called to give you some information," Weber replied.

"Yeah? What's that?"

"Zach Murdoch is sitting in one of my cells right now."

"He is?" The change in Kramer's voice was evident.

"Where did you catch him? Was he hiding out at his mother's just like I said?"

"I didn't catch him. He surrendered himself to me." He knew it was stretching the truth somewhat but didn't care at that point.

"No shit? I'll be there this afternoon to pick him up."

"Well, there's going to be a problem with that," Weber told him. "He's already said he's going to fight extradition back to New Mexico."

"That's bullshit. I'm coming to get him."

"I wish I could help you, but my hands are tied," Weber said. "Best advice I can give you is to go ahead and file papers to extradite him and we'll get him in front of a judge."

"Or, we could just bypass all of the red tape and you could hand him over to me, kind of off the record. Once I've got him back here, he can tell any kind of story he wants, but as far as anybody knows I caught him in New Mexico and you never set eyes on the little bastard. It'll be his word against ours."

"Sorry, I can't do that," Weber said. "We're going to have to do it by the book."

"The book is bullshit! You know it and I know it. All the book does is give pukes like him all kinds of ways to jerk off the system and delay the inevitable. Murdoch is coming back here, and he's going to stand trial, and he's going to get convicted, and then he's going to spend the rest of his life face down on a cell bunk while the other cons take turns with him. And it couldn't happen to a nicer guy. I'd prefer we still had the death penalty and we could just rid the world of him and his kind forever, but I can deal with the other.

"Be that as it may, if you want him a judge has to grant an extradition order."

"Do you think that's going to change anything, Weber? One way or the other, that boy's ass is mine."

"Well, like they say, see you in court."

Kramer was cursing him when Weber hung up the phone.

His next call was to Leslie Hensdell, the woman Zach said was his probation officer. When he told her that he had Zach in custody in Big Lake, she replied, "It didn't take him long to get caught, did it?"

"Actually, he turned himself in," Weber said.

"I just don't understand that kid," the probation officer said. "He kept his nose clean and did everything by the book and he had what, three weeks to go, and he screws up like this?"

"According to Zach, he didn't know there were drugs and paraphernalia in his girlfriend's car when he got stopped."

"How many times have you pulled someone over and they admitted to having contraband, Sheriff Weber?"

"You've got a point there," Weber admitted.

"Though, I have to say, if I was ever going to buy anybody's story about that, it would probably be Zach's."

"Why is that?"

"I don't know, Sheriff. I've dealt with a lot of people in my time, and I think I've probably gotten jaded over the years. You hear so many lies from so many people who swear they're telling you the truth that pretty soon you don't believe anybody."

Weber understood that cynicism, it was something that most cops experienced.

"But with Zach," Leslie continued, "I think he really is a nice kid. I get a lot of people coming to my office and it's yes, ma'am and no, ma'am and all that sort of thing, and how they want to do the right thing. And you know all along that they're just feeding you a line of crap and expecting you to believe it. But with Zach, I don't think he was trying to blow smoke up my ass. I really think he was sincere. He had a good job and his own apartment and was doing well and he screwed up. And he realized it. I think he really did want to do better in life. And as far as him killing that nurse? I would've never seen that coming in a million years."

"Ms. Hensdell, Zach says he didn't kill her. In fact, his story is pretty wild."

"Please, call me Leslie. So what's his story?"

"Well, according to him, Chief Kramer there in Cañon Verde killed her."

"Zach said that?"

"Yes, ma'am." Weber told her the whole story as related by Zach, about how he had been pulled over for a routine traffic stop and the drugs were discovered, how the arrest had gone down without any problems, but how once he got to the police station Chief Kramer had assaulted him, about being taken to the hospital, and about how the police chief attacked Barbara Eibeck when she began taking pictures of his injuries. When he was finished telling her about Zach's escape and him turning up in Big Lake, and how he was certain that if he was released to Kramer the police chief would kill him to cover up his crimes, the woman was silent for a long time. So long, in fact, that Weber wondered if she had hung up.

"Are you still there?"

"Yeah... yeah, I'm sorry. I'm here. I'm just trying to digest all of this."

"So what do you think? Is it a crazy story by a desperate kid trying to get out of trouble or is there a possibility that there's any truth to it at all?"

There was another moment of silence, and then Leslie replied, "Whatever you do, Sheriff Weber, don't turn Zach Murdoch over to Kramer."

"So you think Zach is telling the truth?"

"I don't know how much truth there is to it, but I'll tell you this. I have had more than one probationer who got an ass whipping in Chief Kramer's jail. Last year I had a closed-door meeting with him and confronted him about it, and he didn't deny it for one second. He was proud of the fact that people only stepped over the line one time in Cañon Verde."

"Did you report it to anyone?"

"Oh, yeah, I did. I reported it to my supervisor as soon as I left that meeting."

"And did anything happen?"

"Yes, Sheriff Weber, something happened. I received a letter of reprimand and a personal visit from someone up the chain of command who told me that I was getting soft and I might want to think about putting in my papers next year when I'm eligible for retirement. And it was strongly hinted that I needed to mind my own business until then, or I might be looking for a new career. Kramer's got a lot of influential friends in this part of the state, and they are behind him one hundred percent."

Nick Russell

Chapter 20

When Weber was finished talking with the probation officer he went outside to Parks' trailer.

"What's up, Bubba?"

"I'm going to say something I've never said before, so you mark this day on your calendar, Parks."

"Finally, you're going to tell me I'm brilliant and handsome and the best lawman you've ever known, aren't you?"

"No, not that any of that isn't true, but this is something else."

"Hey, as long as we both agree on what a great guy I am, you don't really have to say it. Just knowing it warms my heart. What's on your mind, Jimmy?"

"I think we should take an airplane ride."

Weber had never been a fan of flying, especially in small airplanes, and though he knew Parks was a competent pilot, he still wasn't comfortable when the little Cessna 172 Skyhawk lifted off the ground. But the butterflies left his stomach before long and he was able to sit back and enjoy the flight. It was not quite 200 miles to Las Cruces and they covered the distance in less than two hours. While Parks tied his airplane down at the general aviation section of the Las Cruces International Airport, Weber went into the office and rented a car. Using the mapping app on his telephone, they had no problem finding the Ford dealership.

It was a big place in an auto mall, and an eager young man with a name tag that identified him as Randy greeted them when they arrived.

"Hello guys, it's a great day at Fisher's Ford. How can I help you?"

Weber was tempted to ask if that was a canned greeting that every employee gave to anybody who called or walked on the lot, but instead he asked for Lee Drysdale. The salesman seemed somewhat disappointed that he wasn't going to get to sell them something, but he said, "That's Lee, over there by that white Focus."

Drysdale was in his late 30s and was already showing a noticeable bald spot on the top of his head. He was a slender man of average height with narrow shoulders. Nothing about him stood out. He was a man who went through life as just another face in the crowd. They approached him and he smiled and said hello. At least he hadn't told them what a great day it was at Fisher's Ford.

Weber was dressed in jeans and a flannel shirt, which had been comfortable at home but was warm down in the desert. He pulled his badge wallet out and showed it to the man and said, "Mr. Drysdale, I talked to you earlier today. I'm Sheriff Weber from Big Lake, Arizona, and this is FBI Agent Larry Parks."

His look of panic told Weber that the man had secrets. Secrets that he wasn't willing to give up. He looked at both of their IDs and then looked around quickly to see if anybody else was nearby. Another salesman was showing an older couple a used minivan nearby. Weber wondered if Drysdale might turn and run, but instead he asked, "What are you doing here? I told you I didn't have anything to say to you."

"I'm sorry, but I think you do."

"Please, just go away."

"Look, Mr. Drysdale, all we want is a few minutes of your time. If it wasn't important we wouldn't be here."

"You don't know what you're asking."

"Like I said, just a few minutes."

He looked around again. Randy, the young salesman they had first encountered, was shaking hands with a young couple and started leading them to a row of parked Mustangs. The other salesman had convinced the couple to get into the minivan and they were pulling out to go on a test drive. Two other salespeople were standing under the dealership's cement awning to stay out of the sun while they waited for customers to show up.

"I can't talk standing out here. There's an Applebee's two blocks down the street. I'll take an early lunch and meet you there in half an hour."

~***~

Weber wasn't entirely certain that Drysdale would show up, but a few minutes after the waitress brought their iced tea he came into the restaurant and looked around. Spotting them, he came to their table and sat down.

"Before anything else, I want to see your IDs again."

They both handed him their credentials and he studied them carefully before passing them back. The waitress came back to ask if he wanted something to drink or if they were ready to order, and Drysdale waved her away.

"You've got five minutes. What's this all about?"

"It's about the Cañon Verde Police Department, and about Chief Kramer in particular," Weber told him.

"I told you on the phone this morning, I don't have anything to say about that place."

"Yeah, you told me that. But why don't you want to talk about it?"

"I don't know what you guys are looking for, but you're not going to get it from me."

"Mr. Drysdale, I promise you that you're not in any kind of trouble," Weber said.

The man looked at him with misery on his face.

"You have no idea what trouble is, Sheriff."

"Oh, I know a little bit about trouble. I've seen some of it in my time. And I know that whatever happened over there in Cañon Verde must have been pretty bad from the way you're acting."

"I don't mean to be rude, but how about you two do me a favor and go back where you came from and forget you ever saw me?"

"Like Sheriff Weber said, we're not looking to jam you up," Parks told him.

"You guys don't get it, do you? You just being here, me just talking to you... no, I don't want to get involved in anything that has to do with Cañon Verde."

"We know bad things are going on over there," Weber said. "We know Chief Kramer is dirty. We just need you to tell us anything you can about your time there, or why you left the police department. We're never going to bring your name up in any way at all. You've got my word on that."

"Forget it, guys. You came to the wrong man. I've got nothing to tell you."

"Mr. Drysdale, if you did something over there, we'll work with you. Whatever it is, trust us on that."

"Trust you? I don't even know you guys. Forget it, you're wasting your breath."

He started to stand up and Weber put his hand on his arm.

"What happened over there? What's got you so scared that you won't talk to anybody about it?"

"Let go of my arm, Sheriff. I'm out of here! Those people in Cañon Verde all think Chief Kramer walks on water and can do no wrong. Well, they can have him. I'm done with that place and I never want to hear his name again."

He pulled his arm away and stood up. "I'm sorry you wasted your time coming all the way here to talk to me, but I told you on the phone I had nothing to say."

"You just said the people in Cañon Verde all think Chief Kramer walks on water. But from what I hear, not everybody feels that way."

"Yeah? Well all the ones that matter do!"

He was walking away from the table when Weber said, "Not a woman named Barbara Eibeck. The way I hear it, she stood up to Kramer. And now she's dead."

Drysdale froze, then turned back with a look of shock on his face.

"Barbara's dead?"

Weber nodded his head. "Yes, she's dead. She was killed a few days ago. According to Kramer, a prisoner he took to the medical center killed her and then escaped. That young man is sitting in my jail over in Big Lake and he's got a completely different story about what happened. According to him, Kramer killed her."

"That prick. That no good rotten prick!"

Drysdale was a different man. His jaw was tense and his hands were balled into fists. His whole body language made it seem like there was a surge of electricity going through him.

"Sit down and let's talk," Weber said.

Nick Russell

Chapter 21

"I worked for the police department here in Las Cruces for two years," Drysdale told them. "Then my wife got cancer. She was gone in six months. She was from Cañon Verde and her parents still live there. Mine are divorced. My dad lives in California and my mom married some guy and they moved to Dallas. Stacy's parents kept telling me I should move there and they could help me with the kids. We had two. Jason is nine now, and Heather is seven. I couldn't really afford good care for them on a cop's salary, and you know how the schedule can be. It's hard enough when you're married, but for a single parent... it was just overwhelming. So I hired on with the PD in Cañon Verde. Biggest mistake I ever made in my life."

"Tell us about it," Parks said.

"There are some good guys on the department, don't get me wrong. But there's also some jerks. And then there's Chief Kramer. That guy, there's a word I'm looking for... swaggers. He swaggers through life and he walks right over anybody who gets in his way, and he doesn't give it a second thought. If you're Mexican, if you're a young person with long hair or tattoos and don't come from the right family, you've got a problem."

"What kind of problem?"

"You're not welcome in Cañon Verde. More than once I've seen Chief Kramer run people out of town for no reason except that he didn't like their looks. And more often than not, they got a good ass kicking before they left, to make sure they never came back."

"Who did the ass kicking? Chief Kramer?"

"He wasn't the only one, there were a couple of guys who didn't hesitate to lay into somebody for any excuse at all. And forget it, I'm not naming names. But Chief Kramer, it was like he enjoyed it. Sometimes they'd bring in some poor kid, or some Mexican who hadn't done anything, and Kramer would just work them over. He always said he was tuning them up because they had a bad attitude. And there were times when I actually saw him go out looking for someone, anyone, so he could kick their ass. He'd see somebody and decide he didn't like their looks, and he'd pull them over and that was it. Before they knew it they were locked up in a cell and he was making them sorry they were ever born."

"Lee, can you give us any specifics? Anything at all?"

He shook his head stubbornly. "I told you, that's not going to happen. You can call me a coward or whatever you want, I don't care."

"What happened there? Why did you leave the department?"

"Officially, I left because I wanted to come back to Las Cruces to make more money than a small town cop earns. And I do, working at the Ford dealership. I'll never get rich, but I'm able to take care of my kids, and I'm home every night with them. That's all that matters to me."

"That's the official story," Weber said. "What really happened?"

The man wouldn't reply, but Weber could tell that whatever it had been, it had made a deep impact on him.

"What can you tell me about Barbara Eibeck?"

"Barbara's a nice lady. Or was, I guess. I can't believe she's dead."

"Did you know her well?"

"We weren't close friends or anything like that, but you know how it is. You get to know the people in the ER when you're a cop. She was really good to work with."

"Do you know if there was ever a problem between her and Chief Kramer?"

"I know that she didn't think much of him at all. A couple of times when we took a prisoner in who had been roughed up, she asked him a lot of questions about how it happened. Of course, according to him, they always got hurt while they were resisting arrest. You could tell she didn't believe that for a minute. A couple of times she asked too many questions and he got pissed off and told her that if she knew what was good for her, she would mind her own damned business."

"Let me ask you something," Weber said. "We know Kramer has stepped way over the line in abusing prisoners in the past, but do you think he'd go so far as to kill somebody like Barbara Eibeck?"

Drysdale was quiet for a long time, staring at the table, and Weber thought he was going to tell them again that he had nothing more to say. But instead, he nodded his head.

"Lee? Are you saying you think he would do something like that?"

The former policeman raised his head and looked at them and said. "If Chief Kramer thought he had to kill somebody to cover his ass, he wouldn't hesitate for a moment."

"I don't doubt he'd take out one of those people you were talking about that don't matter to him, an Hispanic person or some poor young longhair," Parks said. "But do you really think he would go so far as to kill somebody like Mrs. Eibeck?"

"Yeah, he would."

"You seem pretty sure of that. Why is that, Lee?"

There were tears in his eyes when he looked at them and said, "Because I watched him hold a gun to my five-year-old daughter's head and pull the hammer back and tell me that if I ever tried to cross him, if I ever did anything to cause him any kind of problems, he was going to kill her right in front of my eyes. Kill her, and then kill Jason, and then kill me. That's why I left, and that's why I didn't want to talk to you guys. He was gonna kill my kids!"

It took a few minutes for Drysdale to compose himself, but then he told them the story.

"I'd seen enough to make me uncomfortable and it didn't take me long to realize that I'd made a big mistake coming to Cañon Verde. But I just tried to keep my head down and mind my own business because I really did think it was better for my kids to be there where their grandparents could help take care of them. But then one night one of our cops named Warren Moon pulled over a car for speeding. There was a young couple in it, and there's no question that they had a bad attitude right from the start. The driver refused to give Moon his license or registration and was mouthing off. Moon called for backup and when I pulled up he had them both out of the car and with their hands on the trunk. They were talking a lot of shit, calling us pigs, you know the routine. We handcuffed the guy but when we tried to cuff the girl she went off on both of us. She smacked me in the face and my nose started bleeding, then she kicked Moon in the nuts. She was a handful, but we finally got her subdued and cuffed. When we searched the car we found a bunch of paraphernalia and some meth. So we arrested them and took them to the station. And that's when things got really ugly."

"What happened, Lee?"

"Even when he's off duty, the chief monitors his radio 24/7. He came in wanting to see the woman who had assaulted two of his officers. Like I said, that girl was out of control, which was bad enough to start with. But when Chief Kramer got there, it escalated big time. He was screaming at her, telling her she was going to do hard time for assaulting police officers and for the drugs, and she spit in his face. That was like tossing a match in a can of gasoline. He started beating on her and I thought he was going to kill her right there. But he didn't, instead he took her back and put her in a cell with four guys. Four really bad ass guys. He told them they were getting an early Christmas present. Then he walked out and locked the door behind him and told the other officers to stay out of there."

Weber felt his stomach turn and when he looked at Parks he could tell his friend was feeling the same thing.

"What happened to her, Lee?"

"What you think happened to her? They used that poor girl in ways I can't even describe. I kept telling Chief Kramer and Moon that that was wrong, and they both just laughed at me. I couldn't take it and I started back to the cellblock to put an end to it. Chief Kramer stopped me. He told me that if I knew what was good for me I would just go home and keep my mouth shut. I took off my badge and dropped it on the floor and told him I was done."

Drysdale was speaking in a monotone now as he recalled that horrible night. "I went to my in-laws' house and I picked up the kids and I went home. I put them to bed and I started packing right then, because the sooner I got out of that town, the better. An hour or so later I came out of my bedroom with a suitcase in each hand, and Kramer was sitting there on the couch, and he had one of my kids on each side of him. They were half-asleep, and he had a .357 Magnum in his hand. He put it up to Heather's head and cocked the hammer, and that's when he told me that if I ever crossed him, if he ever heard a word from me again, he was going to kill both the kids, then me."

It was all Weber could do to keep himself from walking out of the restaurant and getting in his rental car and driving straight to Cañon Verde to confront the man who had bullied so many people and disgraced his badge.

"I'm very sorry that happened to you," Parks was saying. "Believe me, Lee, we're going to take this guy down. Once and for all."

"I really hope you do," Lee replied. "But I'm telling you both, right here and right now, you're going to have to do it without my help. I've never told anybody about this before, and I shouldn't have told you now. I'm already regretting it."

"Don't," Weber told him. "I can't imagine what that must have been like for you, Lee. I truly can't. But I can tell you that Kramer is not going to get away with the things he's done. Your testimony would sure help."

Drysdale stubbornly shook his head. "I'm sorry, guys I can't. We all know how the law works. He could walk on all of this. He could walk, and someday I could come home and find him sitting on the couch again with his gun and my kids. That's not a chance I can take."

They were silent on the drive back to the airport. While Weber returned the rental car, Parks made sure his airplane was topped off with fuel and then did a preflight check. They taxied to the side of the runway and had to wait while a business jet landed before they got clearance to take off. Weber's mind was so occupied with the story that Lee Drysdale had told them that he didn't have the usual queasy feeling in his stomach.

Once they were airborne, he said to Parks "Why don't we just fly to Cañon Verde and find Kramer and shoot his ass?"

"I love you like a brother, Jimmy, but I've got to be honest, I'd rather spend the rest of my life sleeping with Marsha instead of sharing a cell with you. We're going to take this guy down, but not that way. He's not worth it."

Weber wasn't sure he agreed with his friend. At that point, in his mind, it would have been worth any sacrifice it took to make sure that Arthur Kramer got what he had coming to him.

Chapter 22

"Just so you know, Chief Kramer is in town and Chet's on the warpath," Mary Caitlin said when Weber returned to the office that afternoon.

"It didn't take him long to get here."

"No, I think he probably ran lights and siren all the way. He came in here demanding to take Zach back to New Mexico with him and I told him he was going to have to have a court order to do so. So he handed me this."

Mary gave Weber a legal form, which he opened and read. A request for extradition of Zachary Murdoch to the State of New Mexico to face charges of first-degree murder, assault on a police officer, and escape.

"Then what happened?"

"Coop and Chad were here, and they told him that you are out of town and that he wasn't taking anybody anywhere without your say so. He started raising hell and they escorted him out of the office. Half an hour later Chet was in here demanding that we turn the prisoner over to him. Meanwhile, Juliette had retained a lawyer from down in Phoenix, and he faxed a paper to stop extradition to us. I guess he sent one to Judge Ryman, too, because the judge called and wanted to talk to you as soon as you got back to town. So what I'm telling you, in a nutshell, is that the shit has hit the fan, Jimmy. Did you find out anything in New Mexico?"

"Oh, yeah," he told her.

"Enough to convince you that Zach is telling the truth?"

"Enough that if Kramer walked through the door right now, I might be tempted to pull out my weapon and start squeezing the trigger, and not stop until the magazine's empty."

As it turned out, it was Mayor Chet Wingate who came through the door, and he was fuming.

"Sheriff Weber, you're in trouble. Big trouble!"

"How about we just cut to the chase and I tell you to go to hell, Chet? I'm too busy to waste time with your nonsense today."

"You can't talk to me that way!"

"Obviously I can, because I just did."

"I'm relieving you of duty, Sheriff."

"Okay, let's make it official. Go to hell, Chet. You can't relieve me of duty. It takes a majority vote of the entire Town Council."

"Oh, I can do it. You abandoned your post and left town without my permission."

"I don't have to have your permission to do a damn thing, Chet."

"We'll just see what the Town Council has to say about that!"

Councilwoman Gretchen Smith-Abbott, the mayor's trusty sidekick, seemed more concerned with his rising blood pressure than with the sheriff's supposed misdeeds. "Calm down, Chet. Your heart."

"My heart is just fine," the mayor snapped at her.

Everyone in the room knew that his heart was not fine, that the mayor had already suffered a couple of cardiac incidents in the past, and while Weber did not want to aggravate his condition, having once before had the mayor collapse in his office, he wasn't going to back down either.

"Go talk to the Town Council or whatever you need to do, Chet. I've got work to do."

"What you need to do is release that prisoner of yours to Chief Kramer. How dare you try to circumvent the legal process?"

"Chet, you're the one trying to circumvent the legal process. You and Kramer. Paperwork has already been filed to contest the extradition order."

"I want to see that paperwork."

Weber handed him a copy of the fax from the attorney Juliette Murdoch had hired and while the mayor was reading it, he called the courthouse.

"Chief Kramer from New Mexico is here now," the court clerk told him. "The judge wants you to come over as soon as you can."

"I'm on my way."

"You're not going anywhere until we settle this," the mayor said, stepping in Weber's path to block him.

"Chet, I can walk through you or over you, it's up to you."

"You're done in this town, Sheriff!"

Weber shoved him aside and left the office.

~***~

It took a lot of effort not to physically attack Kramer when Weber saw him at the courthouse. Judge Ryman wasted no time taking them both into his chambers.

"Chief Kramer, I've looked at your extradition request, and at this time I'm denying it because the defendant in this case has filed a motion to resist."

"Sir, with all due respect, the defendant in this case has a record of drug convictions in the past. And from what I hear, he was in trouble here for burglary. We're not talking about some Sunday school kid. He's a murderer."

"The way I understand the law, he's innocent until he is proven guilty."

"And he is going to be proven guilty once I get him back to New Mexico."

"Bullshit," Weber said. "You and I both know you're going to kill him before you ever get back to Cañon Verde. There's no way you're going to let him live."

"Sheriff, watch your language," the judge said sternly.

"I'm sorry, Your Honor. But that's exactly what's going to happen."

"I don't know what kind of fairytales that kid's been telling you, but..."

"That's enough," the judge said holding his hand up. "I'm setting a hearing for 10 o'clock tomorrow morning. Chief Kramer, you can state your case then."

"I want to talk to Murdoch, right now."

"That's not going to happen," Weber told him.

"Judge, will you order him to let me talk to my prisoner?"

"Sorry, Chief Kramer, at this point he's Sheriff Weber's prisoner. If he doesn't want you talking to him, you're not going to talk to him. Now, I've got other things to do besides sitting here listening to you two argue. Save it for court tomorrow."

They left the judge's office, and when they were out in the parking lot Kramer turned and pointed a finger in the sheriff's face. "When this is over, you and me are going to settle things between us, Weber. You're gonna find out that nobody screws with Art Kramer and gets away with it."

"No, when this is over, you're going to spend the rest of your life in a prison cell," Weber told him. "I've done some digging, Kramer. I know all about you, and how you do things over there in New Mexico. Trust me, those days are over. Enjoy your freedom while you can, because like I said, you're headed for prison, which is right where you belong."

Weber didn't know it at the time, but his prediction would never come true.

~***~

"We're all used to Chet sticking his nose in Sheriff's Department business," Coop said an hour later. "But telling you to release a prisoner just like that? That's extreme even for him."

"Chet's been mad at Juliette Murdoch ever since Snowdaze," Mary Caitlin said. "After that whole Santa Claus fiasco, he tried to blame her because everything fell apart. To hear him tell it, it's even her fault that Jill Cotter's body turned up floating in the lake in the middle of the event."

The Snowdaze winter festival, held a few months earlier, had been a fiasco right from the start, when the mayor's plan to have a mannequin of Santa Claus parachute into the middle of the opening festivities had gone wrong, the mannequin exploding on impact. Forever after, the mayor was known as The Man Who Killed Santa Claus. But always eager to take all the glory when something went wrong, Mayor Wingate was just as quick to try to place the blame on somebody else when it didn't. In this case it was Juliette Murdoch, the Chamber of Commerce director, who had come up with the idea of Snowdaze in the first place. When she had dug in her heels and refused to be responsible for something that he had thought up, she had made an enemy. The mayor was an unforgiving man who carried a grudge a long time.

"Mad enough that he would let Kramer take her son out of here, knowing what he's likely to do to him?"

"I don't think he has any clue about that part of things," Weber said. "When it comes to Chet, the less he knows, the better."

"So what's the deal with this Kramer guy, Jimmy? Is he as bad as Zach Murdoch says he is, or is the kid just trying to cover his ass?"

"Dolan, from what I've been able to find out so far, he's even worse than I thought. He's a very dangerous man."

"This isn't just based on what Zach is telling you?"

"No, it's not. Parks and I talked to a former officer who worked under him. He told us some things that would make your skin crawl."

The office door opened and Archer came in with two Styrofoam containers containing the prisoner's evening meal.

"I'll take them back to him," Weber said.

Zach was sitting on the bunk in the cell and when he looked up Weber could tell the strain was getting to him.

"I brought you something to eat, Zach. How are you doing?"

"My mom said that Chief Kramer is back in town."

"Yes, he is. But don't worry about it, he's not getting anywhere near you. Your mom hired an attorney, and there's going to be a hearing tomorrow about the extradition."

"Do you think he's gonna be able to take me, Sheriff?"

The young man's voice and body language showed his fear.

"No, he's not taking you anywhere. You need to listen to me, Zach. I believe everything you told me, and come hell or high water, Kramer is never going to lay a hand on you. I promise you that."

"You believe me? You really do?"

"Yes, I do. I've done some looking into the way Kramer does things over there in Cañon Verde and I have no doubt that he killed that nurse, not you."

The look of relief on Zach's face was one Weber would always remember. It was the expression of a man who had walked up to the brink of the abyss and peered into it but had been able to step away. It was the expression of a young man who realized that no matter how grim his situation might be, someone believed in him and was there to help. Someone who he believed *would* help. And Weber knew that no matter what he had to do, he wasn't going to let Zach Murdoch down.

Chapter 23

"I've ain't never met Zach, but I know Miz Murdoch, and she's a real fine lady," Kallie Jo Wingate said. "She really cares about this town and the business community. Why, do you know that with all she's got to do at the Chamber office and all that, and goin' to meetin's and talkin' to the business class at the high school tryin' to get those kids interested in coming back for a business career right here at home instead of takin' off someplace when they graduate from high school or college, she also volunteers out there at SafeHaven?"

"No, I didn't know that," Weber said, though he wasn't surprised that Juliette Murdoch put in time at the women's shelter helping those less fortunate. They may have had their problems in the past, but there had never been any question in his mind that the Chamber of Commerce director loved their little mountain community and was one of its strongest boosters.

"And you know what else? I'll tell you what else," Kallie Jo said in her rapid-fire Georgia-laced manner of speaking, "That Miz Murdoch, she ain't afraid of hard work. No, sir, she's not! Couple weeks ago we had a delivery truck come in and Darrel was out sick, and Norma was upfront takin' care of customers, so it was just me and the truck driver unloadin' it. And he was complainin' 'bout how bad his back was and he weren't supposed to be liftin' anythin', so guess who was doin' all the work? Now, don't get me wrong, Sheriff Jimmy, I ain't afraid of hard work and I done my share of it back home on the farm. But it was a lot of stuff to unload and I ain't that big a girl, as you might have noticed. My daddy, he used to say I weren't much more than a popcorn fart in the wind. I know that may sound crude, but that's what my daddy used to say. 'Course, he knew I was a hard worker, too. You grew up on a farm or ranch, right? So you know what I'm talkin' 'bout. Everybody has to pitch and get the job done."

Weber had given up trying to hold a real conversation with Kallie Jo a long time ago. When she launched into one of her homespun dialogues, the best thing to do was just nod your head once in a while. So he just nodded his head.

"Anyway, what was I sayin'? Oh yeah, I was talkin' 'bout Miz Murdoch. She came in to talk to me about somethin', now what was that? The fundraiser for the volunteer fire department? No, I don't think it was that. I know what it was! It was about those bricks they're goin' to put in the park. Did you hear about that? For $150 you get a brick with your very own name on it. Now, I know what you're thinkin'. You're thinkin' you could buy a whole lot of bricks for $150, ain't you? But see, this is a fundraiser to help pay for playground equipment at the park. That's the kind of thing Miz Murdoch is always doin' to help this town. Now, Mr. Chet, he'd, well he'd poop a brick if he know'd I spent money on somethin' like that. Excuse my French, but that's somethin' else my daddy used to say, too. Well, not poop a brick, he'd use the S word. Not that Daddy is a man given to cussin' because he usually ain't. Well, no more than any other man, and a lot better than a whole bunch of 'em."

In spite of her mile a minute manner of speaking, everyone loved Kallie Jo, a tiny, dark haired bundle of energy that Archer had met online. She had even won over Archer's father, the mayor, who had started out believing she was no more than a gold digger when she showed up in town unannounced to claim her man. Won him over to the point that he had turned over the day-to-day operations of the family hardware store to her when his heart condition had become a problem. Though he had made a good recovery in spite of the fact that he refused to follow his doctor's orders to maintain a proper diet and not to stress out all the time like he was prone to do, Kallie Jo had turned things around at the store to such an extent that he left her to run things. Kallie Jo had quickly set to work, eliminating old stale stock that had set on the shelves for years and replacing it with items the customers wanted. Mayor Wingate, a born skinflint, had not always agreed with the way she did things, but he did like making money. Customers were happier, morale among the store's employees was at an all-time high, and profits were up. Even Chet, who wore a perpetual frown, couldn't argue with those results

Kallie Jo wrinkled her forehead for a moment and said, "I wonder why we say excuse my French like that? Because poop or brick ain't neither one no French word, are they? I mean, I'm sure they got words in that language for both of them things, but why do we say excuse my French? And we don't just say it for those words, we say it for other words, too, if you know what I mean."

Sometimes when Kallie Jo was on a roll just listening to her gave Weber a headache. He wasn't sure if it was because it had been a long day, or the airplane ride down to such a low elevation at Las Cruces and then back up to the mountains, or maybe because Kallie Jo was talking so fast, but he could feel something in the back of his skull starting to ache.

"Like I was sayin', I was out back unloadin' that truck pretty much by myself, what with that truck driver sayin' he's got a bum back. Well, Miz Murdoch, she just pitched right in and helped me get that thing unloaded! Yes, sir, she did! Now, that weren't no part of her job, but that's the way she is. A nice, hard-workin' lady who cares."

Kallie Jo emphasized her last statement with a noticeable nod of her head.

"Yeah, she's a nice lady," Weber said. "No question about that."

"That's right, she is," Kallie Jo said. "And I just don't believe that no lady like that, bein' a single mom and all that, I can't believe she's goin' to raise a son that would do somethin' terrible like that man is sayin' her boy Zachary did."

"I think you're right, Kallie Jo," Robyn said. "And we're going to do everything we can to prove he's innocent."

The office door opened and Archer lumbered in.

"There's my man," Kallie Jo said excitedly and ran to throw her arms around her husband. Of course, Archer was so big and she was so small that those arms didn't have much of a chance of getting all the way around, stopping somewhere in the vicinity of his ribs.

"I'm here for extra night duty like you told me, Jimmy."

"Well, this is not going to be very hard, Archer," the sheriff said. All you've got to do is stay here in the office and make sure that nobody goes back into the cellblock, okay?"

"All night long?"

"Yes Archer, all night long. We had this conversation, remember? You didn't want me to dock your pay to pay for the window you broke in your car, so this is how you do it. One shift of extra duty."

"I sure hope I can stay awake."

"Archer, you *will* stay awake. You know what they do to sentries who fall asleep on guard duty in the Army, don't you?"

Archer shook his head. "You know I was never in the Army, Jimmy."

"Well, what they do is they shoot them, Archer. I really don't want to have to shoot you. So do us both a favor and stay awake, will you?"

"Don't you worry about it, Sheriff Jimmy," Kallie Joe assured him. "I'm goin' to stay right here with him for a while to keep him company. And Archer, I brought you a basket with all kinds of your favorite snacks. There's pastrami sandwiches, and some leftover fried chicken drumsticks, and some beef jerky, and I even brought you some of my homemade potato salad. And two Pepsi's, and there's coffee, so you're gonna be fine."

Weber wasn't sure which surprised him more, how much food Kallie Jo considered a snack, or the fact that there were ever any kind of leftovers at their house.

"Okay, it's 10 o'clock, and I need to go home. I've got to be in court in the morning. Don't forget what I said, Archer, nobody goes back in the cellblock."

Archer nodded his head as he bit into a drumstick. He chewed loudly, smacking his lips, then wiped the back of his hand across them and asked, "What if it's one of our guys, Jimmy? What if Dan or Buz brings in a prisoner or something like that? They can't put them in a cell?"

"Archer, don't worry about it. Everybody knows that we're not bringing anybody in unless it's an extreme case, okay? They're just gonna cite them and tell them to see the judge at the appointed time."

"But what if it is an extreme case? Then what?"

Weber sighed. Kallie Jo wasn't the only person who could give him a headache.

"Archer, eat your drumstick. And stay awake. Don't worry about anything else, okay?"

"Whatever you say, Jimmy. But if somebody brings in a prisoner in the middle of the night, I'm calling you to find out what you want me to do about it."

"Fine, Archer. You do that."

Weber walked outside and looked up at the night sky. It had warmed up in the last few days and there were a lot of stars out. Maybe winter was finally over at last.

Chapter 24

"We are here to show cause as to why the defendant charged with multiple felony crimes should not be extradited back to Cañon Verde, New Mexico to stand trial," Judge Ryman said when court convened the next morning. "I believe we have a representative from the Eddy County Attorney's office in New Mexico here. Is that correct?"

A stocky bald man in a gray suit stood up and said, "Yes, Your Honor. I'm George Harwood. And this is Cañon Verde Police Chief Arthur Kramer."

"Chief Kramer and I have met," the judge said, then turned to a man seated on the other side of the aisle. "And you, sir, are here to represent the defendant?"

A well-groomed man in a tailored suit and professionally styled hair stood up and said, "Yes, Your Honor. Adam Turner for the defense. Mrs. Murdoch has retained my office to represent her son."

"It's nice to meet you both," the judge said. "Sheriff Weber, is the defendant here?"

"Yes, he is, sir."

Weber went to a door on the side of the room and knocked, and Deputy Dan Wright escorted Zach Murdoch in, wearing an orange jail jumpsuit with his hands and legs shackled. He began shaking visibly when he saw Chief Kramer. Dan led him to a seat and put a comforting hand on his shoulder as he sat down.

"All right then, let's get started. Mr. Harwood, you first."

"Your Honor, Chief Kramer himself witnessed the defendant attack and savagely murder a woman named Barbara Eibeck, an emergency room nurse at the medical center in Cañon Verde. At the time, the defendant was in police custody for possession of drugs. In addition to murdering Mrs. Eibeck, he then violently assaulted Chief Kramer and attempted to murder him before escaping custody. He then fled across state lines and came here to

Big Lake. The State of New Mexico wants him back to face justice for his horrendous crimes and can find no reason why he should not be extradited at this time."

"Very well. Thank you, Mr. Harwood. Mr. Turner, what is your response?"

Standing up, Turner said, "Your Honor, Zachary Murdoch is innocent of the crimes alleged against him, except for the original charge of driving a car that had a small amount of marijuana and a bong in it. He readily admits to that. However, he attests that those items were not his and he was not aware they were in the vehicle."

"Yeah, right," Kramer said, earning him a sharp look from the judge, who raised his finger in warning.

"Furthermore, not only did my client not murder Mrs. Eibeck, he actually witnessed Chief Kramer assault and murder her. When the chief then attempted to kill him, my client fought back in self-defense. Yes, he did flee, but only because not doing so would have resulted in certain death for him. We contend that not only is my client innocent of the felony murder and assault charges against him, but that if he is released into Chief Kramer's custody, we have reason to believe that he will never make it back to Cañon Verde alive, based upon threats that Chief Kramer has made."

"Ridiculous, Your Honor," Harwood said. "Who heard these alleged threats? Or is this just based upon the defendant's lies to avoid justice?"

"Your Honor, those threats were made to Deputy Ted Cooper of the Big Lake Sheriff's Department. Deputy Cooper is prepared to testify that Chief Kramer told him that the next time he laid eyes on the defendant he would, and I'm quoting here, 'blow him away'."

"Your Honor, objection. That is ludicrous," Harwood said. "To even allege that a man with Chief Kramer's long and distinguished reputation as a law enforcement officer could be capable of such crimes is not only an insult to him personally, but to every man and woman who has ever worn a badge. The defendant's wild fabrications are just that, Your Honor, fabrications. A story he made up to try to save himself from facing the justice he deserves. Given his previous criminal history, there is no cause to believe anything he has to say."

"Mr. Harwood, are you insinuating that one of our deputies would also lie about what Chief Kramer told him he would do if he saw the defendant again?"

"Your Honor, those were the words of a frustrated public servant who found his efforts to do his job blocked by Sheriff Weber, nothing more than that."

"I see," the judge replied. "I have to say, I'm rather concerned about a public servant that can become so frustrated, as you call it, to make a comment like that. Especially when he carries a gun."

"Your Honor, Chief Kramer is not the one charged with any crimes here. Zachary Murdock is."

"Very well, Mr. Harwood," the judge said. "Chief Kramer, tell me about this assault and murder that Mr. Murdoch is alleged to have committed."

After being sworn in, Kramer told his story, relating how Zach Murdoch had been arrested after drugs were found in the car he was driving, how he had been injured resisting arrest, and how when taken to the Medical Center for treatment he had attacked and murdered nurse Barbara Eibeck, and then attacked Kramer himself before escaping.

After listening to him carefully, the judge asked, "Chief Kramer, why was the defendant taken to the Medical Center in the first place?"

"During the course of his original arrest he resisted my officer. While lawfully subduing him, he got a cut lip and a few scrapes."

The judge looked at Zach. His bruises were beginning to fade but were still very evident.

"Sir, approach the bench, please."

Dan led him to the judge's podium, and the defendant was instructed to open his mouth.

"All right, take him back to his seat, Deputy. Thank you."

"Chief Kramer, I've looked at the report from Dr. Patel at our Medical Center, noting Mr. Murdoch's injuries, and I've seen the bruises on this young man and how much damage has been done to his teeth. That's a lot more than the cut lip and a few scrapes you described."

"Your Honor, please, this is ridiculous," Harwood said. "Those injuries were sustained in the violent struggle with Chief Kramer while he was escaping after the defendant killed Mrs. Eibeck. Yes, they look bad, and they are. But you have to understand that Chief Kramer was fighting for his very life."

"Mr. Turner, is your client prepared to tell his side of the story at this time?"

"Yes, he is, sir."

As he was speaking the door to the courtroom opened and Special Agent Larry Parks and a woman who looked vaguely familiar to Weber entered.

"Your Honor, Mr. Murdoch will not be testifying at this time."

"I beg your pardon? And just who are you, ma'am?"

"Your Honor, my name is Sandra Dunnsire. I'm an Assistant U.S. Attorney based out of Phoenix. I have an order here from Federal Judge Anthony Weinman down in Phoenix to take Zachary Murdoch into protective custody pending a full investigation into allegations of abuse and misconduct made against Police Chief Arthur Kramer."

"What? This is ridiculous, Your Honor!"

"That's enough, Mr. Harwood. Ms. Dunnsire, let me take a look at that order, please."

She approached the bench and handed him a folder of legal forms. The judge picked up his reading glasses and put them on to look through the paperwork. When he was finished, he took the glasses off, folded them and set them down, then said, "Everything looks to be in order. Sheriff Weber, would you please release the prisoner to the custody of Ms. Dunnsire and Special Agent Parks?"

"Objection, Your Honor. You can't just..."

"I'm sorry, Mr. Harwood. You need to take it up with the U.S. Attorney's office and Judge Weinman. It's out of my hands\."

He rapped his gavel and said, "Court is adjourned."

Kramer launched himself out of his seat and started toward Zach with a look of pure hatred on his face. "You're dead, you little maggot!"

Weber and Dan both stepped in front of him to block his way.

"I can't believe you're going to believe this little puke over me! He comes in here and tells a bunch of lies to make me look like I'm the bad guy? Bullshit! I'm not going to stand for that, and I'm not gonna roll over and play dead because all of you want to protect this little asshole!"

"That's enough," Judge Ryman ordered. "You stop right now, Chief Kramer!"

He ignored the judge and tried to push his way past Weber and Dan. He didn't get far. Kramer was a big man, and he may have spent a lifetime fighting with criminals, and maybe those who didn't deserve his special brand of justice, but he was no match for Weber and Dan, who had played college football. The deputy swung his feet in front of the police chief's, knocking them out from under him. Kramer crashed to the floor with Dan and Weber on top of him.

"Stop struggling, Kramer," Weber said pulling his arm behind him.

"Let go of me!"

"Stop it," Weber ordered, pulling harder on his arm while Dan put a knee in the small of the man's back and pushed him down as he tried to rise up. "I'm not telling you again. Stop resisting. You can walk out of here like a man and go back where you belong, or I swear to God, we'll hogtie you and drag you out of here. It's your choice. Which is it going to be?"

"I'll kill you, Weber. I swear to God, I'll...."

"Shut up, Art," Harwood said. "That's enough. Don't worry, we'll get this all sorted out. That kid is going to face justice for what he did. But in the meantime, you're just making things worse."

Kramer finally stopped struggling and they jerked him to his feet. Weber took the man's pistol from his holster, then patted him down, finding a small Kel-Tec .380 semiautomatic pistol in one of his trouser pockets.

"Ms. Dunnsire, do you want Chief Kramer detained at this point?"

"No, Sheriff, we will be talking soon enough," she said.

"Okay, you get him out of here and you take him back to New Mexico right now," Weber told Harwood. "Kramer, if I see you around this town again, you've had it. Go back where you came from and stay there."

"I want my guns back."

"You can have your guns, but I'm keeping your ammo," Weber said. He pulled the magazines from both pistols and emptied them, then carefully ejected the rounds from the chambers. Then he took the two extra magazines for the chief's duty weapon from their pouch on his belt and emptied them, too. "Where's your vehicle?"

"Out in the parking lot. Where else do you think it would be?"

"Give me the keys."

Kramer reluctantly handed him the keys to the Tahoe.

Weber gave them to Dan and said, "Go out and search his ride. If there are any weapons in it unload them and take the ammunition. Make sure you get all of it."

"Is that really necessary, Sheriff?"

"Yes, Mr. Harwood, it's necessary. You've already seen how out of control Chief Kramer is. He's threatened to kill Mr. Murdoch more than once and he just threatened to kill me. If I were you, and if I wanted to cover my butt from what's going to be coming down from all this, I would be talking to the folks back home and telling them exactly what to expect. The farther you distance yourself from this jerk, the better off you're going to be."

Chapter 25

Back at the Sheriff's office, they allowed Juliette Murdoch a few minutes with her son. She was visibly shaken after the incident with Kramer.

"What happens to Zach now?"

"Special Agent Parks is going to transport him down to Phoenix and we're going to hold him in protective custody while we interview him about everything that happened at Cañon Verde," Sandra Dunnsire said. "Within 24 hours I expect the FBI will be all over that town."

"It's hard to believe things like that can still happen in this country in this day and age," Weber said.

"It sickens me," she told him. "How can somebody get away with something like that for so long?"

"I'm just glad it's finally coming out in the open. Kramer needs to be locked away for a long time. He's one scary dude."

"Trust me, Sheriff Weber, that's exactly what's going to happen to him."

~***~

Late that afternoon Weber had just left the office and was climbing into his Explorer when Mary Caitlin came out and stopped him.

"There's a phone call I think you need to take, Jimmy."

"Please tell me it's not Chet Wingate. And if it is, would you just save me the trouble and tell him to go to hell for me?"

"No, it's not Chet," Mary said. "It's a woman who says she's Barbara Eibeck's daughter."

Weber followed her back into the building and picked up the phone, pushing the button with the flashing light. "Sheriff Weber here."

"How could you? How could you protect that maniac that killed my mother?" The woman was shouting and Weber had to hold the phone away from his ear.

"I'm sorry, who is this?"

"My name is Tabitha Eibeck. Barbara Eibeck was my mother."

"I'm sorry for your loss, Ms. Eibeck."

"You're sorry for my loss? Sorry? You say you're sorry but you're protecting the man who killed her?"

"Ms. Eibeck, I don't know where you're getting your information from, but if you'll just hear me out."

"What? Listen to you repeat the same lies that the guy who killed her is spouting off to get himself out of trouble? No, thank you! My mother is dead and you're protecting her murderer."

"I don't believe Zachary Murdoch killed your mother, Ms. Eibeck."

"You don't believe it because you're sleeping with *his* mother, right?"

"That's not true at all," Weber told her. "Again, I don't know where you're getting your information, but..."

"Oh, Chief Kramer has told us all about how things are there in Big Lake. He went over there to try to bring that man back to face trial and you and that whole town turned him away so you could protect that murdering little bastard."

"Ma'am, with all due respect, you don't know what you're talking about. All I can say is you're going to have to wait until this whole thing plays out."

"Oh, I'll wait, Sheriff Weber. I'll wait, and I'll wait, and I'll wait as long as it takes to see that man convicted of my mother's murder. And then I'm going to stand up in court and tell him exactly what I think about him. And someday I'd like to see you, so I can tell you face-to-face just what I think about you, too!"

With that, she hung up. Weber stared at the phone in his hand for a moment before placing it back on the receiver. He almost wished it had been Chet Wingate calling instead. Chet he could deal with. But the grieving daughter of a murdered woman who believed the lies Arthur Kramer had told her about her mother's death left him feeling unsettled. While he was convinced that Zach

Murdoch was telling the truth that Kramer was a bully cop who had killed an innocent woman in a fit of rage, he knew that even knowing the real facts about her mother's death would never ease Tabitha Eibeck's pain.

Tabitha's enraged call was not the only one the Big Lake Sheriff's office would receive from people in Cañon Verde who supported Police Chief Arthur Kramer. The dispatcher was overwhelmed with calls from Cañon Verde citizens that evening and into the next morning demanding that Sheriff Weber turn the murderer of one of their most respected citizens over to Chief Kramer so he could face justice. Weber, Mary Caitlin, and the dispatchers gave up trying to tell them that it was now a federal matter and out of their hands, instead just thanking them for their calls and hanging up.

"My God, that man has got a lot of people behind him over there," Mary Caitlin said after answering three calls in a row from Cañon Verde. "You'd think it was election time and every candidate was calling, trying to get votes."

"This is more important than any election, as far as Kramer is concerned," Weber said. "He knows that when this all comes out, he's done for."

"How does a guy like him, who rides roughshod over everybody in his path, get so many people to blindly believe he's the good guy in all of this? It just boggles my mind," Chad Summers said.

"I know, it's like he's got his own cult or something over there," Robyn replied.

"Those are the one's we're hearing from. But he's bound to have made a lot of enemies. Maybe they're afraid of saying anything right now," Weber said, "but I think if the FBI does launch that investigation that Sandra Dunnsire said was coming, we're going to start hearing from them, too. It's just like when some famous movie director or politician or whatever who is accused of sexually harassing women. It seems like they get away with it for a long time, but once one woman has the courage to come forward and tell her story more of them suddenly open up."

The Sheriff's office wasn't the only place getting calls about Zach Murdoch. Weber had expected Chet Wingate to come around, along with his trusty sidekick Councilwoman Gretchen Smith-Abbott, but when they did they were accompanied by Councilwoman Janet McGill and Councilman Adam Hirsch.

"Sheriff Weber, do you realize the can of worms you have opened? Our telephones are ringing off the hook with calls from irate citizens from Cañon Verde. You have to do something!"

"Do you have any idea how the law works, Chet? Just what is it you expect me to do? The matter is out of my hands. Zach Murdoch is in the custody of the U.S. Attorney's office."

"He wouldn't be if you would have just done your job and turned him over to Chief Kramer in the first place," Councilman Hirsch said.

"No, Adam, he'd be dead," Weber replied.

"That's nonsense, Sheriff Weber. Do you really believe a man with Chief Kramer's reputation could be guilty of the things Zach Murdoch says?"

"When did you become head of the Arthur Kramer Fan Club, Ms. McGill?"

"I don't know what you're talking about," she snapped. "I've never even met the man."

"You've never met him, but you know what a great reputation he has. That's interesting."

"Whatever you're insinuating, I don't appreciate it, Sheriff Weber."

"I'm not insinuating a damn thing," he told her. "I'm flat-out saying you don't know what the hell you're talking about. You've never met Kramer, but you know what a fine person he is. Well, I *have* met him. I've met him, and I can tell you right now, he's a psycho. What kind of lawman tries to attack a prisoner right in a courtroom and has to be taken down and put on the floor to stop him?"

"All I'm saying..."

"Shut up. Shut up and get out of my office. All of you, just get the hell out."

"How dare you? Who do you think you are?"

"I know who I am," Weber said. "I'm the man running this department. If you don't like the way I'm doing things, the four of you can march your asses out of here right now and go call an emergency Town Council meeting and take a vote to fire me. But in the meantime, I'm done listening to your bullshit. Out!"

When they were gone, Mary Caitlin said, "Jimmy, I know you're doing the right thing. But I'm not sure that was the best way to handle it."

"What do you mean, Mary?"

"I mean that there are four of them. That makes up the majority of the Town Council. They could do just what you said, Jimmy. They could call a special session and vote to fire you."

"Let them do it. I'm sick and tired of having to justify everything I do to Chet Wingate. If those four airheads want me gone because I stood up for what was right and wouldn't let Kramer take that kid out and kill him they can have this damn job!"

"Settle down, Jimmy, I'm not the one you're mad at."

Weber realized he had been shouting and felt bad about it. "I'm sorry. I didn't mean to yell at you. It's just this bullshit goes on and on and there never seems to be an end to it."

"Well, hopefully when word gets out about what really happened in Cañon Verde and the way Kramer has been running things for so long, they'll back off."

"Maybe so. But even if they do this time, you're right, Mary. The four of them do make up the majority of the Town Council, and eventually they may get their way and kick me to the curb. I don't know, maybe I ought to start thinking about doing something else. I'm still young enough that I could..."

"You stop that nonsense right now," Mary said sternly, pointing her finger at him. "Don't you *ever* start thinking or talking like that, Jim Weber! When Pete retired, he chose you to take his place because he knew you were the right man for the job. I've been married to that old fart for most of my life, and he can be a real pain in the ass sometimes. He's stubborn as a mule, he never wipes his feet when he comes in the door, I'm always picking up after him because he doesn't know what a trash can is for, he tells the worst jokes in the world, and I don't care what he says, there *is* more to life than tying flies and catching trout. But one thing he has always been is a damned good judge of character. There's a reason you're wearing that badge. It's because Pete pinned it on you when he took it off. And no matter what Chet and his little band of idiots think, you're the only man I know fit to wear it. End of discussion."

And with that she turned and answered the phone to listen to yet another person calling from Cañon Verde, New Mexico complain about the Zach Murdoch case.

Chapter 26

Weber was restless and irritable, and he knew he wasn't going to accomplish anything at the office except step on the toes of the people who supported him, so he left and paid a call on Kirby Templeton. He found the senior town councilman arranging a display of decongestants on an end cap in his pharmacy.

"It looks like you're working hard, Kirby."

"With the weather turning warm so quickly, it won't be long before people are going to be sneezing and rubbing their eyes. Happens every spring."

"That it does."

Virginia Weaver came up to them and demanded to know where Kirby had moved the Dr. Scholl's innersoles.

"They're right there on aisle seven, Miz. Weaver. Right where they've always been."

"No, they're not. Honestly, Kirby I don't know why you keep moving things around. Customers like to come into a store and find what they need without having to search up and down every aisle."

"No, ma'am, I haven't moved them," Kirby said patiently. "They're right there on aisle seven on the right-hand side, right where they've always been."

"I know what's going on, Kirby Templeton. It's all that marketing stuff they talk about. I saw something on television just last week about how the reason grocery stores keep the milk in the back is so you have to walk through the whole store to get to it, and you wind up buying other things you don't need along the way. Well, I won't have it! I want to find things where they always have been. If I have to spend half the day just looking for my husband's innersoles, I might as well drive to Show Low and go to the Walmart."

Kirby excused himself and took her to aisle seven where he showed her the innersoles were in their proper place. Instead of acknowledging that she was wrong, Mrs. Weaver said, "I don't know what you're trying to pull, Kirby, but they weren't there five minutes ago! That's it, from now on I'm taking my business to Walmart."

"Yes, ma'am. You do what you think you have to do."

He started to hang the innersoles back on the wire shelf and she asked, "What are you doing? I need those! They're the only thing that helps my husband's feet."

"I thought you were going to Walmart."

She jerked them out of his hand and said, "I am from now on. You've lost my business. I don't appreciate such poor customer service."

She turned on her heel and marched to the front counter to pay for her purchase.

Kirby shook his head. "I've known Virginia Weaver since we were kids. She was hard to get along with back then and old age hasn't improved her attitude one bit."

He resumed stocking the end cap with decongestants and said, "I assume you're here because of your visit from the Fearsome Foursome."

"You heard about that, did you?"

"Oh, yeah. When they left your office they came right here demanding that we have an emergency meeting today to discuss your many sins."

"It's going to take longer than one day to cover all of those," Weber told him.

Kirby chuckled and said, "I don't doubt that."

"Mary Caitlin tells me I'm skating on thin ice since those four make up a majority of the Town Council."

"Well, you know that if Chet and Gretchen and Adam had their way, you'd have been gone a long time ago. And now with Janet on the council, she seems to be leaning hard in their direction."

"I don't know what I did to piss her off," Weber said.

"She's from California, Jimmy. What can I say?"

Like many old-timers in Big Lake, Kirby had a dim view of many of the people who had moved to town from out of town and out of state. They came because they were looking for a small laid-back community where life was perfect and thought they had found it. Then they quickly grew dissatisfied and started trying to change things to make it more like the place they had just escaped from.

"So is this special meeting they want going to happen? Do I need to be looking for another job?"

"Not on my watch," Kirby said. "You didn't do anything wrong, Jimmy. You followed the letter of the law in not turning Juliette Murdoch's son over to that guy from New Mexico until there had been an extradition hearing. No matter what Chet and that crowd likes or doesn't like, you were doing your duty. Nothing more and nothing less. I already talked to Bob Bennett and he concurs. So don't sweat it, okay? If they want to have their meeting, we'll have it, and Bob's going to tell them that as the Town Attorney they are way out of line."

"I appreciate your support, Kirby."

"I'm just doing my job, Jimmy, just like you. And now I'd better get back to it, because this stuff isn't going to put itself on the shelves."

As Weber turned away, Kirby said, "Hey, Jimmy, for what it's worth, me and Frank Gauger and Mel Walker, and a lot of other people in this town, appreciate the job you're doing. Keep that in mind, okay?"

Weber felt somewhat better after leaving the pharmacy, but he was still unsettled. So he went to see the one man he could always depend on to put things in perspective.

"I figured you'd show up here before too long. How's it hanging, Jimmy?"

"To the left the last time I looked."

Pete Caitlin finished wrapping a bit of red thread around a hook that was adorned with a small feather, deftly tied the knot, and then sat upright from his jig pushing the thick magnifying glasses up onto his forehead as he took the fly out and inspected it before setting it aside.

"Looks like you're getting ready for fishing season."

"Oh hell, son. I was born ready for fishing. Ain't no getting ready to be done. I'm just stocking up. You and me need to get our asses out on that lake and get our lines wet."

"I'm looking forward to it," Weber said.

Pete and Mary Caitlin had been close friends with his parents, and Weber and his sister had always considered them to be like an uncle and aunt. After their parents were killed in a traffic accident when Weber was a young soldier, Pete and Mary had helped fill the void left in their lives. When Weber took a hardship discharge from the Army to come back to Big Lake to take care of his teenage sister and the family ranch, they had been there to support both of them. And when he had sold off the stock and leased the land, Pete had hired Weber as a deputy. A few years later, when it came time for him to retire, he had chosen him to be his successor.

"I hear tell things are a bit tense down at the office these days," Pete said, taking off the glasses and stretching his arms to relieve his back.

"Yeah, I guess Mary probably told you about Chet and his crowd showing up this morning."

"Don't worry about them, Jimmy. You did what was right and I'm proud of you."

"Thanks, Pete. That means a lot to me. I can't believe how many people are calling from New Mexico, supporting this Kramer."

"You can bet your ass the story he told back there is a lot different than what went down here, and a lot different than what actually happened to that nurse. And it sounds like he's working hard to spread the word so everybody knows he's a good guy."

"I know the truth is going to come out eventually," Weber said. "But in the meantime, I don't know what to tell those people when they call."

"Don't tell them a thing," Pete said, shaking his head. "Most of them aren't going to believe you anyway."

"Yeah, I know."

"You remember that old saying that the best defense is a good offense? That's what Kramer is doing, Jimmy. Maybe you should take a lesson from his playbook."

"What do you mean?"

"I mean that maybe instead of waiting for everything to come out, you might help matters along a little bit."

"And how do I do that?"

"Well, as I recall, you've got some history with a certain hotshot reporter down in Phoenix. When's the last time you talked to her?"

"You know, at one point I actually told Kramer I was going to give her a call," Weber said.

"Maybe you should. How many times have you and I walked into the middle of a barroom brawl to break it up, Jimmy?"

"More times than I care to remember."

"That's right. And when we had to get physical to get the job done, did you ever see me pull any punches?"

"No, sir, I didn't."

"That's because when you're in a fight, you use every weapon you have to your advantage."

"I think you may be onto something there, Pete."

"You *think*? Jesus, boy, you're almost as bad as that old woman of mine. Trust me, if I say it, just take it as gospel. It'd make life better for all of us."

Weber laughed and said, "Okay, I'll try to remember that."

"Here's something else you need to remember, Jimmy. I chose you to take my place because you were the right man for the job. And no matter what the bag of wind Chet Wingate says, you're still the right man for the job."

"Mary said the same thing," Weber said.

"Well what do you know? After all these years that old gal finally agrees with me about something. It's a red-letter day in my life, Jimmy."

Chapter 27

It took him a few minutes of waiting on hold until Lisa Burnham came on the line.

"Sheriff Weber, what a surprise. How are you doing?"

"I'm good," he told her. "How about you?"

"Oh, the usual. Traffic accidents, idiots sticking up liquor stores, people having babies, kids drowning in backyard pools, the economy sucks, better times are coming. You know the routine."

"Life goes on, doesn't it?"

"It does. I assume this isn't a social call, since you never make social calls. What's up?"

As Pete Caitlin had said, Weber and the good looking blonde reporter for News Channel Six in Phoenix had some history between them. Lisa could best be described as a ball buster mover and shaker with her eye on a network anchor slot, and she was not above doing anything it took to get there. That included using her beauty and her feminine wiles to get the inside line on a news story if that's what it took. She and Weber had butted heads on a couple of occasions in the past, but over time they had somehow formed an uneasy alliance. While Weber was never a fan of the news media, he had come to realize that at times it was nice to have a friend with someone like Lisa's access to the public.

"No, it's not a social call. You might want to get your pen and a piece of paper out and start taking some notes, because I've got a story to tell you."

~***~

The story broke on the 5 o'clock news with a graphic in the background that said *Chaos In The Courtroom.*

"As this startling security footage from the courtroom in Big Lake shows, things got out of hand when the police chief from Cañon Verde, New Mexico became enraged after extradition

159

proceedings were halted on a fugitive accused of murdering a woman there. According to Big Lake's Sheriff Jim Weber, Police Chief Arthur Kramer wasn't going to take no for an answer when the U.S. Attorney's office halted the proceedings and took the defendant, Zachary Murdoch, into protective custody pending an investigation into allegations of misconduct and prisoner abuse by Chief Kramer and other officers with the Cañon Verde Police Department. As this video shows, Sheriff Weber and one of his deputies had to physically restrain Chief Kramer when he tried to attack the defendant. We've bleeped much of the audio from the incident due to the profanity Chief Kramer was using in his tirade, in which, among other things, he threatened to kill the defendant and Sheriff Weber. "

The courtroom video showed the confrontation and Kramer being taken to the ground and handcuffed, then disarmed.

"When asked about this bizarre incident, Sheriff Weber would only say that this isn't the first encounter the Big Lake Sheriff's Department has had with Chief Kramer in the past, nor is it the first time his deputies have had to restrain Chief Kramer when he had one of his outbursts of temper like the one you just saw here. When I spoke to Assistant U.S. Attorney Sandra Dunnsire about the incident with Chief Kramer and the allegations of misconduct against him, she would only say that her office and the Federal Bureau of Investigation has been interviewing Mr. Murdoch, and that the case is pending. Calls to the mayor's office and the police department in Cañon Verde were answered with a simple 'no comment.' We will follow up on this story and keep you informed."

The graphic on the screen changed to an image of a crumpled car at a railroad crossing and the camera shifted to Burnham's co-anchor, who talked about yet another senseless tragedy when someone ignored the flashing lights and drove around the barriers to try to beat a train.

"As much as I don't like that woman, I have to say that knowing her comes in handy now and then," Robyn said.

"You just don't like her because she wants Jimmy's body," Marsha teased.

"You're right. And I let her know that she'd better keep her hands and her eyes off of him."

"If it makes you feel any better, she didn't really want my body, she just wanted a story," Weber said. "Her coming on to me was just a means to an end."

"Yeah? Well after she and I had our little talk, she knows that if she does it again I'm going to get mean and that will be the end of her."

"Hey, don't complain. At least your man is here," Marsha said. "Parks tells me that once they're done interviewing Zach Murdoch down in Phoenix, he's headed to New Mexico. You two will be cuddling up and whispering sweet nothings to each other, and it'll just be me and that big old empty bed."

"What do you think's going to happen now?"

"Oh, I'll get through the night," Marsha said. "Don't worry about me. I'll just be alone."

She gave an exaggerated sigh and Robyn said, "I was talking to Jimmy about things over in New Mexico. Get over yourself."

"It's always nice to have my girlfriend there for me when I'm in need," Marsha said.

"I know what kind of needs you have, and forget it, I'm not that kind of girlfriend."

"As far as New Mexico, Lisa Burnham told me that two television stations there were picking up her feed, so I think things are going to get pretty crazy in Cañon Verde. I don't care how many good old boys with deep pockets over there like Kramer and have been able to ignore what's been going on for so long. A story like this is going to get people talking all over that area. I'd be willing to bet a month's pay that he's going to regret he ever saw Zach Murdoch, or Big Lake."

~***~

Parks stopped briefly at Weber's office the next morning to say that he had come home to pick up some clothes before heading to Roswell, New Mexico to meet with Special Agents Mayfield and Boyer and a representative of the U.S. Attorney's Office.

"Isn't Roswell where that UFO was supposed to have crashed all those years ago?"

"That's the place," Parks said. "Have you ever been to Roswell, Jimmy?"

"No, I don't think so."

"Well, I've driven through it, and I have a theory."

"You've got a theory about most things. What was that one you had a while back about somebody poisoning the water system because you're starting to get some gray in your temples and you think it's arsenic or something like that?"

"I never said arsenic, I just said something was doing it. Look at me, do I look like I should have any gray hair?"

"I know I didn't have any before I met you. You've aged me, Parks."

"No, I've helped you mature. And you're welcome."

"So what's this theory you have about the UFO in Roswell?"

"I think that if a UFO actually did crash there, it was a suicide mission. I mean think about it, you leave your home planet a gazillion light-years away and you travel through the whole universe, and you wind up in Roswell instead of Miami Beach or Rio or someplace like that? If I did that I'd commit suicide, too. I mean, don't get me wrong, I'm not saying anything bad about Roswell. But it sure isn't Club Med."

"Well, just in case, try not to get abducted, okay?"

"Don't you worry about that, I'm going to be too busy busting Kramer to mess with any of those little pointy-headed aliens."

"So this is going to happen?"

"Oh, it's happening already, Jimmy. That news story that Lisa Burnham broke last night really got the ball rolling. I know a couple of stations in New Mexico carried it, and I think one in El Paso, Texas did, too. I know that people have already started calling the Bureau and the U.S. Attorney's office with stories to tell about things that have happened there. It's only a matter of time before we've seen the last of Kramer. You can bet your bottom dollar on that."

As it turned out, Parks was wrong. Dead wrong.

~***~

When Parks left, Weber went across the street to the newspaper office to pick up a copy of the new addition hot off the press.

"Didn't I tell you I had a big story for you?"

"Yeah, but I sure wish you would've given me more time to work on it, Jimmy."

"I'm sorry, Paul, but there just wasn't time. To be honest with you, I actually told Lisa Burnham about it first, because I wanted it to make the evening news. Then I realized it was deadline day for you and hustled over here as quickly as I could."

He could tell his old friend was miffed at him and felt bad about it.

"Look, there was a reason I called her first."

"Yeah, because she's drop dead gorgeous. Me, I'm just drop dead."

"Don't be that way, Paul. This Kramer is a bad guy and I needed to get the story out there as quickly as I could. Chet Wingate is hot to trot to call a Town Council meeting and get rid of me, and right now he's got a majority that I think will side with him. I thought if word got out about Kramer and everything he's been doing they might back off."

"So it was a political move?"

"I guess you could say that, as much as I hate to play politics. And I've got to admit, I wanted people to know what Kramer has been up to. Not just here, but over there in Cañon Verde. You do a good job of covering the local news, but when I dropped this stone in the water, I needed it to make ripples that would reach out a long ways."

Paul seemed somewhat accepting of his explanation and said, "There's no way that Chet can fire you over this."

"That's what Bob Bennett says, too. Until now the Council's been pretty evenly divided between Chet, Gretchen, and Adam on one side and Kirby, Frank Gauger, and Mel Walker on the other, with Ladonna Jordan always stuck in the middle and being the swing vote. Usually she was pretty reasonable, but I think she got tired of all the bickering and that's why she resigned. Now, with Janet McGill taking her place, it seems like they've got a majority."

"If Bob Bennett says you were in the right, how can they fire you?"

"Maybe they can't on this one, Paul, but if Chet gets McGill solidly in his camp, sooner or later they could find some reason to do it.

"Nope, it's never going to happen," Paul said, shaking his head. "Too many people know how much you've given to this town, Jimmy. Folks like the fact that you tell it like it is, and that you do the job without regard to who's toes might get stepped on. Yeah, sometimes they piss and moan when it's their toes, but overall, you've earned a lot of respect around here. And this may be just a little newspaper, just a little ripple in the pond, but I'm behind you all the way. You know that, right?"

"Even if I called Lisa Burnham before I called you."

"Oh hell, Jimmy," his friend said, dismissing the comment with a wave of his hand. "If I was in your place and I had my choice of calling someone who looked like her or someone with a fat ass like mine, I'd have done the same thing, no matter who made the biggest ripple."

Chapter 28

Even with everything that was happening, Chet Wingate and his allies insisted on holding a special meeting of the Town Council that afternoon to discuss Weber's alleged misconduct. The mayor launched into a long diatribe about the sheriff's history with the town and his constant stubbornness and refusal to cooperate with the mayor or Town Council, then he moved on to the most recent incident when, as he put it, Weber had defied not only the mayor but a long tradition of law enforcement working together for the common good. He ended by calling for a vote to dismiss Weber for his lack of professionalism and malfeasance in office. Councilman Adam Hirsch quickly seconded the motion, but before a vote could be taken, Town Attorney Bob Bennett stood up and said, "Hold on a minute. Mr. Mayor, didn't you just say that you ordered Sheriff Weber to release the prisoner to Chief Kramer?"

"Yes, I did," Chet said primly. "And like he does all the time, Sheriff Weber ignored my order."

"Just for the record, why were you involved in it, Chet? How did you even know about it?"

"I knew because Chief Kramer contacted me asking for my help when Sheriff Weber refused to turn Zach Murdoch over to him."

"And that's your reason for calling this meeting? You want Sheriff Weber removed from office because he disobeyed your order?"

"Yes, among other reasons. The sheriff has always been disrespectful and he has always..."

"Hold on a second. Forget all that," Bennett said, waving his hand. "I'm talking about this meeting right here and right now. You want Sheriff Weber fired because he didn't obey your order in the matter of Zach Murdoch, is that correct?"

"That's what I said," snapped the mayor. "Now, let's take a vote."

"Before you people move forward, you'd better listen to what I'm telling you," Bennett said. "Sheriff Weber upheld the law when refusing to turn Zach Murdoch over to Chief Kramer so he could take him back to New Mexico. Under federal and state law, a defendant has the right to fight extradition and no government entity or law enforcement agency can deny them that right. That's a violation of his civil rights. So, Mr. Mayor, when you colluded with Chief Kramer and then ordered Sheriff Weber to release the prisoner to him, you committed a conspiracy. A conspiracy that is punishable under law."

"What are you talking about? Nonsense!"

"What part of it is nonsense, Chet? You just said that you talked to Chief Kramer and then ordered Sheriff Weber to release the prisoner to him, didn't you?"

"Don't try to twist my words, Kirby."

"I'm not twisting your words, Chet. Those were the words you just said."

"I didn't do anything wrong."

"Yes, Chet, you did. And if anybody on this Council votes to remove Sheriff Weber from office because he didn't cooperate with your conspiracy, that makes them a party to it. You all might want to think about that before this goes any further."

Templeton looked each council member in the eye. Gretchen Smith Abbott stared back at him defiantly, as did Adam Hirsch. But then the man dropped his eyes and shook his head. Councilwoman McGill said, "I want it stated for the record that I had no idea what the background was behind all this."

"You had no idea what it was about, but you went to the Sheriff's office with the mayor and two other council members to try to pressure him just the other day. Isn't that right?"

"Like I said, I had no idea..."

"Janet, if you're going to be on this Council, maybe you'd better start investing the time and energy to find out what's going on before you jump the gun like that," Councilman Frank Gauger chastised her. "We've got enough petty bickering going on all the time with the mayor's constant barrages against the sheriff."

"I was taking the mayor's word for it. If we can't trust the mayor, who can we trust?"

166

The woman's face colored and she looked away.

"I think we're finished here," Gauger said. "I make a motion that we adjourn this meeting."

"No."

Everybody turned to look at Kirby Templeton.

"Beg pardon, Kirby?"

"I said no, we're not adjourning this meeting. Not yet. I have something to say."

The room was silent and all eyes were on him.

"Chet, every week we come in here and we listen to this nonsense, over and over and over. You've got such a grudge against Sheriff Weber that you can't see straight. And why? Because he won't stroke your fragile ego?"

The mayor started to say something, but the look on Kirby's face told him to think better of it.

"And Gretchen, if Chet said the sky was green and the grass was blue, you'd back him up on it. Loyalty is a fine thing in a person, but blind loyalty is dangerous."

The councilwoman's face twisted in anger, but she didn't say anything.

"As for you, Adam, grow up. Some girl in high school liked Weber instead of you and you've still got your panties in a wad over it? My God man, how many years has it been? Are you really that shallow?"

There was an uncomfortable silence in the room.

"I'm going to make a motion," Kirby said, without waiting for an answer from any of them. "I make a motion that this Council take a vote of no confidence in Mayor Chet Wingate right now, based upon his continued pettiness toward the sheriff and his own admission in this meeting that he conspired to violate the law and the civil rights of Zach Murdoch."

There was silence for a moment, then Councilman Mel Walker said, "I second the motion."

"A motion has been made that this Council take a vote of no confidence in the mayor. All in favor of that motion, say aye. I'll be the first," Kirby said. "Aye, I favor the motion."

"Aye, me too," Mel Walker said, followed by Frank Gauger.

"Nay," said the mayor.

"You can't vote on this, Chet."

"Why not? I'm the mayor!"

The Town's Attorney ignored the question as one might the constant questions of a child.

Councilwoman Gretchen Smith-Abbott and Councilman Hirsch also voted against the motion. All eyes turned to Councilwoman Janet McGill. She looked at all of them uncomfortably, then shook her head and said, "There's too much going on here that I don't know about. I think I'm in over my head, and before I could vote either way with a clear conscience, I need to know some of the history that we're discussing."

"So you're abstaining from voting, is that right?"

"Yes, Councilman Templeton. I don't know what else to say at this point."

There was silence for a moment, then Kirby said, "Let the record show that the motion passed with a majority of votes, with the mayor's vote invalidated and one councilmember abstaining. With that being said, Councilman Gauger, I second your motion to adjourn this meeting. All in favor, say aye."

The answers were subdued and the meeting broke up on a solemn note.

Outside on the sidewalk, Paul Lewis said, "Wow. I didn't see that coming."

"Kirby asking for the vote at all, or the way it turned out?"

"Both, I guess. No matter how the vote went, Jimmy, he damn sure got it on the record how he felt about things. I just wish that they'd have had this damn meeting yesterday. It's going to be hard to wait until next week to get it in the paper. I may put out a special edition just for this!"

"It's just politics, Paul, that's all it is."

"No, Jimmy, it's not. It's a lot more than just politics. Those three council members voting that they had no confidence in Chet? That's big news. You talked about how that police chief over there in New Mexico walked all over people and he's finally getting his comeuppance. Well, Chet may not be physically brutal to people, but he's been a bully who's walked all over people in this town for a long time. He keeps getting reelected because so many people owe him money or owe him favors. But after this meeting I really think his days are numbered. The no confidence vote could lead to a recall to replace him."

~***~

The emergency Big Lake Town Council meeting wasn't the only one of its kind taking place. Just as Parks had predicted, the pressure on the Cañon Verde City Council brought about by the media concerning Police Chief Arthur Kramer's actions at the extradition hearing for Zachary Murdoch in Big Lake, along with calls that were coming in from citizens about the chief's actions in the past, left that body with no alternative but to have their own hotly debated meeting. It was followed the next day by a second closed-door session. Kramer may have had a lot of friends, but one thing politicians on every level of government, from small towns in the West to Washington D.C., know how to do is to cover their rear ends. The meeting ended with a decision to suspend Chief Kramer with pay, pending the outcome of the FBI investigation being directed by the U.S. Attorney's Office.

Nick Russell

Chapter 29

The next morning, Councilwoman Janet McGill was waiting for Weber when he arrived at the Sheriff's office.

"Good morning. What brings you here, Councilwoman?"

"Can we talk privately, Sheriff?"

"Sure, let's go in my office."

She took a seat next to his desk and Weber asked, "How can I help you? "

"I owe you an apology, Sheriff Weber. When the mayor called me and asked me to come to your office the other day with him and the others, I didn't take the time to acquaint myself with the issues at hand. Since then I've learned a lot about the history between you and the mayor, and about how things work here in Big Lake. I've done a lot of thinking about that. When I was in California I was somewhat of an activist, I guess you could say, and when I came here I really thought that by being on the Town Council I could help this community. I know many people come here from someplace else and immediately want to start changing things. That's not what I want to see happen. I fell in love with this town the first time I saw it, and I don't want it to change if change means condos and uncontrolled growth."

"I'm afraid you might be a little too late for that," Weber said. "It's already changed a lot."

"Maybe so, but that doesn't mean it has to continue. I know it's going to grow, I'm no fool. But it doesn't have to turn into just another elitist resort town like Aspen or Lake Tahoe."

"I sure hope it doesn't get to that point," Weber said.

"Neither do I. So, like I said, I got involved because I wanted to help this community preserve its natural charm. But at the same time, there's a lot of underlying conflict here that I never realized."

"I think you'd probably find that anywhere, big city or small town."

"I'm sure you're right, Sheriff. I didn't expect this place to be a utopia. And sometimes conflict is good because it brings about change. Hopefully, positive change. However, by jumping onto Mayor Wingate's bandwagon without doing my own due diligence, I added to the negativity of the conflict. That's inexcusable. I think I made a mistake running for a seat on the Town Council. I've already shown I may not be the best person for the job."

"You made a mistake," Weber said. "We all make mistakes. The idea is to learn from them and not make the same ones again."

"And maybe the best way to do that is to step aside and let somebody more in step with the community take my seat."

"You don't strike me as a quitter."

"I just want what's best for Big Lake. And right now, I'm not sure that's me."

"I disagree," he said.

"Really? I should think you'd want me gone before I caused more problems."

"Do you think you'd blindly accept anything Chet, or anyone else on the Council says again?"

She shook her head ruefully. "Oh, no. What's that they say, fool me once?"

"You said something about due diligence. You're obviously an intelligent woman, and just by coming here this morning you've shown a lot of integrity. I respect that. We need people like you on the Town Council. Stick around. I think you'll be good for Big Lake."

"Do you really think so?"

"Once you get to know me, I think you'll figure out that I don't say things just to make people feel better. I'm kind of a tell it like it is guy and let the chips fall where they may."

She thought about what he said for a moment, then nodded her head."

"Thank you for that, Sheriff. Maybe I will. And I promise you that me coming in here with the mayor and the others without knowing both sides of the story won't happen again. I'm not saying we will always agree about everything, because I think you and I are two very different people with very different outlooks on the world. But I want you to know that I won't just rubberstamp everything that Mayor Wingate puts in front of the Town Council."

"That's all I could ever ask for," Weber told her. "And I appreciate you coming here, Ms. McGill."

"How about we just forget all the formalities and you call me Janet."

"Fair enough, if you call me Jimmy."

"Very well then, Jimmy. There's something else I don't understand. It doesn't have anything to do with the business at hand, but I'm just curious why your title is Sheriff instead of Police Chief. Isn't a sheriff an elected county official?"

"It is in most places," Weber said. "But as you're coming to realize, Big Lake isn't like most places. One of the first settlers around here was a fellow by the name of Mike Washburn. Everybody called him Big Mike. He was one of those larger-than-life people that you always hear about. He came here in the 1880s and spent years carving a large cattle ranching and logging operation out of a wilderness. He fought off Indians, rustlers, and squatters, and he wound up with an empire."

"He sounds like quite a man. Some might say a ruthless man," Janet said.

"Maybe so, but it was a different world back then, and maybe it took ruthless men to get the job done. Anyway, Big Mike became a legend in this part of the country. He wasn't a fan of big government, and when he founded the town of Big Lake and donated the land it sits on, he wanted things done a certain way. When he drew up the Town Charter he specified how he wanted things done, and that if at any time in the future the town tried to change those things, the land Town Hall sits on, the courtroom, the schools, the parks, and any other public property would revert back to his family. Among those things was that there had to be a school, at least two churches, that there be hitching posts for horses like the ones you see in front of some of the businesses, and that there would always be public access to the lake. Something else he specified was that the town have a sheriff, not a police chief. I don't know why, maybe it was just a throwback to the Old West. But at any rate, in reality, I'm a police chief they call Sheriff."

"Big Mike sounds like a fascinating man," Janet said. "Why am I picturing John Wayne?"

"He was gone before my time, but that's probably not too far off the mark," Weber told her.

"Whatever happened to him?"

"The way I hear it, on his 70th birthday, back in about 1935, he downed most of a bottle of Jack Daniels, ate a big steak from a steer he had butchered himself, and then climbed onto the back of a stallion none of his cowboys could break and told them to watch how the old man taught a horse a few manners. It threw him into a corral post and broke his neck."

"Wow. If there isn't a book about him, there should be."

"I think you're probably right."

"Well, I've taken enough of your time, Sheriff. I mean Jimmy. Thank you for talking to me today."

"Anytime, Janet. My door's always open."

She extended her hand and they shook, then he led her to the door. As she was going out, she turned back and looked at him and asked, "Really? That much ammunition?"

Weber laughed and said, "Wait until you hear about the tank I want to buy."

"A tank?" She looked at him incredulously, then saw the twinkle in his eye and laughed. "The next thing I know, you're going to be telling me you want to put a battleship in the middle of the lake."

"I don't know about that, but I'll admit that back in high school I did take a girlfriend or two out to the lake to watch the submarine races."

She laughed and shook her head as she left.

"Well that was interesting," Mary Caitlin said as she handed Weber a cup of coffee. "What did she want?"

"She came to apologize for jumping the gun and going along with Chet when she came in here with him the other day."

"As far as I'm concerned, she's just another Californicator," Buz Carelton said. "An airhead from the land of quakes and flakes who wants to come here and make us into another suburb of Los Angeles."

"That was my first impression when I met her a while back," Weber said. "Now, I think maybe I was wrong about that. I've got a feeling she's going to be a good addition to Big Lake."

"The whole town's talking about Kirby Templeton's vote of no confidence in Chet," Mary said. "Did you know that Paul Lewis put out a four-page special edition about the Town Council meeting last night?"

"He said he might do that."

"This could be big, Jimmy. Kirby has drawn a line in the sand and made it clear that he's fed up with Chet and the way he's been doing things."

"Paul said this could lead to a recall election."

"It could," Mary said. "And if it does, I think it's going to get ugly."

"You might be right."

"Speaking of ugly, what the hell were you doing telling Pete I agreed with something he said? Christ, I'll never live that down!"

"You guys have been married since Christ was a corporal. You must have agreed with him at least once somewhere along the line, haven't you?"

"Maybe, but if I did, I damned sure didn't let him know about it. You make a note of that for once you two get hitched, Robyn. If you start agreeing with everything they say, it upsets the whole balance of power. Draw the battle lines right from the start."

"Does it have to be a war all the time?"

"No, honey," Mary said, putting her arm around Robyn's shoulders and hugging her. "Not *all* the time. But if you're not fighting, you're not making up. And trust me, making up can be a lot of fun!"

Robyn's face colored, and Mary laughed and said, "Just remember that whole balance of power thing, okay?"

~***~

People were indeed talking about the town council meeting and the vote of no confidence all over Big Lake. Over coffee and their morning croissants at the Sweet Seductions bakery, during

175

lunch at the Frontier Cafe, across the counter at the shops and stores and backyard fences, everybody had something to say about the showdown that was sure to come.

Weber had expected the mayor to come out swinging in response, but instead nobody had seen Chet. Weber assumed he was holed up someplace planning his strategy in response to what he was sure to see as a betrayal by the three longtime council members and plotting his revenge. Whatever the little bully was up to, as long as he was out of sight, Weber was happy to go about his business undisturbed by the mayor's constant interruptions.

Chapter 30

At the end of his third day in New Mexico, Parks called with an update.

"So the aliens haven't abducted you yet?"

"Oh, they tried to," Parks said. "They wanted to take me back to their planet and make me king. But I'm an active guy, I'm just not cut out to spend my life sitting on a throne."

"Really? That surprises me because when you are staying at my place you seemed to spend a lot of time sitting on the throne."

"Hey, I didn't work for over eleven hours today just so I could come back to my motel room to call you and be abused. I plan to call Marsha for some long-distance abuse once I'm done talking to you. It's not as good as in person, but sometimes a man's got to take what he can and be satisfied."

"What's happening over there?"

"Lots of things are happening, Bubba. When we first got here it was what one might call a hostile work environment. Nobody wanted to talk to us, and when they did they let us know that they weren't going to stand for us railroading Kramer. But between the television and newspaper coverage, things started happening. New Mexico's governor ordered the State Attorney General to start their own investigation. We've got over two dozen people who have come forward and are willing to testify to being assaulted by Kramer and two of his officers. Both of those officers have clammed up and refused to cooperate with us, but there have been a couple others with a change of heart. They're probably just trying to cover their asses, but at any rate they have also given statements about things they've seen happen."

"What about Kramer? Have you guys talked to him yet?"

"Nope. We tried to and he told us that he wasn't willing to say anything without an attorney present. He's not going to go down easy. Don't get me wrong, he's going down, no question about that. But he's going to fight all the way."

"What kind of things have you guys been hearing about what happened over there?"

"A lot of it's just like Zach Murdoch and Lee Drysdale told us. Somebody gets in trouble for a minor infraction and Kramer beats the hell out of them just for grins and giggles. And sometimes people didn't even have to do anything wrong to get his attention. One fellow who actually lives in Lubbock, Texas called and told us he was passing through town and stopped at a convenience store for gas and a cup of coffee. He said there was a police car sitting in the parking lot and he didn't pay it any attention. But he said when he came out and started to get back in his car Kramer stopped him and asked for his ID. He asked what the problem was, and Kramer told him he was the one asking the questions and he wanted to see the damned ID. The guy, whose name is Terry Gallivan, showed it to him and he said after Kramer ran a background check on him, he said something like that he needed to get out of Cañon Verde and never come back. Gallivan said he told Kramer that as far as he knew it was still a free country. According to him, Kramer had started to hand his driver's license back to him, but instead dropped it. He said when he bent over to pick it up, Kramer kneed him in the face and knocked him down, then kicked him in the ribs three or four times. Then he handcuffed him and took him to jail and he spent the next two days there."

"Damn."

"And it's not just this Gallivan telling pretty much the same story. There's no question that this kind of abuse has been going on for a long time, and there's no question that a lot of people in Cañon Verde knew about it."

"Knew about it, and still let it continue," Weber said. "That's the part I just can't stomach."

"There are still a lot of people who think Kramer is the best thing since sliced bread," Parks told him. "Maybe they didn't all know about the abuse, but they believe in him. I talked to a young woman named Tabitha Eibeck. She's the daughter of the dead woman, and she was about as hostile as a badger on crack. She can't believe we're protecting Zach Murdoch when everybody knows he killed her mother. She called me things I haven't heard since Navy boot camp or when I was a new recruit at the FBI Academy. She's definitely on Kramer's side, all the way."

"Yeah, I heard from her, too," Weber said. "I tried to reason with her but she wasn't hearing any of it."

"No, and there are still a lot of people around here just like her. To hear them tell it, the people who are complaining are just a bunch of losers and malcontents looking for a way to stick it to a good man who has dedicated his life to the community."

"Have you heard how Zach is doing?"

"He's still down in Phoenix and they're keeping a lid on him. I do know that they let him call his mother twice, but he wasn't allowed to tell her where they're holding him. I don't even know for sure where he's at, but wherever it is, it's a lot better than being here sitting in Kramer's jail."

"Any idea how much longer you're going to be there?"

"I'm not sure. Why, do you miss me?"

"I miss a bad toothache I had one time, Parks. I miss a mean-spirited horse we had back on the ranch when I was a kid that tried to kick me or bite me every time I came near it. But you? No, stay away as long as you need to. I'll be okay."

"That hurts me, Jimmy. It really does."

"You'll get over it," Weber told his friend. "Seriously, make sure you guys cross every t and dot every i. When you take Kramer down, I want him to stay down."

"Trust me, we're covering all the bases. I'll be in touch."

~***~

Weber was leaving his office at the end of the day when he heard a horn honk in the parking lot. He looked up to see Mayor Chet Wingate sitting behind the wheel of his champagne-colored Cadillac Escalade.

He walked up to the open driver's side window and asked, "What's up, Chet?"

"Jimmy, I wanted to talk to you off the record."

Weber was instantly on guard. The mayor never called him by his name unless he was up to something. Of course, Chet was always up to something, but this kind of familiarity was out of the norm.

"What is it?"

"Listen, about that silliness with that policeman from New Mexico and poor Zach Murdoch. How about we just put all of that behind us, okay?"

"Oh, so now you agree with me that turning Zach over to Kramer would have been a bad idea?"

"Have you seen the news reports about that man? My God, he's crazy!"

"Yeah, I tried to tell you that, Chet. But you didn't want to listen to a thing I said. As I recall, you were going to fire me because I wouldn't let him take Zach out of here."

"Okay, maybe I overreacted a little bit. But that's in the past. Right?"

"*Maybe* you overreacted a little bit?"

"Fine. I was out of line. Now are you happy? The point is, the past is the past. Let's let it stay there."

"I see. Just let bygones be bygones. Is that what you're saying, Chet?"

"Exactly. We need to show this community a united face as we move forward and deal with the challenges ahead."

"Challenges? Challenges like that vote of no confidence that the Town Council passed?"

"Oh, that was just Kirby being grumpy. Come on, Jimmy, you know how he can be."

"So this united face we're supposed to put on, Chet, you and me are supposed to be on the same side, right?"

"Side? What side? Isn't it everybody's goal to make Big Lake a better place to live? We can't do that if we're all fighting amongst ourselves. And as far as that silly stuff that Bob Bennett was saying, about me being part of a conspiracy and all that, that was just a big misunderstanding. That's all. The last thing this town needs is for something like that to be spread all over. Why, look how that town over in New Mexico is being torn apart right now, what with the FBI and the U.S. Attorney's office over there doing all of their investigations. No, we don't need that here."

"What are you getting at, Chet?"

"I'm just saying that this was all a big misunderstanding. A failure to communicate. I didn't actually *order* you to release Zach Murdoch to Chief Kramer. Like Bob Bennett said, that would be denying him his constitutional rights. You know I would never do something like that, Jimmy. I think you just misunderstood me."

"Oh, I get it," Weber said, chuckling. "This is about covering *your* ass, isn't it Chet? You didn't *order* me to do anything, I just *misunderstood*."

"Exactly, Jimmy. We need to put a stop to all of this before it gets blown out of proportion."

"So then what you're telling me is that you want me to become part of a *new* conspiracy by lying about our conversation which led to the possibility of the first conspiracy charge against you for colluding with Kramer."

"What? No, that's not what I'm saying at all. What I'm saying is..."

"Chet, I'm going to give you a word of advice and as hard as it is for you to do, I really think you should follow it. Shut your mouth, start your car, and get the hell out of here. Because if you don't, I'm going to march you inside my office and I'm going to lock you up in a cell, and then me and the FBI and the U.S. Attorney's office are going to have a long talk about conspiracies. You can take my advice and leave and I can forget we had this conversation, or else you won't have to worry about a recall election, because you'll be too busy trying to stay out of the federal penitentiary to worry about anything else."

The mayor started to open his mouth to say something, but Weber raised a cautionary finger.

"Not one word, Chet. Not one word."

The little man glared at him, then started his SUV, backed out of his parking spot, and drove away.

Nick Russell

Chapter 31

"A few days ago News Channel Six told you about the outburst a police chief from New Mexico had at the Big Lake Courthouse," Lisa Burnham said in a special report the next morning as Weber was eating breakfast. The background showed the video of the scene in the courtroom when Kramer tried to attack Zach Murdoch, with Weber and Dan Wright subduing him. "We have an update on that story this morning," Lisa Burnham said. "After a series of meetings to discuss the incident, and other allegations made against Police Chief Arthur Kramer, which has led to an investigation of his actions by the Federal Bureau of investigation and the U.S. Attorney's office, as well as the New Mexico Attorney General's office, late last night the Cañon Verde City Council fired Chief Kramer, citing his conduct unbecoming of an officer, betraying the public trust within the community, his blatant disregard of the law and abuse of authority. In a press release issued by the City of Cañon Verde, Mayor James Wickstrom said that Kramer has become more of a liability than the city could afford to bear, and that he and the entire City Council are both appalled and ashamed that things went on this long without their knowledge."

A commercial for a car dealership came on and Robyn said, "They are appalled and ashamed now. But all these years they let him get away with what he was doing and nobody cared then."

"I guess it's better late than never," Weber said. "I wonder if the FBI is going to take him into custody now."

As it turned out, Weber found out that wasn't going to happen anytime soon when Parks called him an hour later at the office.

"Did you hear about Kramer getting shit-canned?"

"Yeah, it was on the news here a little while ago."

"As soon as it was announced here, it's like a dam broke. Not only police officers, but also civilian employees who work for the PD suddenly want to get their stories told so they're on the record as being on the right side. And we're getting even more calls from people who want to tell us about abuse they've either experienced firsthand or know about."

"Have you heard anything from that woman that Lee Drysdale told us about? The one that Kramer locked in a cell with those other prisoners?"

"No, nothing about that," Parks replied. "I don't know if she's so traumatized that she doesn't want to relive it, or if she's even around anymore. I did mention it to one of the officers who was in here spilling his guts to us, and he said that he was there when it happened, too. Of course, he said he tried to keep Kramer from doing it, but he ignored him."

"When are you guys going to lock him up?"

"Not yet, but it's coming."

"The sooner, the better," Weber said.

"Don't be impatient, Jimmy. It's going to happen. The U.S. Attorney we're working with here is a fellow named Brett Grothier and he's sharp. By the time he's ready to file formal charges against Kramer, we're going to have enough evidence against him that he'll never see daylight again. And believe me, that evidence is piling up right now."

"Have you seen Kramer?"

"No. According to his attorney he's in seclusion while they deal with the, and I'm quoting here, the backlash from our 'witch hunt.'"

"If it's a witch hunt, can we burn him at the stake once it's all over with?"

"That would be too good for him," Parks said. "No, that man needs to spend every day of his life in prison for the things he's done."

"However long that may be. We both know cops don't live long in prison."

"I really hope somebody doesn't shank him," Parks replied "That would be too quick and too easy. I want him to grow old sitting in a cell knowing he is never going to breathe free air again. Knowing that he isn't the big fish in a small pond anymore, he's just a little guppy swimming in a pool full of sharks, day in and day out, forever. I never want him to have a good night's sleep because I want him to lay awake and wonder if every footstep he hears, every sound, is somebody coming to show him what it feels like to be the victim for a change."

"The more I think about it, the more I think you're right," Weber said. "And don't start getting a swelled head on me, Parks. Even a blind pig finds an acorn now and then."

His friend laughed and said, "Fair enough. I'll tell you what Jimmy, as much fun as it is busting this guy's world wide open, and as much as I'm looking forward to putting the handcuffs on him, I'll be glad to get back home."

"I wish I was there to see you put those cuffs on him," Weber said. "It would be the second-best thing to me doing it myself."

~***~

After a long day of dealing with paperwork that had backed up while he was busy dealing with Zach Murdoch in the aftermath of him showing up in Big Lake, Weber was driving home when a red Toyota Camry ran a stop sign and pulled directly in front of him, a mile from his cabin. He slammed on his brakes and turned the steering wheel hard to the right to avoid a collision, ending up in a ditch and slamming his forehead into the steering wheel.

"Son of a bitch!" He looked up and the Camry was just going out of sight, headed back toward town. The Explorer's engine had stalled and he restarted it, then shifted into gear, feeling the tires spin as they tried to get purchase in the muddy ditch. Cursing, he shifted into four-wheel-drive and feathered the throttle slowly until the SUV was able to crawl out of the ditch and back onto the pavement. Looking both ways to make sure nobody was coming, he made a U-turn and headed in the direction the Camry had gone, turning on his roof lights.

Pulling his microphone from its clip on the dashboard, he said, "Dispatch, this is Big Lake One. If you can get anybody headed out of town on the east side of the lake, tell them to be on the lookout for a red car with a loud stereo. I think it's a Toyota but I'm not sure. He just ran a stop sign and I almost T-boned him before I ended up in the ditch."

"10-4, Sheriff. Are you injured?"

"Negative, I'm back on the road and in pursuit.

"Sheriff, I'm at Lake and Cochise Street, headed your way. If I see him, I'll pull him over," Deputy Jordan Northcutt said.

"10-4."

Weber wanted to floor it and catch up with the offending car, but he knew his tire treads were caked with mud and would not give him enough traction to do so safely until it wore off. Still, he made good time and a few minutes later he spotted flashing lights up ahead of him.

"I've got eyes on the vehicle. It's a red Toyota, and I'm pulling him over," Jordan said over the radio. "Looks to be one person in it, a male, I think."

"Coming up behind you."

Weber stopped behind Jordan's patrol car and got out, walking up to where his deputy was standing at the driver's door of the Camry. Music was blaring from the car, the big speakers booming with the bass so strong the air seemed to vibrate.

"Turn that damn noise off," Weber ordered.

"What's your problem, man?"

"I said turn the radio off. I'm not going to tell you again."

"Whatever," said the young man behind the wheel as he reached over to turn the radio off. "Why are you guys stopping me, anyway? I didn't do anything."

"Did you even see me when you ran that stop sign back there?"

"What stop sign? I didn't run any stop sign."

"Yeah, there was a stop sign, and you blew right through it. I almost broadsided you."

"I think you've got me confused with somebody else."

"No, it was you," Weber said. "Your music was just as loud then, too."

"What? You don't like music?"

"I don't like people who run stop signs and endanger other drivers like you did."

"Nope, it wasn't me," the young man said smugly.

"I've got a dash cam that says it was you," Weber told him.

"I don't care what you've got. I've got a dad who's a lawyer."

"You've also got an attitude," Weber said. He opened the car door and said, "Get out."

"I don't think so."

"It wasn't a request, it was an order," the sheriff said, grabbing him by the arm and pulling.

"Get your damn hands off me!"

"I said get out of the car. I'm not going to tell you again."

"No!"

Weber reach past him to try to unbuckle his seatbelt and the young man put both hands over the latch to prevent him from doing so.

"Okay, we can do it your way. Weber looped his arm around the driver's neck and started pulling him backward.

"Ouch! Stop it, that hurts!"

"I told you to get out and you wouldn't obey."

"My dad's going to own you when this is over with!"

Weber ignored him, and with Jordan's assistance they got the seatbelt released and the driver out of the car. He tried to struggle but the sheriff applied pressure with his arm around his neck and led him to the back of the Toyota, where he pushed him facedown onto the trunk lid. Jordan pulled his handcuffs from the pouch on his belt and locked them on the driver's wrists.

"Oww! They're too tight."

"That's because they're brand-new," Weber told him. "Don't worry, they'll stretch after a while."

They put him in the back of Jordan's car and then the young deputy said, "According to his driver's license his name is Jeffrey Stapleton, and he's from Tempe, Arizona. Dispatch says his license is suspended."

"Go ahead and arrest him for driving on a suspended license, running a stop sign, and failure to yield. And throw in resisting arrest. That way his daddy, the lawyer, will have plenty to work on."

His deputy opened the back of his car and told Stapleton he was under arrest, then read him his Miranda rights.

"You guys can't do this to me! I was minding my own business. You can't just pull people over and start messing with them for nothing."

"Save it for the judge," Weber said. "You got things under control, Jordan?"

"No problem, Sheriff. Are you okay? It looks like you're going to have a welt on your forehead."

"Yeah, I'm okay. Hit the steering wheel when I went down in the ditch. I'm surprised the damn airbag didn't inflate."

"Do you need to get checked out?"

"No, I'm fine. I just want to go home and kick my shoes off and watch TV for a while and then get a good night's sleep."

"Roger that. I'll take Mr. Stapleton here in and arrange for a tow truck for his car. You get some rest, boss."

"That's exactly what I plan to do," Weber told him, having no idea how little rest he was going to get that night.

Chapter 32

Weber was sleeping soundly when his phone rang. It took him a moment to pull himself out of the depths of a dream in which he was standing on the edge of Big Lake watching the sun rising over the water as a dragonfly prowled the cattails along the shoreline. He glanced at the digital clock on his nightstand, the red numbers showing it was 12:11 a.m. He knew a call at that time of night wasn't going to be good news, and it wasn't.

"I'm sorry to wake you, Sheriff," the dispatcher said, "but we've got a shooting. Dolan says one fatality confirmed."

"Where at?"

"It's at Judith Murdoch's house on Alderbrook Way."

Weber felt a sense of déjà vu when he pulled up in front of the Murdoch home on Alderbrook Way. Police cars with their flashing lights reflecting off the neighboring houses blocked the street, people stood on the curb talking amongst themselves, and the front door was kicked in again. Inside, a distraught Juliette Murdoch was sitting on her couch wrapped in a blanket. But this time there was something very different. Along with a smashed chair and other items knocked to the floor, the body of Arthur Kramer was lying on its side in the hallway leading to her bedroom.

"I didn't want to shoot him," she cried out when she saw Weber. "I swear I didn't. But he was acting so crazy that I was afraid he was going to kill me!"

Coop and Dolan Reed were standing near the body. Weber joined them and asked, "Any idea what happened?"

"Looks pretty cut and dried to me," Dolan said. "According to Mrs. Murdoch, she was in bed and just falling asleep when she heard a loud noise and she said it felt like the whole house shook. She jumped out of bed and started into the front of the house and was confronted by Kramer trying to knock her door down. She said he was screaming at her and telling her that it was all because of her kid. She said she told him to get out and he told her that she was going to be just as dead as Zach was going to be when he found him. She said she tried to keep him from getting in but he kicked the front door open. She turned and ran back to the bedroom to get her phone to call 911 and he chased her. She said she pulled that chair there in front of him as she passed, hoping it would slow him down, but he picked it up and smashed it against the wall. According to her, all the while he was telling her that she was a dead bitch. She grabbed the phone and tried to dial, but her fingers were shaking so bad she couldn't hit the buttons. Meanwhile, Kramer was heading toward the bedroom. So she grabbed her gun out of the nightstand and shot him."

"Damn."

"Neighbors had called to report a disturbance and we both headed this way," Dolan said. "Mrs. Fuller from next door was out in the yard when we got here and she said she heard gunshots. The people in the two-story house on the other side were out there, too. They're the ones that first called it in. Coop and I made entry and when we got inside Mrs. Murdoch was sitting on the floor with her back against the door jamb in the bedroom doorway and Kramer was lying here."

"Does she have any injuries?"

"She said her wrist feels like it's sprained from trying to hold the door shut when he was kicking it in."

"Where's her gun?"

"I've got it," Coop said, holding up a plastic evidence bag with a four-inch barreled Taurus .38 revolver in it. "I checked it, two rounds have been fired, and Kramer looks like he's got two bullet holes in him."

"We also found this stuck in his belt," Dolan said, showing Weber another evidence bag, this one with a Sig Saur .40 semiautomatic pistol in it. "And if that wasn't enough, this was in the console in his car parked out there on the street." A third evidence bag held a short barreled Smith & Wesson Model 19 .357 Magnum revolver with a matt-black finish and a round butt. Weber couldn't help but wonder if it was the same gun Kramer had held to the head of Lee Drysdale's daughter when he threatened to kill her.

Deputy Tommy Frost joined them and said, "Ambulance is here. So are Buz and Robyn."

"Have Robyn take Mrs. Murdoch out to the ambulance so they can check her wrist," Weber said. "Also, tell Robyn to read Mrs. Murdoch her rights, as a formality. If the paramedics say she's okay, have Robyn transport her to the office. And tell Buz to come in here and help Dolan process the scene. And when you're done with all that, start taking statements from all of the neighbors, Tommy."

"10-4, Jimmy," Tommy said and left.

"So what's your gut reaction, guys?"

"Given what we know about Kramer, I think it went down just like the lady said," Coop replied. "I think his back was against the wall and he flipped out and decided that if he was going down, he was taking somebody with him. And since he couldn't get to Zach, his mother was the next best thing. If he couldn't hurt Zach physically, he would hurt him by taking his mother away from him."

"So you think he would have killed her?"

"Do you doubt it, Jimmy?"

"No, not at all. It looks like a good shooting to me. Or at least as good as any shooting can be."

~***~

Dolan and Buz were the most skilled deputies Weber had at processing crime scenes and he left them to do their job when he drove to the Sheriff's office to interview Juliette Murdoch. She had calmed down and now seemed to be totally drained. Weber had seen other people who had dealt with violent situations or tragic accidents react the same way. Once the adrenaline rush was over they didn't have anything left in them.

"Juliette, I know you've been through a terrible ordeal," he said when he sat across from her at the table in the interview room. "And I really hate to put you through this right now, but it's important that we get a statement from you, if you're willing to talk to us, okay?"

She nodded her head woodenly.

"I believe Robyn read you your rights. Is that correct?"

She nodded her head again and Weber said, "Juliette, we're videotaping this and I need you to say yes or no."

"Oh, I'm sorry. Yes."

"And having been advised of your rights, are you willing to talk to us without an attorney present."

"Am I under arrest?"

"No, ma'am. I just want to cover all the bases, for your sake."

"Yes, I'll talk to you. I'm not trying to hide anything. I didn't want to shoot him, but I had to. He was going to kill me."

"Let's take it from the beginning," Weber said. "Just tell me what happened as well as you can remember."

"I was in bed. I went to bed about 11 o'clock and I was just starting to fall asleep when there was this big noise and it felt like the whole house shook. At first, I thought a tree fell on the house, just like the first time it happened when he showed up. I didn't think it was possible he would come back, not with everything going on."

"When you say he, do you mean Arthur Kramer?

"Yes. I couldn't believe he would come back again. But when I got to the front of the house, there he was, kicking and slamming his shoulder into the door. It was starting to open and I tried to push it back to keep him from getting in. But he just kept slamming into it and yelling that I was going to die. Me and Zach, both. At some point when I was trying to hold the door closed I felt something hurting in my wrist. I thought he had broken it."

She held up her left wrist, which seem to be swollen more than the other one.

"What did the paramedics say about your wrist?"

"They said it was probably just a bad sprain."

"Do you want to go to the Medical Center and get an X-ray, just to be sure nothing's broken?"

"No, it's okay. Just tender."

"Okay. So you were at the door and Kramer was trying to force his way in. Then what happened?"

"I kept telling him to leave, kept telling him I was going to call the police, but he wasn't listening. The door started to fall apart and I realized I couldn't keep him out, so I ran back to my bedroom for the telephone. By then he was in the house and he was chasing me. I think I tripped and got back up, I'm not sure, it all happened so fast. I picked up my phone and I couldn't get the buttons to work. I just kept hitting the wrong ones or something. And he was getting closer all the time. That's when I grabbed the gun."

"Where did the gun come from, Juliette?"

"It was in the nightstand next to my bed. I've had it for a long time, ever since the boys left home. I used to keep it in a zippered case on the top shelf of my closet, but after Kramer broke in the first time, I got it out and loaded it and put it in the nightstand. God, I never thought I'd have to use it."

She began to cry, and Weber gave her some time to compose herself.

"What happened then, Juliette?" he asked gently.

"He was so out of control. He wasn't just yelling, he was raving, going on about how hard he had worked and how he had done so much to make life better for everyone and how they had turned their backs on him. About how Zach had ruined his life and it was time for payback. And he kept coming. I told him to stop, and he wouldn't. So I shot him."

"How many times did you shoot, Juliette?"

She shook her head. "I'm not sure. I think it was more than once, but I don't know. Why don't I know that? How can I not know how many times I pulled the trigger?"

"It's okay," Weber assured her. "Juliette, when you shot Arthur Kramer did you truly believe your life was in danger?"

"Yes! He kept saying he was going to kill me. Kill me and kill Zach. And he would've done it. I'm sure of it."

"After the incident at your house when he broke in the first time, have you seen or spoken to Kramer?"

"I saw him at court when he tried to attack Zach. That's the only other time I saw him. I didn't say anything to him then."

"And had he called you, anything like that?"

She shook her head. "No. I thought with everything going on, they probably had him locked up already. Why was he even out, Jimmy?"

Weber remembered what Parks had told him about the wheels of justice grinding slowly, but knew that would be of no consolation to the woman.

"I don't know, Juliette. I'm so sorry you had to experience this."

"What happens now? Am I going to go to jail?"

"No. From everything I can see and what you've told me about what happened, and knowing what happened with Kramer before, there's no way in the world you're going to be charged with anything, Juliette. This was self-defense. You did what you had to do to stay alive."

She looked at him with tears in her eyes and asked, "If that's true, why do I feel so terrible? Arthur Kramer was an animal and he wanted to kill my son, and he wanted to kill me. So why do I feel so bad for shooting him, Jimmy?"

Weber knew what she was feeling, because he had been in the same position himself. And he knew that no matter what he could tell her, no matter how justified her actions were, her nightmare had only just begun. She was in for a lot of sleepless nights as she questioned her own actions over and over.

"Juliette, taking another person's life, no matter what the circumstances are, is always a terrible thing. You know you did what you had to do, and I know it, and Robyn here knows it, too. But that doesn't make it any easier."

She put her face in her arms atop the table and began to cry.

"Why is this happening? What did I do to make this happen? I want this to just be a bad dream. I want to wake up and I want to be back in my bed and I want Zach home and I want none of this to have ever happened."

Robyn looked at her and then at Weber. She knew about the nightmares, too. She had been with him when he woke up screaming, when he bolted upright in bed, his whole body shaking, unable to tell her what he was going through. And she did the only thing she could do, the same thing she had done with him so many nights. She moved to the other side of the table and sat down beside Juliette and put her arms around her and held her while she sobbed.

Nick Russell

Chapter 33

The first glimmers of daylight were showing in the East by the time the deputies had finished photographing, measuring, and recording the scene at Juliette Murdoch's house. Weber stood in the middle of the living room as people went about their business, most of his deputies coming in on their off-duty hours to help. He sipped from a Styrofoam cup of strong coffee and thought about the horror that Juliette Murdoch had experienced here not once, but twice, at the hands of the rogue cop from New Mexico. It was almost 6:30 when he dialed Parks' cell phone number. His friend picked up on the third ring.

"If you're calling this early in the morning, you either need me to be your alibi because you were out partying all night or else you've got news to tell me. And at this time of morning, I don't think it's going to be good news."

"I guess it depends on how you look at things," Weber said. "Arthur Kramer is dead."

"No way!"

"I just watched them cart his body out of Juliette Murdoch's house a couple of hours ago."

"What the hell happened?"

"Kramer showed up here sometime around 11 o'clock or so last night, kicked her door in, and told her he was going to kill her. Kill her and Zach both, if he found him."

"Wow!"

"Yep. Juliette tried to keep him out, and then when he came after her she picked up a .38 from her nightstand and shot him. Two rounds. One caught him in the upper left shoulder and the other one was dead center in the heart."

"Couldn't have happened to a nicer guy," Parks said. "How is Mrs. Murdoch doing?"

"About as shook up as you would expect for someone who's been through something like that. I think she sprained her wrist a bit trying to keep the door closed when Kramer was trying to kick it in, but other than that, she's okay physically."

"I'm glad to hear that. I really think he would have killed her, Jimmy."

"No doubt in my mind about that," the sheriff said.

"I've got to let my people here know about this. Damn! I never saw this coming."

"Neither did I. What happens now with your investigation?"

"Hell if I know," Parks told him. "Obviously, with Kramer out of the picture, that changes things. But he wasn't the only one doing wrong over here. Sure, he was the worst of the bunch, and probably the instigator for a lot of it, but that doesn't let the rest of them off the hook for their part in things that happened here, or for being willing to look the other way while it was going on. I need to make some phone calls, Jimmy. I'll get back to you."

~***~

Since she would not be allowed to return to her home until the shooting scene was processed, Juliette's sister Catherine had picked her up at the Sheriff's office and taken her to her house when Weber was finished interviewing her. Sometime around 11 AM he drove there to check on her.

"I was hoping she would get some sleep, but she can't," Catherine said. "I don't know what to do for her, Sheriff. We're not the kind of people who get involved in things like this, and I feel so helpless."

"I understand," he told her. "Do you think Juliette is up to talking to me?"

"I am," Juliette said from the doorway into the living room.

"How are you doing?"

She walked to a sofa and sat down, her movements slow as she did so. "I'm so tired I can't keep my eyes open, and my brain feels like I'm in this really thick fog, if that makes any sense. But when I try to sleep, I just keep going through the whole thing in my head. I keep seeing him, and I keep thinking there has to be something I could have done differently. I just keep playing it over and over again in my head."

"I know," Weber said, sitting down beside her. "I want you to know that I talked to Bob Bennett, the Town Attorney, and I talked to somebody from the Attorney General's office down in Phoenix. I faxed them down everything about what happened with Kramer previously, and last night, with my recommendation that no charges be filed against you. They all seem to agree that it was justifiable homicide."

"Homicide? Doesn't homicide mean murder?" Catherine looked concerned as she asked the question.

"It's a legal term," Weber explained. "It means that while someone has taken somebody else's life, their actions were justified and therefore legal. Arizona has what is known as the Castle Doctrine, which says that a person can use deadly force if they reasonably believe that doing so is the only way to prevent themselves or an innocent third party from being seriously injured or killed. Your sister obviously felt that way last night, and the neighbors reported hearing Kramer say he was going to kill her while he was busting in the door. So she's not going to be charged for what happened."

"Oh, that's such a relief," Catherine said, putting her arms around Juliette. "See, honey? It's all going to be okay."

Weber didn't have the heart to tell them that it wasn't going to be okay, that it was never going to be okay again. Instead, he pulled a business card from his pocket and handed it to Juliette.

"This is Molly Bateson. She's a psychiatrist over in Springerville, Juliette. She's good. She helped me a lot when I was dealing with the aftermath of shooting Steve Rafferty. Give her a call, okay? She can help you."

"Is it going to be like this forever, Sheriff? Am I going to feel this way forever?"

"I wish I could tell you that this is one of those things that time is going to heal," he replied. "But based on my own experience, I'd be lying to you. I will tell you this though, you do learn to cope with it. It's not easy, and it doesn't happen overnight, but over time you learn to wall it off in a back corner of your mind, and you learn how to keep it there. Most of the time, at least. Give Molly a call. I told her she'd be hearing from you."

He started to stand up and Juliette grasped his arm.

"What about Zach? Is he okay?"

"Yes, ma'am, he's okay."

"Catherine called Josh and told him about what happened. He's stationed at Lackland Air Force Base in Texas and he's going to come home as soon as he can. He said he'd talk to his commanding officer and he thought he could be on the road sometime today. But does Zach know yet?"

"Yes, he does. I talked to Larry Parks and he talked to Sandra Dunnsire, that Assistant U.S. Attorney. She set it up so that Zach could call me, and I told him what had happened and that you are safe."

"Can I talk to him?"

"I'm sorry, not yet," Weber told her. "He's still in protective custody, and even though Kramer isn't a threat anymore they can't just drop everything and pretend it never happened. He's still a material witness in everything else that happened over there, all the abuse and other activities that were going on in Cañon Verde."

"But they know he didn't do anything, right? They know that it was Kramer that killed that nurse, not Zach."

Weber hated telling her what he had to say next. "I'm sorry, Juliette, but it doesn't work that way."

"What do you mean?"

"There's still an open murder charge against Zach. That has to be addressed."

"But he didn't do it! Kramer did. Can't they see that now?"

"I don't think anybody can deny that Kramer was some kind of a psychopath, not after what he did in the courtroom and then busting in your house like he did. But that doesn't change the fact that he charged Zach with murder."

She started to say something and Weber held up his hand to cut her off. "Here's the thing, the only witness to the event was Kramer. He's the only one that said Zach killed that woman. And obviously he's dead, and whatever credibility he may have had, which wasn't much, died with him. So I don't believe there's any way they're going to be able to convict Zach. But they're still going to have to go through the motions."

"That's ridiculous," Catherine said. "Why?"

"Because that's the way the law works," Weber replied. "And, there's still the charge for the drugs that were found in the car Zach was driving, and he violated probation, and I imagine there's an escape charge. Now, I'm pretty sure most of that's going to go away. But I have to be honest with you, he's not out of the woods yet."

"It just seems so unfair."

"It is unfair, Catherine. But you and I both know that sometimes life isn't fair. The good news is, when Zach does have to go back to New Mexico to face any of those charges, he won't be in danger from Kramer."

"No, but he's got friends over there. Friends in that police department. Who's to say they won't do something to Zach?"

"Believe me," Weber told her, "those people over there are all in so much trouble that Zach is the least of their worries. In fact, the last thing they want is for something to happen to him. But just to be on the safe side, Sandra Dunnsire also said that she will recommend a change of venue to the Attorney General there. That means that Zach won't be held in custody in Cañon Verde, and he won't stand trial there."

"I just wish he could come home. I just wish he could be here and I can put my arms around him."

"I know you do," Weber told her. "Right now, the best thing you can do for him, and for yourself, and for Josh when he gets here, is to try to be as strong as you possibly can. I know it's hard, Juliette, but you're one of the strongest women I've ever known. And you're not alone. A lot of people in this town respect you and care about you. And I do, too. If you need somebody to talk to, you call me. Day or night, I don't care. I mean it, okay?"

She nodded her head and said "Sheriff... Jimmy, you don't know how much I regret all the years I was so mad at you after my boys got in trouble so long ago. I owe you an apology for that. I'm so sorry."

He hugged her, thinking that two women had apologized to him lately, and maybe life would be a little better around Big Lake in the future.

Chapter 34

The day had raced by in a blur of telephone calls from Sandra Dunnsire, the FBI, representatives from the New Mexico Attorney General's office, and the mayor and two city councilmen from Cañon Verde. There had also been calls from news media in New Mexico and Arizona. Mary Caitlin had typed up a press release giving the bare details about the shooting that had taken the life of Arthur Kramer and used it as a response to the many reporters' questions, following up with anything else they asked with a simple "No comment at this time."

The only exception had been Lisa Burnham from News Channel Six. Weber took that call himself.

"For a small town, you guys sure generate a lot of news," she told him.

"Unfortunately, we seem to do that," Weber replied.

"So aside from the generic facts in your press release, what else can you tell me about what happened last night?"

"I'll email you copies of our preliminary reports, for your eyes only," he said. "But basically, Kramer broke into Juliette Murdoch's house and threatened to kill her. She was in danger and feared for her life, and she shot him in self-defense. I've talked to our Town's Attorney and to the Attorney General's office down in Phoenix, and no charges will be filed against her."

"You'd think with all the trouble he was already in, Kramer would've been lying low and trying to keep his head down."

"A reasonable person might do that, but he wasn't exactly reasonable. If he was, none of this would have happened in the first place."

"Can I quote you on that, Sheriff?"

"Help yourself. You and I both know that Kramer was a loose cannon."

"Loose cannon yes, but to go to this extent? What did he hope to accomplish?"

"The mayor over there in Cañon Verde suggested that maybe Kramer thought he could kidnap Zach Murdoch's mother and that would cause the kid to shut up and not tell the investigators anything else. Personally, I think he just saw his whole world crumbling around him and didn't give a damn anymore. From what I've seen of him, he struck me as the kind of guy who lashes out without considering the consequences."

"I've got to be honest with you, Sheriff Weber, there was a time when I thought that about you, too."

"And now?"

"Let's just say that I've come to appreciate the kind of man you are, even if I don't always agree with your methodology. Not that you're perfect. Not by a long shot. But you're somebody I respect. And I don't say that about many people. Especially cops."

"I'll take that as a compliment," Weber told her.

"Good, because it was meant as one." There was silence for half a minute and then she said, "This is the part where you're supposed to tell me that the feeling is mutual."

"How about I say I respect your abilities as a reporter, even if I don't always agree with your methodology?"

Lisa laughed and said, "I won't lie to you, there's times I wish that that little moment we had in your parking lot had gone farther. But you're just not that kind of guy, are you?"

"No, I'm not."

"That's something else I respect about you, believe it or not. And just so you know, if things were different, I'd make that same offer again, with no strings attached."

"That's flattering," Weber told her. "But nothing's changed."

"Robyn's a very lucky woman. I hope she knows that. Even if she does scare the hell out of me."

"For what it's worth, sometimes she scares the hell out of me, too."

She laughed again and said, "You take care of yourself, Sheriff. And thanks again. I owe you."

As he often did when he was worn out but not ready to call it a day and go home, Weber stretched out on the couch in his office. He was almost asleep when Mary knocked on the door.

"Sorry to bother you, Jimmy."

"You say that, but you're still here bothering me."

"I've got a Mr. Stapleton here. His son Jeffrey was arrested yesterday and with everything going on we never did contact the judge and take him to court to face the charges against him.

"What time is it?"

"Almost 4:30."

"Okay," Weber said, sitting up with a sigh. "Send him in."

Frank Stapleton was a big bellied man with thin, curly blonde hair and a pattern of broken veins around his nose that indicated he might be a drinking man.

"Sheriff, I understand you've got my son Jeffrey locked up."

"Yes, sir, I do."

"Can you tell me why?"

"Did he tell you what the charges were against him?"

"He did. He also says he was driving along minding his own business when you and one of your deputies pulled him over for no reason at all."

"We're not in the habit of pulling people over for no reason at all, Mr. Stapleton. But if you'd like, I'd be happy to show you my dash cam video of your son running a stop sign and pulling out in front of me, and the body cam video of us arresting him."

"If you don't mind, Sheriff, I would like to see that."

Weber wasn't as accomplished with the computer as he should be, so he had Mary Caitlin come into his office and pull the videos up for the attorney to review. When he was done watching them, Stapleton sat back and nodded his head.

"Pretty much what I expected."

"What you mean by that, sir?"

"Jeffrey is a punk, Sheriff. A spoiled brat whose mother thinks he could never do anything wrong. He's 22 years old, he dropped out of college, and he doesn't have a job. So he spends his time sitting in his room playing video games, out drinking with his buddies or who knows what else? This isn't the first time he's gotten himself in trouble with his big mouth and his bad attitude and expected me to pull his chestnuts out of the fire. And I'm about tired of it. I sent him up here to get our summer place opened up and ready for the season. Instead, he pulls this bullshit."

"I can call the judge and take him over now, and I'm sure he'll be released on your recognizance," Weber said.

"We can go see the judge," the attorney replied. "But I don't want him released on my recognizance. As far as I'm concerned, you can keep his ass in jail for as long as humanly possible. In fact, I'd consider it a personal favor, Sheriff. Maybe it would finally teach him a lesson and make him realize that there are consequences for the things he does."

Weber laughed, relieved to see a parent who actually expected his son to take some responsibility for his actions for a change. All too often, it went the other way, with the parent screaming about how their kid had been wronged and demanding that they be released immediately.

"Mr. Stapleton, I'd be more than happy to make sure that happens."

~***~

When Weber finally made it home at the end of a very long day, he was so tired that every joint and bone in his body ached, and his eyes felt like they were filled with sand. That guy was still inside his head, but he had given up pounding on the anvil with his sledgehammer and was attacking the Sheriff's skull directly. In fact, Weber thought there might be a platoon of them, all trying to beat their way through to the surface.

He hung up his gun belt, sat on the bed to pull his boots off, and strongly considered just flopping on his back and going to sleep. But he hadn't changed clothes in close to twenty hours and he smelled like a goat even to himself. So he managed to strip and get into the shower, where he stood for a long time lathering and rinsing his body off over and over. When the water turned cold he got out and toweled himself dry, then climbed into bed. He was asleep so fast he didn't remember closing his eyes, and fortunately, no dreams interrupted his slumber.

Chapter 35

Late the next day Weber was at his desk when Mary knocked on his door and said, "There's somebody here to see you."

When the young man first came into his office he thought Zach Murdoch had been released and was back in town, then realized it wasn't Zach, but his brother Josh. Weber stood up and shook his hand.

"You're looking good, Josh. Military life must agree with you."

"It does, Sheriff. I really enjoy it. In fact, I'm thinking about making it a career."

"I came close to it when I was in," Weber told him. "If things hadn't happened here at home that brought me back, I think I probably would have. But it all worked out in the long run. How's your mother doing?"

"She's having a hard time of it. It looks like she's aged twenty years since I saw her two months ago."

"She's been through a lot. And there's a lot more she's going to have to go through."

"My aunt Catherine said she's not to be charged for shooting that guy?"

Weber shook his head. "No, it was self-defense. There's no question about that. But there are bound to be some psychological and emotional things she's going to have to deal with. I gave her the name of a psychologist friend of mine, I really hope she talks to her. It helped me a lot."

"It just seems so weird that my mother killed somebody. My mother."

"She didn't have a choice, Josh. I dealt with Arthur Kramer myself, and there is absolutely no doubt in my mind that it was him or her."

"What's going to happen with Zach? Mom said he still has to stand trial for murdering that woman?"

"I don't know if he's going have to stand trial or not, Josh. With everything that has come out about Kramer, there's more than a little room for doubt that any of it happened the way he claimed it did. But they can't just make it go away because he's dead, or because of the way he died. However, since he was the only witness, it would be very hard to make a case against Zach stick. And again, that's if they even do bring it to trial."

"What about the other stuff, the escape, and stealing the car, and jumping probation and all that?"

"Again, it's hard to say. Zach can state his case that he escaped because Kramer was going to kill him. That's a heck of an extenuating circumstance. As for stealing the car, I don't know that a charge has even been filed about that. And the probation thing, we'll just have to wait and see how it all comes out. Technically, he did violate probation by driving the car with the drugs in it. But really, compared to everything else that he was potentially facing, it's pretty minor."

"Is there any way I can see him, or at least talk to him?"

"I'm sorry, but I don't even know where he is except that he's down in Phoenix. The U.S. Attorney handling his case arranged for me to talk to him so I could tell him about what happened with your mother and Kramer, but they're pretty close-lipped about things. I don't even have a way to talk to him directly without going through channels. That's a good thing, because it was set up that way to protect him from Kramer getting to him one way or another."

"I guess that makes sense," Josh said. "Do you know if he's okay?"

"He is, as far as I know. He was pretty shook up about what happened with your mom, which is understandable. But I think he's going to be just fine. And as for all these charges against him, don't worry about them too much, okay Josh? Like I said, I don't think they can make a strong case in that woman's murder. And right now he's a lot more valuable to the government as a material witness about everything that happened over there in Cañon Verde than he is as a defendant in any kind of trial."

"That's a relief. What can I do right now to help Zach or my mom, Sheriff?"

"Just be there for her," Weber said. "If she wants to talk, let her talk. If she needs to keep quiet, that's okay, too. You might try to encourage her to go see Molly Bateson, that psychiatrist I mentioned. But probably the best thing you can do is just let her hold you. I know when guys get to be your age they don't always feel comfortable having their mother hold them. But this is about her, not you. I think that might be the best medicine in the world for her right now."

"You got it." Josh stood up, then said, "Thank you, Sheriff Weber. Thank you for being there for my mom and my brother. Thank you for believing Zach. And thank you for what happened a long time ago when him and me were being idiots. We owe you a lot."

"Josh, all you owe me is to continue to be the man you've become, okay? I'm proud of the way you turned out."

~***~

Mayor Wingate seemed to have decided to take a proactive stance in the wake of the Town Council's vote of no confidence in him. After a few days of hiding out, he was suddenly all over town, stopping at businesses to shake their owners' hands and compliment them on the success of their stores and shops, showing up at restaurants to glad hand diners, and stopping people on the street to chat them up.

"About the only thing he's not doing is kissing babies," Mary Caitlin said.

"That's just as well," Weber replied. "We don't want a bunch of kids keeping their parents awake with nightmares all night long. It's bad enough they've got the bogeyman hiding under their beds."

"Not to mention the werewolf in the closet," Coop added.

"Chet actually flagged me down today, just to tell me how proud he was of the job I was doing," Dolan Reed said. "And not just me, the whole department. Including you, Jimmy."

"Yeah, he made a point of running into me at lunch yesterday and telling everybody in the restaurant I deserved a round of applause for being such a great public servant."

"I guess a little ass kissing now and then is okay," Mary Caitlin said, "but if he keeps it up he's going to start leaving hickey's."

"Any word on whether or not there's going to be a recall election?"

"There's a lot of talk about it," Mary replied. "It wouldn't surprise me at all if it happens."

"What would Big Lake be without Chet Wingate as mayor?" Robyn asked. "He's been in office forever, hasn't he?"

"Just about. As to what the town would be like without him, I can only think it would be better," Weber told her, then asked, "Aren't you and Marsha supposed to be going down to Phoenix to shop for wedding dresses or something like that today?"

"Tomorrow, Jimmy, don't rush it."

"I thought every girl looked forward to picking out her wedding dress.

"We're picking up my mother because she wants to be part of it. And you know how much I'm looking forward to that."

"Your mother and Marsha together? It would be worth taking a day off work just to see that happen," Weber told her.

"Yeah, and I'm going to be stuck in the middle. Just shoot me now, would you?"

The telephone rang and Mary answered, then put the call on hold and said, "It's for you, Jimmy. Someone from the Attorney General's office down in Phoenix."

Weber went into his office to take the call, and a man's voice said, "Sheriff, this is Reynaldo Salazar, I'm an assistant to the Attorney General. I wanted to let you know that after reviewing everything you sent us about the Arnold Kramer case, our official determination is that Juliette Murdoch acted in self-defense, just like you said, and there will be no criminal charges against her."

"Thank you for letting me know, Mr. Salazar. I'm sure that's going to be a big relief to Mrs. Murdoch."

"Of course, this doesn't mean that somebody from Mr. Kramer's family might not file a wrongful death claim in civil court or something like that. It happens quite often. You might want to make Mrs. Murdoch aware of that, just in case.

"I'll tell her. And thanks again, Mr. Salazar."

~***~

Josh Murdock was attempting to hang a new door on his mother's house when Weber got there, and from the looks of it he was not having much success.

"Need a hand?"

The young man shook his head in frustration and said, "I can rebuild a jet engine and put it back in a plane, but I'm no carpenter. The darn thing won't close all the way and I'm not sure what I'm doing wrong."

Weber inspected the job and said, "Here's the problem. It looks like this door is just a little wider than the original. You see these shims around the frame? Let's take the door off and pull those out and see if that helps."

It did, and within just a few minutes they had the door re-hung and closing properly and latching securely.

"There you go. All done."

"Thanks, Sheriff."

"Yes, thank you, Jimmy," Juliette said.

"How are you doing?"

"I'm... I'm hanging in there. I'm not sure if being back in the house is good for me or bad. Josh came over and cleaned everything up. I just couldn't face that."

"No problem, Mom, I'm here for you."

"I know you are, honey," she said, squeezing his arm affectionately.

"Have you talked to Molly Bateson?"

Juliette nodded her head. "I did. I've actually seen her twice. I think it's helping, but it's a process. You know that better than anyone."

"I do. The reason I came by was to give you some good news."

"I can use all the good news I can get," Juliette told him.

"I got a call from the Attorney General's office down in Phoenix. They've reviewed everything and there are not going to be any criminal charges filed against you."

She let out a sigh of relief. "I know you said that was going to happen, but hearing it officially is such a relief."

"There is one thing," Weber continued. "I don't know what kind of family Kramer had, if any. But there's always the possibility that somebody from his family could try to file a wrongful death suit against you, civilly."

"What does that mean?"

"Well Josh, it means that if Kramer had a wife or kids or somebody like that, they could try to sue your mother for damages."

"That doesn't make any sense at all. If she's innocent, she's innocent, right?"

"There are two sides of the law, Josh, criminal and civil. It's been determined that your mother didn't violate any criminal laws when she shot Kramer. But his family could still try to prove in court that she was at fault in some way."

"That just seems so wrong."

"I know. Even police officers are subject to that if they have to use lethal force. It doesn't mean it's going to happen, and it doesn't mean that even if somebody tries to sue her they will win. I just wanted to make you aware of the possibility so you don't get blindsided if it does happen."

"Thank you, Jimmy," Juliette said. "You're right, it's better to be prepared ahead of time. Or at least aware that something like that could happen."

Chapter 36

"You're kidding me, right? I'm over in New Mexico fighting crime and trying to preserve truth, justice, and the American way, and I finally get to come home and my woman is off having a girls' day in Phoenix *and* a sleepover? What's wrong with this picture?"

"Calm down, Superman. Did you tell Marsha you were coming home?"

"No. I didn't even know I was going to be able to take off until this morning," Parks said. "I wanted to surprise her."

"Well, surprise."

"I'm telling you, this just isn't right."

"What? We're all supposed to be mind readers, or fortunetellers or something, and look into our little crystal balls and predict the future?"

"Hey man, don't be talking about balls, crystal or otherwise. Mine are blue."

"Sounds like a personal problem."

"It is! That's what I'm telling you!"

"Well, the good news is you can take a long cold shower."

"Jimmy, I've been taking more damn cold showers than an Eskimo."

"You'll get over it. Meanwhile, welcome home, for what it's worth."

"It's not worth a hell of a lot right now."

"Are you done over there? The investigations are all over?"

"Oh, there's going to be lots of investigating still going on, but I don't think I have to go back over anymore. Boyd and Mayfield and a couple of people the U.S. Attorney assigned to the case are handling it pretty well after the initial flood of contacts, and the people from the state Attorney General's office are working right alongside them. Besides, I don't think the Bureau wants to keep paying my per diem. The only thing the pencil pushers back in

Washington are more dedicated to than crime-fighting is keeping the budget in check."

"You guys did good over there, Parks."

"It helped a lot when that Lisa Burnham broke the news on television and then the stations in New Mexico picked it up. Before that we were getting a lot of resistance. But then it was like the dam broke and we were up to our necks in people wanting to talk to us. And by the way, you'll never guess who I talked to yesterday afternoon."

"Who?"

"Lee Drysdale."

"You're kidding me?"

"No, sir. He came walking in and I about fell out of my chair. He said that he should've spoken out a lot sooner, and he was embarrassed because he didn't."

"If someone put a gun to my kid's head like that, I think I'd have done the same thing."

"Maybe so. Or maybe you'd say whatever it took to get out of the situation while you could, then you'd come back sometime and blow him away."

"Maybe so, who knows?"

"Anyway, Drysdale gave a full statement about what happened and everything he saw while he was there in Cañon Verde. I guess he figured that with Kramer dead, he could finally do it without worrying that it would cost him his kids' lives."

"Better late than never," Weber said. "I think he's going to feel better about himself now that he did, too."

"I hope so. I think he's a good guy who got caught up in a very bad situation."

"I'll tell you what, Parks. Since we're both batching it tonight, how about I buy you a steak to celebrate your homecoming?"

"Well, it's not quite the hot reception I was hoping for, but it's better than nothing. Let's go."

~***~

"What will it be, gentlemen?" the pretty waitress in the cowgirl outfit and boots asked when they were seated at their table at the Roundup Steakhouse, Big Lake's most popular restaurant.

"I want the biggest steak you've got back there in the kitchen," Parks told her. "And I'm talking big, darling. I want it medium rare, smothered in mushrooms and onions, and I want the biggest pile of steak fries you can carry with it."

"You got it. What kind of dressing do you want on your salad?"

"Salad? Do I look like a rabbit to you?"

The young woman giggled and said, "No, sir. How about you, Sheriff?"

"Same as he's having, but hold the mushrooms and onions," Weber told her.

"And no salad for you, either?"

"Nope, he's not a rabbit either," Parks told her.

"You got it."

She walked away with a bounce, and Weber caught Parks staring after her.

"I could put you in jail for what you're thinking, buddy."

"Me? No way! I'm just admiring some of God's finest work, Jimmy. Just like a beautiful sunset, that's all."

"Uh huh. You can tell your story to the judge. Better yet, you can tell it to Marsha when she gets back in town."

"Hey, that woman doesn't have a problem with me looking, as long as I don't touch. So I wait and do the touching when we're alone."

"That's good to know," Weber told him. "I'd hate to have to lock you two up for public indecency as soon as you lay eyes on her."

Parks started to say something about laying something, but was interrupted when Mayor Chet Wingate came to their table.

"Special Agent Parks, it's so good to have you back in town. How are you doing?"

"I'm good, Mr. Mayor," Parks said as Chet pumped his hand. "How about you?"

"Fine as frog's hair. I was telling Sheriff Weber here how proud we all are of you going over in New Mexico and helping to wrap up all of that nasty business with Police Chief Kramer. That was such a sad, sordid affair."

"Yes, it was," Parks said, rolling his eyes at Weber. "By the way, Mr. Mayor, I understand that you and Kramer had a conversation or two back when this was all going down. Is that right?"

"Ah...we ahh, umm, we..." The mayor was looking everywhere but at Parks, and when he spied Vern Carmichael and his wife Lois at a table across the room, he said, "I'm sorry, I really need to speak to Mr. Carmichael. I hear he's adding onto his guest ranch and I want to tell him how much of an asset his business is to Big Lake. I'm sorry, you're going have to excuse me."

Parks opened his mouth to speak, but the mayor was already making his way rapidly across the room, bumping diners in their chairs along the way. "Oh, Vern? Vern? It's so good to see you and Lois out having a nice meal. I want to thank you for investing not only in your business, but also your community."

Weber laughed and said, "It's worth the price of feeding you just to see him make such a fast retreat."

"He really thinks he's going to get charged with conspiracy, doesn't he?"

"Yeah. You and I know it's not going to happen, but like Mel Walker said, when Chet's busy covering his own ass he doesn't have time to be a pain in anybody else's."

~***~

Robyn and Marsha got back to town late the next afternoon and when she hugged him Robyn said, "I am so glad to be back home!"

"Is that because you missed me or because you couldn't take any more of your mother?"

"Both, actually. But that's not what I'm talking about. When Marsha found out Parks was back she tore up the highway getting here. I swear, if that minivan of hers had wings I think we could've taken flight. I kept hoping some cop didn't stop us and I would have to explain why I was riding with a maniac like her. I don't think my badge would have kept either one of us out of jail "

"Sounds like she was just as eager to get together as he was."

"Eager? She stopped out in front and was almost demanding I get out. I got my suitcase out of the back of her van and she drove away before I could even close the lid!"

"I'd give a lot to be a fly on the wall over there right about now," Weber said.

"Ewww! There are some things I don't want to picture."

"Yeah, I guess you're probably right."

He ran his finger along the inside of her arm from the wrist to the crook of her elbow and asked, "So, how much did you miss me?"

"Not quite that much."

"Really?"

Robyn looked at his face and laughed. "Do you really think those puppy dog eyes are going to work on me?"

"I was kind of hoping."

She grinned impishly and said, "Just because I said I didn't miss you *that* much didn't mean I didn't miss you at all. I just meant we could at least take the time to close the trunk of the car after we put my suitcase in it."

"Yeah, I guess we can do that," he said.

"Then why are you standing here wasting time talking to me instead of throwing the damn suitcase in the trunk?"

Nick Russell

Chapter 37

"So how bad was it?" Weber asked the next morning.

"Worse than I imagined it would be, Jimmy."

"Oh, it wasn't that bad, Robyn," Marsha said. "I had fun."

"I'm glad somebody had fun," Robyn replied as she slid a stack of buttermilk pancakes off the griddle in her kitchen and onto a plate, setting it in front of Parks.

"I've got to tell you, if this bozo ever proposes to me, I'm taking your mother dress shopping with me, too!"

"I don't think my mother ever wants to see you again. As far as she's concerned, you're the kind of bad girl she never wanted me to hang out with when I was growing up."

"Aww... and look at you now."

"What did you do, Marsha?"

"Me? I was just my usual sweet self, Jimmy."

"No wonder she didn't like you."

"Ignore her. Robyn's just exaggerating. I think Mrs. Fuchette thinks of me just like another daughter."

"Before you get too crazy, you can forget me ever proposing," Parks said. "Marriage can ruin a good relationship."

"That's not true! My parents had a great marriage," Marsha told him.

"Mine sure don't," Robyn said. "I feel sorry for my dad. I really do. I don't know how he's put up with that all these years."

"So what did she do this time?"

"Well, let me see, Jimmy. The first thing she did was say she was disappointed that I brought Marsha with me because she thought it was going to be just me and her. This was as soon as Marsha and I got there, with Marsha standing right there in the doorway!"

"Your mother's never been known for her subtlety," Weber observed.

"Then, of course, she had to launch into this long thing about how she never gets to see me because I chose to live up here in the wilderness, and how she never has approved of my career choice and doesn't understand why I couldn't be just as happy being a schoolteacher down there in Phoenix. Of course, she blamed that on you and told Marsha how she doesn't approve of our relationship. And that's before we ever got all the way inside the house!"

"Your mom sounds like a real piece of work," Parks said.

"My mother is an uptight shrew!"

"Wait, she hasn't gotten to the best part," Marsha said. "Tell them what happened at the bridal shop."

Robyn sighed and said, "It was a nightmare. I'm trying on dresses, and no matter what I put on my mother didn't like it. It was too tight, or too short, or too fancy, or not fancy enough. And all the while she's criticizing the poor saleslady that's helping us, and just making a general pain out of herself. And then, for whatever reason, she decided to dig in my purse, which I left sitting on a chair for safekeeping with her and Marsha. My mother decides she needs a breath mint, which was only an excuse to go rummaging around in my purse. The next thing you know, she pulls out my off duty .38 and asks in a loud voice why I have a gun in my purse! The next thing you know women are gasping and looking panicked all over the store. I kept telling them I'm a cop and showed them my badge, and all the while everybody is looking at me like I'm some kind of serial killer. And then...," Robyn had been stern faced but couldn't help breaking into a smile when she continued, "and then she asked Marsha if she carried a gun, too. And this one says..." Robyn started laughing and couldn't continue.

"What? All I did was tell her no, I don't carry a gun, just a big pink vibrator and a bulk pack of magnum sized condoms."

Weber laughed so hard he began coughing.

"You didn't?"

"Oh, yes she did," Robyn said, "and all the while she's got this big innocent look on her face. My mother was so scandalized she went out and sat in the car. Needless to say, dress shopping was cut short. And there wasn't a lot of conversation over lunch, or back at the house."

"Oh, that's wild," Parks said. "So you have to go back and repeat the whole process again to find a dress?"

"You know what? No. I don't want to spend a lot of money on a fancy dress I'm going to wear one time. This whole wedding thing is getting out of hand. I would just prefer to wear jeans and a blouse and go see the judge and get it over with."

"That would break your mother's heart," Marsha said. "She wants this to be such an event."

"My mother doesn't have a heart," Robyn told her.

"I don't care if it's a big wedding or just us standing before the judge," Weber said. "Whatever you want to do is fine with me."

"What I want to do is to forget all about it for right now." Robyn saw the look on Weber's face and quickly added, "I don't mean I want to forget about getting married, Jimmy. Just all this wedding planning and my mother's constant phone calls about flowers and who's going to cater the reception and all that. It's driving me crazy. That's what I want to forget about."

Weber felt a bit of relief. Things had been rocky off and on during their relationship, and more than once Robyn had withdrawn from him when she felt the pressure of a commitment building up. Those days seemed to have been in the past, but he was still wary.

"Can we talk about something else? How is Juliette Murdoch doing?"

"She's coping as best she can," Weber replied. "Her other son, Josh, is back home on a thirty day leave from the Air Force and I think that's helping. And she told me she's been talking to Molly Bateson over in Springerville."

"What about Zach? Where do things stand with him?"

"He'll eventually be going back to New Mexico to answer the charges against him, but I don't think he has much to worry about," Parks said. "We uncovered so much stuff over there that I would think trying to pursue a case against him is the least of their worries

"It was that bad, huh?"

"The best way I can describe it is to say that it was probably not much different than it was in some places in the deep South during the civil rights movement. If you didn't fit into whatever profile Kramer and his guys thought was right, you could be in for a world of hurt."

"But it's all going to change now, right?"

"I think we made a lot of progress, Marsha. But even with Kramer dead, there's still a lot of housekeeping to be done over there. Like I was telling Jimmy, he may have been the worst of them, but he wasn't the only one. And it wasn't just a few bad cops. They can deny it all they want, but the mayor and the city council knew what was going on. And so did a lot of other people in Cañon Verde. And they all either just looked the other way or didn't have the courage to stand up and say something."

"Apparently one woman had the courage to try to put a stop to it. That Barbara Eibeck."

"Yes, she did. And she ended up dead. It makes me wonder if she was the first."

"What are you saying?"

"I'm saying that a guy like Kramer, if anybody stood up to him, if they tried to put a stop to it, I think they would've wound up just as dead as Barbara Eibeck. Look at the way he threatened Lee Drysdale's kids. A guy who would do something like that? He wouldn't stop at anything to eliminate anyone he considered a threat."

"I'm just glad you're back," Marsha said, rubbing the FBI agent's arm affectionately. I hate to admit it, but I missed you."

"Eat your pancakes," Robyn said. "And let him put all the syrup on he wants, Marsha. If I know you, the boy needs his energy."

Chapter 38

It took a week before the news arrived that the U.S. Attorney's office was going to release Zach Murdoch into the custody of New Mexico authorities. A stipulation was made ahead of time that he would not be returning to Cañon Verde to answer to the outstanding charges against him. Instead, he was taken to Alamogordo. Everyone knew that he was an important witness in the ongoing investigation of misdeeds by the Cañon Verde Police Department, and while his mother and Weber both worried that somebody might mistreat him in retaliation, the thin blue line has no use for bad cops, either.

It was determined that there would be a show cause hearing about the murder of Barbara Eibeck to determine if there was sufficient evidence against Zach to move forward with a trial. Because Adam Turner, the attorney Juliette had hired to represent Zach in the extradition hearing in Big Lake was not licensed to practice law in New Mexico, she retained a law firm from Albuquerque that Turner highly recommended to represent her son.

"I don't care if I have to clean out my savings and cash in my 401(k)s and mortgage my house," she told Weber. "I want Zach to have the best defense possible. And I'm going to be there. Every day."

Weber admired her resolve, and knew that she would do everything possible to see that Zach was treated fairly. Weber, Coop, Dan Wright, and even Judge Ryman gave sworn video depositions about Kramer's activities in Big Lake, the threats he had made against Zach's life, his outburst in the courtroom during the extradition hearing, and his ultimate death at the hands of Juliette Murdoch.

"I just don't see how anybody's going to believe anything Kramer said after all of this," Weber said. "I'd be amazed if they don't dismiss the charges against Zach before it ever gets to trial.

And if for some crazy reason they do indict him, there's no way there's any evidence that will hold up in court."

"I think you're probably right," Parks said. "I *hope* you're right. But you just never know what's going to happen. Even though he threatened to kill Zach in public more than once, Kramer maintained all along that it was Zach that killed that nurse, not him. And you know about the woman who accused Zach of being violent toward her, right?"

"No, this is the first I heard anything about that," Weber said, surprised at the revelation.

"Yeah, a woman named Claudia Bukowski claims that Zach assaulted her on two different occasions."

"That name's familiar," Weber said. "Where have I heard it before?"

"She's the gal that Zach was shacking up with before this all happened. It was her car that he was driving when he got busted, and he claimed it was her pot and her bong they found in it, not his. This Claudia is a real piece of work. She's had several convictions for drugs, and she was on probation, too. With all of this going on, you'd think she'd keep her nose clean, but she was too dumb for that. She got busted for possession again, this time up in Roswell, and she's facing a couple of years behind bars. So right away she's wanting to cozy up to whoever she can to try to get off. She's claiming that Zach attacked her twice, and she's willing to testify to it."

"Do you think there's any truth to that?"

"Who knows? By law they shouldn't have even been hanging out together since they are both on probation. But given what I know of Zach and given what I know of this Claudia's history, I don't put a lot of faith in anything she's got to say."

"But that doesn't mean the court over there in New Mexico is going to feel the same way you do, right?"

"I'm afraid not, Jimmy. If they really want to get him, her testimony can help them convince a judge and a jury that he's a good possibility for the murder. If he's already attacked one woman, why not another?"

"Were there ever any reports of domestic violence between them, anything like that?"

"Nope, not a one. In fact, up until now she's been telling the whole world what a great guy Zach is and how he was so loving and so gentle and would never do anything like that. According to her, before she got busted, he wouldn't hurt a fly."

"So she'll lie and throw him under the bus to help herself."

"That's the way it looks," Parks said. "I don't think their relationship is ever going to be made into one of those Hallmark movies."

"Damn, I'm sorry to hear this. There's no question that Zach has made some pretty dumb mistakes in his life, but I sure don't want to see him get railroaded."

"Me, either. When I was a young man back home on the farm, my dad always told me that one rule a guy should always remember is to never screw anybody crazier than he is. I guess nobody ever told Zach about that."

"Then according to your old man, you should still be a virgin."

"Don't be that way, Jimmy. You know I'm everything you want to be."

"Is there any way we can help Zach, besides what we've done already?"

"I don't see how we could. It's all going to come down to whether or not the people in New Mexico want to believe a disgraced cop with a known history of abusing people, or a kid with a minor record who just recently got accused of domestic violence by a woman with a very shady past."

"When you put it that way, things look better for Zach."

"Yeah, but remember, nobody knows what might happen over there until it happens," Parks cautioned. "They could go with Zach's story and put it on Kramer and be done with one clean sweep, or they may decide to go just the opposite direction and try to hang him out to dry so they can say that while Kramer may have stepped over the line a little bit now and then to keep the peace, at least he wasn't a murderer."

"I can't believe they would be that foolish," Weber said.

"There's a lot to consider, Jimmy. As it is now, besides all of the criminal charges that are going to be laid against some of their cops over there, and maybe even some city officials for letting it happen, if it can be proved they were aware of the situation, Cañon Verde is also facing all kinds of civil suits from people who were victims of Kramer and his way of doing things. Do they want to also have to defend themselves against a wrongful death suit from Barbara Eibeck's family? One way or the other, before this is all said and done, that town's going to be bankrupt, no matter what kind of insurance they might have."

Chapter 39

Parks had been right in his supposition that Cañon Verde might try to execute some damage control by pursuing a case against Zach Murdoch. And almost immediately, things looked bad for the young man. Judge James McFadden, a small balding man who viewed the world through thick glasses with a perpetual frown, immediately refused to allow any of the statements from Weber or anyone else in Big Lake to be admitted into evidence at the hearing. Nor did he allow any testimony about how former police chief Arthur Kramer had been killed while breaking in and trying to assault the mother of the defendant in her own home.

"Arthur Kramer is not the one charged with this crime," he said when Zach's attorney tried to introduce the evidence. "We are here to determine whether or not there is cause for Mr. Murdoch to be indicted for the murder of Barbara Eibeck."

"Your Honor, I respectfully argue that the statements made by Mr. Kramer, and his ultimate death, have a large bearing on the veracity of his claim that my client is responsible for the victim's death."

"Save it for the actual trial, Mr. Stevens. As I said before, Arthur Kramer is not the one charged with this crime."

Weber and Parks, who had gone to New Mexico in an unofficial capacity to support Zach and Juliette Murdoch, looked at each other and shook their heads.

"Well, I guess we know which route they're going to take," Parks said in a low voice to the sheriff.

Apparently his voice wasn't low enough, because the judge glared at him and said, "Sir, if you can't remain quiet and conduct yourself appropriately in my courtroom I'll have the bailiff escort you out."

Given the restrictions the judge had put on testimony, allowing only Chief Kramer's report of the incident at the Cañon Verde Medical Center that resulted in the death of Barbara Eibeck and Zach's escape and flight to Arizona, it didn't take long for an indictment to be issued. When the judge adjourned the hearing, Juliette Murdoch sat stoically while she watched a police officer put handcuffs on Zach and take him back to jail.

"This is a setback," Mark Stevens, Zach's attorney told her. "But we knew it was a possibility. Don't worry, Juliette, I'm confident that once a jury hears all of the background on Kramer and the things that he had been doing all along, nobody is going to believe that report of his blaming Zach for the woman's death."

"I didn't believe they would indict him in the first place," she replied. "What happens when it gets to court for the actual trial if they do the same thing? What if they don't allow the testimony about Kramer then, too?"

"That's not going to happen," Stevens assured her.

"It happened here, didn't it?"

"Yes, Juliette, it did. But there's a lot of difference between this hearing and a felony murder trial. I *will* be able to get that all admitted into evidence. And even if for some crazy reason the judge denies it, it still comes down to the word of a dead man over Zach."

"A dead police chief that Zach's mother killed!"

"You have to trust me," Stevens told her. "You have to trust the system to work."

"The system? The system didn't work right from the start! If it did, we wouldn't be here."

Parks looked at Weber and nodded his head, knowing that what she said was true.

~***~

Neither one of them had much to say on the flight back home. The weather had warmed up considerably, producing thermals that made for a bumpy ride. Weber was wishing he had skipped lunch, but Parks seemed to ignore the occasional jolt.

Both men had dedicated their lives to the criminal justice system, and both had believed in it throughout their careers. Weber didn't know about Parks, but right now, just like Juliette Murdoch, he couldn't help but think that sometimes the system he had served for so long seemed broken.

Landing at the new grass airstrip at Big Lake, Parks taxied to his tie down spot and shut the Cessna's engine off. The propeller stopped spinning and they sat there for a moment.

Finally, Parks said, "Jimmy, did you ever get the feeling that you're in a kayak trying to paddle your way uphill at Niagara Falls? There are so many bad guys in the world and you and me and guys like us lock them up, and more often than not some judge gives them a slap on the hand and turns them loose again. Then you get a kid like Zach Murdoch who screwed up a little bit along the way but is basically a good person who's trying to get his life back on track, and he's getting railroaded. It just don't seem right."

"I don't know about a kayak, buddy, but sometimes I feel like I'm up the creek without a paddle. No matter how this turns out, even if Zach gets off, which I have to be honest with you I'm beginning to doubt, it's going to cost his mother everything she has. What's fair about that?"

"I guess all we can do is hope for the best. I really didn't think they would indict him, but we both knew all along that it was a possibility."

While Parks tied the airplane down, Weber called the office and asked the dispatcher to send someone to pick them up. A few minutes later Tommy Frost arrived and welcomed them back home.

"How did it go?"

"Not good," Weber replied, "They indicted him."

"How could they be that dumb, Jimmy?"

"Don't ask me," the sheriff said. "I've been asking myself the same question all the way back here."

Weber had a surprise waiting for him when he arrived at the office. After sharing the news about Zach's indictment and listening to Mary and Robyn's incredulous responses, Mary said, "Things have been kind of exciting around here, too."

"Oh, yeah? What's up? And if Archer wrecked another car or did something else stupid, please don't tell me. I've had enough bad news for one day."

"No, nothing like that. But it is about a member of the Wingate family," Mary said with a cat that ate the canary look.

"What?"

"Someone started circulating a petition for a recall election against Chet, and in just 24 hours they've got almost the required number of signatures of qualified voters to make it happen."

"You're kidding me? Who started it? Kirby?"

"No. Your new best friend, Janet McGill."

"Wow! Talk about jumping in with both feet. She said something about being an activist back in California before she moved here, but I didn't see this coming."

"I don't think anybody did," Mary said.

"How's Chet taking that news?"

"Well, first he wanted to have a Town Council meeting to have her thrown off, but Kirby and Frank Gauger put a stop to that. Then I guess he went over to the newspaper and demanded that Paul put out a special edition talking about what a great public servant he's been, and how the recall petition was so unfair and it was only supported by malcontents and riff raff."

"I bet that went over well with Paul. He's never been a fan of Chet."

"No, apparently not. It was a closed-door meeting in Paul's office, but according to Margie, when it was over with Chet went storming out the door and never even said goodbye to her. She said she was hoping he would at least pause long enough to see a copy of the petition sitting on the front counter."

"Who knows? Maybe there's at least a little bit of sanity left in the world after all," Weber said.

That notion was dispelled instantly when the door opened and the mayor came in.

"Sheriff Weber, could I have a minute of your time?"

"If you're here to bitch about me going to New Mexico for Zach Murdoch's hearing, I took a personal day off, Chet."

"Oh, no, nothing like that. I'm glad to see that you're supporting Zach and Juliette. Lord knows those poor people have been through so much already. Can we talk in your office?"

Weber didn't really feel like talking to the irritating little man, but he led him into his office and sat down behind his desk.

"What do you need, Chet?"

"I don't know if you heard about it, but there's a faction in this town that seems to be causing trouble."

"What kind of trouble are we talking about?"

"Oh, it's nothing to concern yourself about. These are just a bunch of rabble-rousers. But they have started this ridiculous petition to have a recall election. Don't get me wrong, Jimmy, that's their right and you know I support the American way of life all the way. I just want to ask your opinion about something."

There the mayor went, calling him by his first name again.

"What's that, Chet?"

"Do you think this nonsense is going to go anywhere? Do you think that there's any possibility of a recall? Be honest with me."

"Honestly? Yeah, Chet, I think there is a possibility of it. A good possibility."

"And what do you think the results would be?"

"Well, you've made some enemies in this town over the years."

He expected the mayor to disagree and launch into a long monologue about how much he had done for Big Lake, and how unfair it was that some people didn't appreciate him. Instead, he surprised Weber by saying, "I guess it's possible. I've been thinking about that a lot, Jimmy, and maybe it's time."

The sheriff didn't see that coming. Faced with Kirby Templeton and the Town Council's official declaration of no faith in him, was Chet going to spare himself the embarrassment of a recall election and resign from office gracefully?

He should have known better, and that idea was quickly dispelled when Chet continued.

"With the heart problems I've been having and everything else going on, well, Jimmy, I'm not a young man anymore. Maybe it's time I stepped aside and made way for some new blood. Somebody younger and with more energy."

Surprised, Weber said, "I guess that time comes for all of us, Chet."

"It does," the mayor replied soberly. "And that's where you come in, Jimmy."

"Me? What do you mean, Chet?"

"Listen, I know we've had our little differences in the past, but that's all behind us. The truth is, even though we may go about it in different ways sometimes, we both care about this community and we both want what's best for it. And I think what's best is a younger man with new ideas sitting in the mayor's office. Somebody who wants just that, what's best for Big Lake. And that's why I'm here talking to you right now. I think you and I both know who that man is, don't we Jimmy?"

"I'm flattered, Chet, but I have to be honest with you, I have absolutely no interest in being mayor. I'm perfectly happy with the job I have now."

The mayor looked at him with wrinkled eyebrows that showed his surprise and said, "I'm not talking about you!"

"You're not?"

"Of course not. I'm talking about Archer. I'm thinking about appointing him to fill my seat if I resign for health reasons."

Chapter 40

"Archer as mayor? Get outta here!"

"I couldn't believe it either, Hillbilly, but that's what he said, sitting right there in my office. He wants to appoint Archer to replace him."

Christine Ridgeway, the director of Big Lake's SafeHaven women's shelter, crossed her arms and sat back in her chair, looking at Weber incredulously.

"No way! Not even Chet's that dumb."

"Apparently he is."

"Can he even do that? Appoint his son to succeed him in office?"

"I don't know what the legalities are," Weber said. "But he seems to think he can."

"Good Lord! What's this world coming to?"

"According to Chet, Pete Caitlin set a precedent when he picked me to be sheriff before he retired."

"Yeah, but it still had to be approved by the Town Council, right? I mean, Pete strongly recommended you and told them you were his choice, but did they have to follow that?"

"No, they didn't. But things were different back then. We were a much smaller town and everybody on the council knew and respected Pete, so there wasn't a lot of discussion about it. He nominated me for the job and they voted me in."

"Yeah, but this is a lot different," Marsha said. "First of all, like you said, everybody knows and respects Pete. And while everybody knows Chet, respect is a different thing altogether. The last I heard they've already got all the signatures they need for the recall election. That tells you just how much people respect him. This is just his way of keeping the power. He figures with Archer as mayor he can still pull the strings and control everything."

Salvatore Gattuccio, who owned Mario's Pizzeria, came to their table with a big wicker basket full of breadsticks.

"Here you go, my friends. Your pizzas will be out very soon, I promise."

"And are you going to sit with us while we eat, Sal?"

"Of course, my darling. How could I resist such a beautiful woman and such wonderful company?"

He laid an arm around Christine's shoulder and hugged her affectionately.

"Sheriff Jimmy, Mr. Parks, you two and me, are we not the most lucky men in the world to have such amazing women in our lives?"

"You'll get no argument from me about that, Sal," Weber told him.

"Yes, my friend, we are truly blessed. This one here, my Christine? She has changed my life so much. She has shown me that there is more to life than a kitchen and an oven."

Sal had grown up in the family business, learning to toss dough before most boys his age could toss a baseball, and had taken over the restaurant when his parents retired and bought a motorhome to travel the country they had immigrated to when he was just a baby. While the big man had never met a stranger, he had never shown any interest in a relationship with anyone until Christine had returned home to Big Lake after a career in Southern California. Not a tiny woman herself, Weber's childhood friend and the pizza man quickly formed a bond and seemed very happy in their relationship.

Sal excused himself to go check on their pizzas, and was back soon with one of his employees, setting the pizzas on metal stands on the table. He pulled out a chair to sit beside Christine and said, "Now I take off the apron, and the kids in the back can take care of the restaurant. Let's eat, my friends."

The petition and the possibility of a recall election were on everybody's minds, not just at their table but with other diners as well. From what Weber could overhear, it sounded like Chet Wingate had finally gone too far and was on his way out. He didn't know how many people were aware of the mayor's scheme to appoint his own son to replace himself, but he was sure the word would get out before too long. And when it did, he thought the only thing it would accomplish would be to make Chet seem to be even a bigger buffoon than he already was.

As inept as the mayor was, Weber couldn't picture anybody believing Archer would be a suitable replacement. But he knew that the mayor was just as stubborn as he was unrealistic, and figured that nothing was going to stop Chet from trying to make it happen.

Chapter 41

"No, Daddy, you can forget it. I'm a deputy and that's all I want to be."

"Listen to me, Archer. This is an opportunity you can't pass up."

"I can too. And I'm going to. I don't want to be mayor and I'm not going to be mayor. I don't know where you come up with these ideas sometimes, Daddy, but you can forget about it."

It had taken Archer a long time to get up enough courage to stand up to his father, and Weber couldn't help but grin, sitting on the corner of Mary's desk watching the two debate the issue.

"Who knew Archer had a backbone underneath all that flab?"

"Be nice, Jimmy."

"I'm just saying it's about time he grew a pair. His old man's told him what to do all his life. It's good to see him standing up for himself."

"Well, you can thank Kallie Jo for that," Mary said. "That girl's the best thing that ever happened to Archer in more ways than one."

"You stop all this nonsense and do what you're told," the mayor said, his voice growing strident. "I'm still your father!"

"Yeah, but I'm not a little boy anymore and you can't keep telling me what to do. It's time you figure that out, Daddy."

"Archer was never *little*," Weber whispered, getting a nudge in the ribs from Mary's elbow.

"Oh, you think not? Well let me tell you something, mister..." The mayor punctuated his statements by poking a stubby finger in Archer's chest, his voice growing even louder.

Weber decided it was time to put a stop to things before they got completely out of hand.

"Okay, enough bullshit, Chet. Archer's on duty and the town's not paying him to listen to you go on and on about this."

"Stay out of this, Sheriff. I'm talking to my son."

"No, right now you're talking to my deputy. And if you poke him in the chest one more time, you're going to be arrested for assaulting a police officer. That ought to look real good when that recall election starts."

"Starts? It's going to start? What have you heard?"

"I don't know if it's going to start or not, Chet. Just get the hell out of here, will you?"

"I'm here on official business!"

"No, you're here harassing my deputy. And I'm not going to put up with it. So take a hike."

Chet looked at him and said, "I'm still the mayor in this town."

"You are for now. And I'm still the sheriff. And I'm not going to tell you again to get out of my office."

"Fine! You just blew it, Archer. All your life I've tried to help you be better than you are, and you've never appreciated it. Well, I'm done, do you hear me? Done!"

He stormed out of the office and Archer said, "Why does he think I have to be better than I am?"

There were a million answers to that question, but before Weber could voice any of them Mary jabbed her elbow in his ribs again.

~***~

He was in his office going over the next month's duty schedule two hours later when Mary opened the door without knocking and said, "Parks wants you out in his trailer right now. He said it's important."

Not knowing what was wrong, Weber hustled outside and back to the FBI agent's office.

A young woman with strawberry blonde hair was seated across the desk from Parks.

"Tabitha, this is Sheriff Weber. Jimmy, this is Tabitha Eibeck. Barbara Eibeck's daughter."

"Hello, Sheriff. I think I talked to you before."

"Yes, you did."

"Jimmy, Tabitha came to see me because there's something she wants to share and she didn't feel comfortable talking to

238

anybody back in Cañon Verde. Tabitha, tell Sheriff Weber what you started to tell me."

"I found something," the young woman said. "I found something and I didn't know who else to talk to, so I came over here to see Mr. Parks because I had his card and he was so nice when he interviewed me back home. He was nice to me even though I was pretty rude to him. And to you, too, when I called you about my mother. I'm sorry about that. Chief Kramer was telling everybody that we needed to call and put pressure on you guys to release her killer to him."

"You were emotionally distraught," Weber told her. "No apology necessary."

"With everything that's been going on, I'm afraid to go to the police. So many people are talking about how bad Chief Kramer was but there are still a lot of people that don't believe any of it. They say everybody is just making things up about him. I've heard people talking about how when this is all said and done, when the dust settles, some traitors are going to get payback."

She began to cry and said, "I just don't know who to trust right now. Not even those FBI agents from Roswell. I know you work with them and they're probably good people, Mr. Parks, but they're still cops, and cops are the ones that..." She started to cry again and they gave her a moment, then Parks reached across the desk and put a hand on hers.

"You can trust us," he said gently. "What did you find, Tabitha?"

"A while after my mother was killed, someone from the police department called and said I could come down and get her wedding ring and her watch, and stuff like that. They said they were going to keep her clothes for evidence, but I could come and get the rest. And when I did, her cell phone wasn't there. I asked about it and nobody seemed to know where it was. So I went to the Medical Center and I asked the people there, but none of them had seen it either. Somebody said that maybe Zach Murdoch, that guy they said killed my mother, maybe he took it."

"Not that I'm aware of," Weber said.

"I've heard about this thing called pinging or something like that, where they can track where a cell phone is. I asked the police about that, but they told me it didn't matter since they already knew who killed my mom and he was in custody. They said for all they knew he may have thrown it out somewhere between Cañon Verde and here."

Tabitha Eibeck looked like she was probably somewhere around Zach Murdoch's age, early 20s, but both of them had experienced horrendous things at such a young age, and it showed on her face just like it did on Zach's.

"Anyway, I didn't think a whole lot about it. It's just a phone, right? But then the other day I remembered all of the pictures my mom had on it. She was one of those people who are always taking pictures and videos. Of me and my dad before he died, sunsets, people at work, everything. And now, with her and my dad both gone, I was wishing I had those pictures and videos. Then I remembered that my mom had her phone set up so that it backed everything up to the cloud when she took a picture or video. So I logged onto her account. It took me a while to figure out her password, which was the first three letters of my name and my birthday, but I got in. And when I did, I realized that Chief Kramer had been lying to everybody all along. Zach Murdoch didn't kill my mother. He did."

"What did you see, Tabitha?"

She bent down and picked up a thin laptop computer sitting on the floor next to her chair and opened it up.

"I copied all the files to my hard drive. You can click on that folder there that says Barbara. I'm sorry, I can't look at it again. I couldn't look at all of it to start with. But I saw enough."

"Before we do that, how about I have somebody from my office take you over there so you don't have to see or hear anything else." Weber said.

She looked reluctant, and Weber said, "I promise you, it's going to be okay. You're safe here."

Tabitha nodded her head and he called the office with his cell phone.

"Mary, I need you out here."

A few minutes later, after Mary had shepherded Tabitha to the sheriff's office, Parks clicked on the folder icon Tabitha had indicated. The video opened with a badly beaten Zach Murdoch sitting on a bed in what was obviously a hospital emergency room and a woman's voice asking, "What happened to you, young man?"

"Chief Kramer beat me up at the jail."

"Did you resist arrest or fight with the police?"

"No, ma'am."

"Do you know why..."

The woman's question was interrupted by the sound of a door opening and then closing and Arthur Kramer's voice demanding, "Turn that damned phone off, Barbara."

"This is it, Kramer. This is the last time you're going to do this to somebody. I'm taking this to the..."

"Give me that phone," Kramer's voice said.

There was a yelp from the woman, and the scene jerked as the phone panned to the ceiling of the room and then apparently was dropped. When it landed the image was crooked but showed the upper half of Arthur Kramer's body as he slammed Barber Eibeck into the wall. Once, twice, a third time.

"Leave her alone," Zach Murdoch was heard saying.

Kramer's image blocked the screen for a moment and there was a sound of flesh striking flesh and then Kramer saying, "I'll kill you too, you little prick."

Then he apparently moved again, and this time the screen only showed part of his body and one of the nurse's flailing arms.

"I told you to mind your own business, bitch. But you just wouldn't listen, would you? Nobody crosses Art Kramer and gets away with it!"

They could hear the woman struggling and fighting for breath, and then there was silence.

Kramer was seen stepping away as the woman's body slumped to the floor. Then he moved again and only one of his legs was showing. There was a sound that Weber and Parks both knew well, the sound of somebody unlocking and removing handcuffs.

"You're dead, you son of a bitch," Kramer said.

After that the phone was apparently kicked because it was suddenly showing the ceiling again, but the sounds of a fight was evident. There was a crashing noise, and then the sound of a door opening and slamming shut. A moment later Kramer came into view again as he picked up the phone and shoved it into his pocket.

While there was no video after that there was still the sound of a door opening and closing and then Kramer running down the hall and through another door. It was obvious he was outside, because now there was traffic noise in the background and a moment later what sounded like Kramer making a call from his own cell phone.

"Moon, get your ass over to the hospital right now. I need your help. We need to find Murdoch and get rid of him. Yeah, back parking lot. Hurry!"

It wasn't a perfect video, but it showed enough to know that Zach Murdoch had been telling the truth. Arthur Kramer had killed Barbara Eibeck. It also proved that that his injuries had been sustained before he arrived at the medical center, and that he had been handcuffed during the woman's murder.

"I'll be damned. I've heard of people reaching out from the grave to see justice done, but this is the first time I've ever experienced it myself," Weber said.

Chapter 42

"Why did you bring this all the way here, Tabitha?"

"At first I thought about talking to Warren Moon, because him and his wife live across the street from us and I always considered him a friend. Him and my dad used to watch football games together and drink beer. So I went over and talked to him. I said I had proof that Chief Kramer killed my mother. Right away Warren told me to shut up and not to say another word. He said that was a lie and if I knew what was good for me I'd forget whatever proof I thought I had and never say anything like that again. I had heard that he's as mixed up in all the bad things that were happening as much as Chief Kramer was, but I didn't want to believe it. Now I do. I remembered how nice you were to me, Mr. Parks, even when I was being pretty mean to you. And I figured that since you guys are from over here instead of Cañon Verde, and you're the ones that started the whole investigation, you really do want to do what's right."

"Tabitha, you said you didn't watch all of this. How much did you watch?"

"I had to stop when I saw him attacking my mother. I'm sorry, I just couldn't watch anymore. I threw up."

"I want you to hear something right at the end," Parks told her. "This is after Zach Murdoch escaped and ran outside. You don't have to look at the screen, it doesn't show anything anyhow, but I think it's important that you hear this."

He queued up the sound of Kramer leaving the Medical Center and his call to Officer Warren Moon. As Tabitha listened, her already pale skin turned whiter and she began to shake. Mary Caitlin put her hands on the young woman's shoulders reassuringly.

"Oh my God! He knew. He knew what happened to my mother."

"I think he did," Parks said.

"He was our friend. I knew my mother didn't like Chief Kramer, but he was our neighbor. His wife and my mother used to bowl together. We had cookouts together. He was even a pallbearer at my father's funeral."

"I'm sorry," Parks said.

"If he'd have seen this video, I'd be dead, too."

"I think that's very possible," Parks told her.

"What happens now? I can't go back there. When this comes out they'll kill me!"

"It's okay," Mary Caitlin reassured her. "You don't have to go back there, honey. Not now, not ever again."

Tabitha was crying, and Mary moved to the side of her chair and bent down to hug her. "It's going to be all right. I know it doesn't seem like it right now, but it's going to be all right."

"You did the right thing coming here, Tabitha," Weber said. "It took a lot of courage. But because of you, the truth is finally going to come out. If there's a hero in any of this, Tabitha, it's you."

~***~

"Hi guys," Josh Murdock said when he answered the door of his mother's house.

"Josh, is your mom here?"

"Uhh... yeah. What do you need?"

"We need to talk to her. It's important."

He looked toward the living room, then back at them and lowered his voice. "She's had a couple of drinks. She's not drunk or anything. Not yet, anyway. But the last couple of nights, since we got back from Zach's hearing, she's been hitting the bottle. She says it's the only way she can sleep."

"I understand," Weber told him. "Maybe what we've come here to talk about will help."

Josh seemed reluctant, but he nodded his head and stepped back to let them in. Juliette Murdoch was sitting on the couch in the same place she had been when Weber arrived in response to news of the shooting of Arthur Kramer. She looked at them when they entered the room, and while Weber could tell she had had a couple of drinks, like Josh said, she wasn't drunk.

He sat down beside her and said, "Juliette, I've got news. Good news."

~***~

If Lisa Burnham's original broadcast about Arthur Kramer and the things that had gone on with the Cañon Verde Police Department had caused a ruckus, complete chaos erupted when regular programming was interrupted and she told viewers that the Big Lake Sheriff's Department and the Federal Bureau of Investigation had obtained a cell phone video that clearly showed then Cañon Verde Police Chief Arthur Kramer assaulting and murdering registered nurse Barbara Eibeck at the Cañon Verde Medical Center, and then making a phone call to Police Officer Warren Moon, telling him they needed to find Zach Murdoch and, in the chief's words, "Get rid of him."

"While we haven't seen the actual video ourselves, here at News Channel Six, Sheriff Jim Weber from Big Lake told me that the contents are too graphic for television viewers and are, as he said *'sickening and horrifying.'* When asked how the video had surfaced, Sheriff Weber would only say that he couldn't release that information at this time. As I'm sure you can imagine, this puts a whole new light on the allegations of misdeeds by former Police Chief Arthur Kramer and the members of the Cañon Verde Police Department. Sheriff Weber tells me that he is sure that those responsible for helping to cover up Mrs. Eibeck's murder, along with other crimes against prisoners in custody in Cañon Verde, will finally face justice for their crimes."

"That's an amazing story, Lisa," her co-anchor said. "Is there any new information on what's going to happen with Zach Murdoch, the young man originally accused in Mrs. Eibeck's death?"

"There is, Michael. Just before we went on the air I spoke to someone at the courthouse in Alamogordo, New Mexico, where Mr. Murdoch is being held. I was told that after someone from the

U.S. Attorney's office contacted Judge James McFadden, who presided over a show cause hearing about the charges against Mr. Murdoch, and after he saw the video, he immediately ordered Mr. Murdoch released from custody and said that all charges relating to Mrs. Eibeck's case have been dropped."

"So Zach Murdoch is a free man?"

"That's my understanding, Michael."

"Wonderful," the co-anchor said. "The system does work after all, doesn't it?"

~***~

In truth, while he was out on bond, Zach Murdoch was still not a free man. It took another three weeks for the escape charges to be dismissed, after Mark Stevens successfully argued in court that his client had only fled to avoid certain death at the hands of Arthur Kramer and Warren Moon. In the wake of the revelations about his abuse while in custody, the original charges of possession of drugs and drug paraphernalia were also dropped. A day later, Probation Officer Leslie Hensdell announced that given the circumstances surrounding the case, the State of New Mexico had decided to grant Zach early release from probation, saying, "In my long career as a probation officer, I've dealt with many people, from first-time offenders who had made a mistake and really wanted to put it behind them and get on with their lives as productive citizens, all the way to habitual criminals who were institutionalized from an early age and show little hope of ever making any positive changes. In Zachary Murdoch's case, I saw a young man with a good future ahead of him who did something wrong and owned it, and was on his way to bigger and better things in his life. I think his early release from probation is the right decision."

~***~

Zach came home to Big Lake, telling his mother it was only until he got all the dental work he needed done and had a chance to get his head together and figure out what he wanted to do from then on. There was talk about joining the military, if his prior arrest for drug possession wouldn't interfere, and for a while he toyed with his original idea of trying to get a job on a pipeline crew. But the days turned into weeks, weeks turned into months, and with the healthy settlement he received from Cañon Verde for the abuse he had suffered while in custody there, he was able to repay his mother for everything she had spent trying to get him freed, send $2,000 to the owner of the Honda he had stolen, and still have enough left over to buy a building just off Main Street and open a fully stocked tool and equipment rental business. Interim Mayor Kirby Templeton, appointed by the Town Council to fill the vacancy left when Chet Wingate resigned from office, citing health reasons, was on hand with the rest of the council for the ribbon-cutting at Zach's new business.

Shortly after Zach's Tool and Supply opened, Weber stopped in to inquire about renting a wood chipper to do some cleanup work at the construction site on his parents' old ranch where the new house that he and Robyn would be moving into after their wedding was nearing completion. He was surprised to see the young woman working behind the counter.

"Tabitha? Is that you?"

"Yes, it's me," Barbara Eibeck's daughter said with a broad smile.

"Well, I'm surprised to see you here, to say the least."

She shrugged her shoulders as Zach came out from the back room, wiping his hands on a shop rag. "I just couldn't bring myself to go back to Cañon Verde. With my parents gone and everything that's happened, there was nothing left for me there. Something I did have to do was go to Zach's mom's house and apologize to both of them for everything they went through."

"You didn't owe anybody an apology," Zach said, putting his hand affectionately on hers.

"I was so scared I was shaking because I was sure they'd hate me. But as soon as I told Mrs. Murdoch who I was she put her arms around me and hugged me and told me everything was going to be all right. Anyway, the three of us had a long talk, and I think we all started to heal. It turns out this guy here, he's pretty special. So, I guess I'm going to be hanging around Big Lake for a while."

"I'm tickled to hear that," Weber told them with a big smile. "And I can tell you from my own experience, this is a good place to heal."

Turn the page for a sample of Big Lake Wedding, coming soon from Nick Russell!

Here's A Sneak Preview Of Nick Russell's Next Big Lake Book, *Big Lake Wedding,* Coming Soon!

Chapter 1

While it was one of the most anticipated weddings in the town of Big Lake's history, there is no question that it was also one of the most unusual. The bride wore a traditional modified white A-line dress with lace on the shoulders, a modest scoop at the neck and an open back. The groom wore a simple light gray suit with a dark blue tie over a sky-blue shirt. The bridesmaid was dressed in a dark green dress with a mid-length hem, while the best man also wore a gray suit of a darker shade than the groom's.

As a bride walked slowly down the aisle on her father's arm, the people gathered for the event couldn't help noticing the hastily applied safety pins that were holding the bodice of her dress together, or that her left eye was black and swollen shut. There were bandages on two of the fingers on her right hand, but fortunately, the ring finger was bare.

Standing at the front of the room, the groom's two black eyes made him resemble a raccoon. One of his trouser legs was torn halfway to the knee, a white gauze bandage covered part of his forehead, and dried blood caked his split bottom lip.

When they reached the front, the bride's father kissed her on the cheek, shook hands with the groom, and sat in a chair in the front row. He was by himself because the bride's mother refused to take part in the spectacle, choosing instead to sit outside in their car.

Judge Harold Ryman, who was officiating, looked at the man and woman in front of him affectionately and smiled, then shook his head.

"I've heard of brides or grooms that needed to be dragged to the altar before, but I have to say that this is the first time it looked like both of them put up a fight."

There was laughter from the audience, and from the wedding party. When the groom laughed, he revealed a missing front tooth.

"It looks like these two are off to a rough start," the judge said. "Let's hope that things get better for them. Because I've got to tell you, it doesn't look like it could get much worse."

His comment was greeted with more laughter, the groom putting a hand to his side and pressing against what he was sure was a cracked rib as he did so.

"I've asked both the bride and groom if they wanted to proceed with things today, or if they would prefer to put it off for another time. Both of them have told me this *is* the right time. Actually, I think the bride said, and I'm quoting her here, 'Can we just get this the hell over with?'"

Now the entire room was laughing loudly at the absurdity of the scene before them. Yes indeed, it was like no other wedding the little mountain community had ever seen, and people would be talking about it for a long time afterward.

"Well, all right then. Let us proceed," the judge said. "But before I do, the bride asked me if I was going to go through that whole love, honor, and obey thing. I told her I normally do, it's just part of the tradition, and she let me know that she was okay with the first two, and that she would obey her new husband from 9 to 5, but the rest of the time, that idea was out the window."

In spite of herself, the bride started to laugh so hard that she snorted. By now any sense of decorum had long since left the room and people were wiping tears from their eyes and slapping their legs at the judge's last statement.

When she managed to get control of herself, the bride said, "Like I asked you before, can we just get this the hell over with?"

"Yes, ma'am," the judge told her. "I make it a point never to argue with brides. Especially brides that carry guns."

He went through the usual thing about two people joined together in the eyes of God, talked about the bond they were making to each other forevermore, and then asked if there was anybody who felt the couple should not be joined in holy matrimony. Everyone in the audience held their breath for a moment, wondering if someone would actually raise an objection, and both the bride and the groom watched the door, expecting her mother to storm inside and try to put a stop to the proceedings. But when there was only silence, the judge said, "Very well then, James Alan Weber, do you take this woman, Robyn Abigail Fuchette ...."

Made in the USA
Las Vegas, NV
17 October 2023

79272630R00144